THE CATTLEMEN

Edited by Bill Pronzini & Martin H. Greenberg

FAWCETT GOLD MEDAL • NEW YORK

A Fawcett Gold Medal Book
Published by Ballantine Books
Copyright © 1986 by Bill Pronzini & Martin H. Greenberg

Library of Congress Catalog Card Number: 86-91294

ISBN 0-449-13145-9

Manufactured in the United States of America

First Edition: January 1987

ACKNOWLEDGMENTS

"Tall Men Riding," by S. Omar Barker. From *Rawhide Rhymes*. Copyright © 1968 by S. Omar Barker. Reprinted by permission of Elsa Barker.

"The Silver Dollar," by Thomas Thompson. Copyright © 1949 by The Hawley Publications, Inc. First published in *Zane Grey's Western Magazine*. Reprinted by permission of the author.

"The Seventh Desert," by Frank Bonham. Copyright © 1945 by Liberty Magazine, Inc. First published in *Liberty*. Reprinted by permission of the author.

"The Rancher's Lady," by Elmore Leonard. Copyright © 1955 by Elmore Leonard. Reprinted by permission of the author and H. N. Swanson, Inc.

"The Land Beyond," by Bryce Walton. Copyright © 1960 by Great American Publications, Inc. First published in *Wagon Train*. Reprinted by permission of the author.

"The Big Die-Up," by Steve Frazee. Copyright © 1953 by Flying Eagle Publications, Inc. First published in *Gunsmoke*. Reprinted by permission of Scott Meredith Literary Agency, Inc., 845 Third Avenue, New York, N.Y. 10022.

"They Walked Tall," by T.V. Olsen. Copyright © 1963 by T.V. Olsen. First published in *Pick of the Roundup*. Reprinted by permission of the author and the Lenniger Literary Agency, Inc.

Contents

Introduction

The Cattlemen is the seventh anthology of unusual and entertaining Western fiction to be published as part of our Best of the West series. Readers of the first six volumes were offered a wide variety of stories about sheriffs, marshals, and other law officers (*The Lawmen*); the men who rode the outlaw trail (*The Outlaws*); cowpunchers and trail hands (*The Cowboys*); members of the various Indian tribes as told from their point of view (*The Warriors*); the men who built and operated both the great railroads (*The Railroaders*); and the great Western riverboats (*The Steamboaters*). In this volume, we bring you tales of the ranchers large and small who settled, shaped, and sometimes bloodied the Old West landscape in their quest for freedom, sustenance, and power.

Montana, Wyoming, Texas, Colorado, California, Oregon, Arizona, and New Mexico are the settings of these stories. Action, danger, hardship, and triumph over odds both natural and man-made are their themes. And Owen Wister, Charles Alden Seltzer, Elmore Leonard, Thomas Thompson, Frank Bonham, T. V. Olsen, Steve Frazee, and Norman A. Fox, among others, are their authors. All in all, we think you'll agree that they represent the Best of the West.

In future books in the series, you will find stories about the horse soldiers who fought and died on the Western frontier; the drifters and loners of legend and fact; the gunfighters, the miners and prospectors, the hardy pioneers. These, too, will bear the names of acclaimed western writers—names such as Bret Harte, Jack Schaefer, Clay Fisher, James Warner Bellah, Elmer Kelton, Brian Garfield, A. B. Guthrie, Elmore Leonard, and Dorothy M. Johnson.

It is our hope that these volumes, along with *The Cattlemen* and the six that have preceded it, comprise a tribute to the American West that you'll want to keep as a permanent part of your library.

—Bill Pronzini and Martin
H. Greenberg

The late S. Omar Barker was twice recipient of a Western Writers of America Spur Award, once for his short story "Bad Company" (1955) and once for his poem "Empty Saddles at Christmas" (1966). His collections Songs of the Saddlemen, Sunlight through the Trees, and Rawhide Rhymes contain some of the most poignant verse ever penned about the Old West.

Tall Men Riding

S. Omar Barker

This is the song that the night birds sing
As the phantom herds trail by,
Horn by horn where the long plains fling
Flat miles to the Texas sky:

Oh, the high hawk knows where the rabbit goes,
And the buzzard marks the kill,
But few there be with eyes to see
The Tall Men riding still.
They hark in vain on the speeding train
For an echo of hoofbeat thunder,
And the yellow wheat is a winding sheet
For cattle trails plowed under.

Hoofdust flies at the low moon's rise,
And the bullbat's lonesome whir
Is an echoed note from a longhorn throat
Of a steer, in the days that were.

3

Inch by inch time draws the cinch,
Till the saddle will creak no more,
And they who were lords of the cattle hordes
Have tallied their final score.

This is the song that the night birds wail,
Where the Texas plains lie wide,
Watching the dust of a ghostly trail,
Where the phantom Tall Men ride!

Owen Wister (1860–1938) is widely known for his novels The Virginian *and* Lin McLean; *but his Western short stories are every bit as fine, as such collections as* Red Men and White, Members of the Family, *and* When West Was West *admirably attest. "At the Sign of the Last Chance" is Wister at his most evocative—a story about which Jack Schaefer once said, "It compresses into one quietly moving evening . . . the full authentic flavor of one typical section of the Old West and is the perfect epitaph of its passing."*

At the Sign of the Last Chance

Owen Wister

*M*ore familiar faces than I had hoped to see were there when I came in after leaving my horse at the stable. Would I eat anything? Henry asked. Not until breakfast, I said. I had supped at Lost Soldier. Would I join the game? Not tonight; but would they mind if I sat and watched them till I felt sleepy? It was too early to go to bed. And sitting here again seemed very natural.

"Does it, now?" said Stirling. "You look kind of natural yourself."

"Glad I do. It must be five years since last time."

"Six," said James Work. "But I would have known you anywhere."

"What sort of a meal did he set for you?" Marshal inquired.

5

"At Lost Soldier? Fried beef, biscuits, coffee, and excellent onions."

"Old onions of course?" said Henry. "Cooked?"

"No. Fresh from his garden. Young ones."

"So he's got a garden still!" mused Henry.

"Who's running Lost Soldier these days?" inquired Stirling.

"That oldest half-breed son of Toothpick Kid," said Marshal. "Any folks to supper with you?"

"Why, yes. Six or seven. Bound for the new oil-fields on Red Spider."

"Travel is brisk down in that valley," said Work.

"I didn't know the stage had stopped running through here," said I.

"Didn't you? Why, that's a matter of years now. There's no oil up this way. In fact, there's nothing up this way anymore."

They had made room for me; they had included me in their company. Only two others were not in the game. One sat in the back of the room, leaning over something that he was reading, never looking up from it. He was the only one I had not seen before, but he was at home quite evidently. Except when he turned a page, which might have been once every five minutes, he hardly made a movement. He was a rough fellow, wearing the beard of another day; and if reading was a habit with him, it was a slow process, and his lips moved in silent pronunciation of each syllable as it came.

Jed Goodland sat off by the kitchen door with his fiddle. Now and then he lightly picked or bowed some fragment of tune, like a man whispering memories to himself.

The others, save one or two that were clean-shaven, also wore the mustaches or the beards of a day that was done.

I had begun to see those beards long before they were gray; when no wire fence mutilated the freedom of the range; when fourteen mess wagons would be at the spring roundup; when cattle wandered and pastured, dotting the endless wilderness; when roping them brought the college graduate and the boy who had never learned to read into a lusty equality of youth and skill; when songs rose by the campfire; and the dim form of the night herder leaned on his saddle horn as under the stars he circled slowly around the recumbent thousands; when two hundred miles stretched between all this and the whistle of the nearest locomotive.

And all this was over. It had begun to end a long while ago. It had ebbed away slowly from these now playing their nightly game as they had once played it at flood-tide. The turn of the tide had come even when the beards were still brown, or red, or golden.

The decline of their day began possibly with the first wire fence; the great ranch life was hastened to its death by the winter snows of 1886; received its mortal stroke in the rustler war of 1892; breathed its last—no, it was still breathing, it had not wholly given up the ghost. Cattlemen and sheepmen, the newcomers, were at deeds of violence with each other. And here in this place, at the poker table, the ghost still clung to the world of the sagebrush, where it had lived its headlong joys.

I watched the graybeards going on with this game that had outlived many a player, had often paused during bloodshed, and resumed as often, no matter who had been carried out. They played without zest, winning or losing little, with now and then a friendly word to me.

They had learned to tolerate me when I had come among them first; not because I ever grew skilled in what they did, either in the saddle or with a gun, but because they knew that I liked them and the life they led, and always had come back to lead it with them, in my tenderfoot way.

Did they often think of their vanished prosperity? Or did they try to forget that, and had they succeeded? Something in them seemed quenched—but they were all in their fifties now; they had been in their twenties when I knew them first.

My first sight of James Work was on a night at the Cheyenne Club. He sat at the head of a dinner-table with some twenty men as his guests. They drank champagne and they sang. Work's cattle in those days earned him twenty per cent. Had he not overstayed his market in the fatal years, he could be giving dinners still. As with him, so with the others in that mild poker game.

Fortune, after romping with them, had romped off somewhere else. What filled their hours, what filled their minds, in these days of emptiness?

So I sat and watched them. How many times had I arrived for the night and done so? They drank very little. They spoke very little. They had been so used to each other for so long! I had seen that pile of newspapers and magazines where the man was reading grow and spread and litter the back of the room since I was twenty.

It was a joke that Henry never could bring himself to throw anything away.

"I suppose," I said to him now, as I pointed to the dusty accumulation, "that would be up to the ceiling if you didn't light your stove every winter with some of it."

Henry nodded and chuckled as he picked up his hand.

The man reading at the back of the room lifted his magazine "This is October 1885," he said, holding the shabby cover toward us.

"Find any startling news, Gilbert?"

"Why, there's a pretty good thing," said the man. "Did you know signboards have been used hundreds and hundreds of years? 'Way back of Columbus."

"I don't think I have ever thought about them," said Henry.

"Come to think about it," said James Work, "signboards must have started whenever hotels and saloons started, or whatever they called such places at first."

"It goes away back," said the reader. "It's a good piece."

"Come to think about it," said James Work, "men must have traveled before they had houses; and after they had houses; travel must have started public houses, and that would start signboards."

"That's so," said Henry.

A third player spoke to the reader. "Travel must have started red-light houses. Does he mention them, Gilbert?"

"He wouldn't do that, Marshal, not in a magazine he wouldn't," said James Work.

"He oughtn't," said Henry. "Such things should not be printed."

"Well, I guess it was cities started them, not travel," surmised Marshal. "I wonder whose idea the red light was."

"They had signboards in Ancient Rome," answered the man at the back of the room.

"Think of that!" said Henry.

"Might have been one of them emperors started the red light," said Marshal, "same as gladiators."

The game went on, always listless. Habit was strong, and what else was there to do?

"October 1885," said Marshal. "That was when Toothpick Kid pulled his gun on Doc Barker and persuaded him to be a dentist."

"Not 1885," said James Work. "That was 1886."

"October 1885," insisted Marshal. "That railroad came to Douglas the next year."

"He's got it correct, Jim," said Henry.

"Where is Toothpick Kid nowadays?" I inquired.

"Pulled his freight for Alaska. Not heard from since 1905. She's taken up with Duke Gardiner's brother, the Kid's woman has," said Henry.

"The Kid wanted Barker to fix his teeth same as Duke Gardiner had his," said Work.

"I don't think I've seen Duke Gardiner since '91," said I.

"When last heard from," said Henry, "Duke was running a joint in El Paso."

"There's a name for you!" exclaimed the man at the back of the room. "Goat and Compasses! They had that on a signboard in England. Well, and would you ever guess what it started from! 'God encompasseth us'!"

"Think of that!" said Henry.

"Does it say," asked Work, "if they had any double signs like Henry's here?"

"Not so far, it doesn't. If I strike any, I'll tell you."

That double sign of Henry's, hanging outside now in the dark of the silent town, told its own tale of the old life in its brief way. From Montana to Texas, I had seen them. Does anybody know when the first one was imagined and painted?

A great deal of frontier life is told by the four laconic words. They were to be found at the edges of those towns that rose overnight in the midst of nowhere, sang and danced and shot for a while, and then sank into silence. As the rider from his roundup or his mine rode into town with full pockets, he read, First Chance; in the morning as he rode out with pockets empty, he read, Last Chance. More of the frontier life could hardly be told in four words. They were quite as revealing of the spirit of an age and people as Goat and Compasses.

That is what I thought as I sat there looking on at my old acquaintances over their listless game. It was still too early to go to bed, and what else was there to do? What a lot of old tunes Jed Goodland remembered!

"Why, where's your clock, Henry?" I asked.

Henry scratched his head. "Why," he meditated— "why, I guess it was last January."

"Did she get shot up again?"

Henry slowly shook his head. "This town is not what it was. I guess you saw the last shootin-up she got. She just quit on me one day. Yes; January. Winding of her up didn't do nothing to her. It was Lee noticed she had quit. So I didn't get a new one. Any more than I have fresh onions. Too much trouble to mend the ditch."

"Where's your Chink tonight?" I inquired. Lee was another old acquaintance; he had cooked many meals and made my bed often, season after season, when I had lodged here for the night.

"I let Lee go—let's see—I guess that must have been last April. Business is not what it used to be."

"Then you do everything yourself now?"

"Why, yes; when there's anything to do."

"Boys don't seem as lively as they used to be," said Work.

"There are no boys," said Henry. "Just people."

This is what Henry had to say. It was said by the bullet holes in the wall, landmarks patterning the shape of the clock that had hung there till it stopped going last January. It was said by the empty shelves beneath the clock and behind the bar. It was said by the empty bottles that Henry had not yet thrown out. These occupied half one shelf. Two or three full bottles stood in the middle of the lowest shelf, looking lonely. In one of them the cork had been drawn and could be pulled out by the fingers again, should anyone call for a drink.

"It was Buck Seabrook shot up your clock last time, wasn't it, Henry?" asked Marshal. "You knew Buck?" he said to me; and I nodded.

"Same night as that young puncher got the letter he'd been asking for every mail day," said Work.

"Opened it in the stage office," continued Marshal, "drew his gun, and blew out his brains right there. I guess you heard about him?" he said to me again, and I nodded.

"No," Henry corrected. "Not there." He pointed at the ceiling. "Upstairs. He was sleeping in number four. He left no directions."

"I liked that kid," said Stirling, who had been silent. "Nice, quiet, well-behaved kid. A good roper."

"Anybody know what was in the letter?" asked Work.

"It was from a girl," said Henry. "I thought maybe there would be something in it demanding action. There was nothing beyond the action he had taken. I put it inside his shirt with him. Nobody saw it but me."

"What would you call that for a name?" said the reader at the back of the room. "Goose and Gridiron."

"I'd call that good," said Work.

"It would sound good to a hungry traveler," said Stirling.

"Any more of them?" asked Henry

"Rafts of them. I'll tell you the next good one."

"Yes, tell us. And tell us when and where they all started, if it says." In the silence of the cards, a door shut somewhere along the dark street.

"That's Old Man Clarke," said Henry.

"First time I ever heard of him in town," said I.

"We made him come in. Old Man Clarke is getting turrible shaky. He wouldn't accept a room. So he sleeps in the old stage office and cooks for himself. If you put him in New York, he'd stay a hermit all the same."

"How old is he?"

"Nobody knows. He looked about as old as he does now when I took this hotel. That was 1887. But we don't want him to live alone up that canyon anymore. He rides up to his mine now and then. Won't let anybody go along. Says the secret will die with him. Hello, Jed. Let's have the whole of 'Buffalo Girls.' " And Jed Goodland played the old quadrille music through.

"You used to hear that pretty often, I guess," said Henry to me; and I nodded.

Scraping steps shambled slowly by in the sand. We listened.

"He doesn't seem to be coming in," I said.

"He may. He will if he feels like it, and he won't if he feels like not."

"He had to let me help him onto his horse the other day," said Marshal. "But he's more limber some days than others."

Presently the scraping steps came again, passed the door, and grew distant.

"Yes," said Work. "Old Man Clarke is sure getting feeble."

"Did you say it was Buck Seabrook shot your clock the last time?"

"Yes. Buck."

"If I remember correct," pursued Stirling, "it wasn't Buck did it, it was that joker his horse bucked off that same afternoon down by the corral."

"That Hat Six wrangler?"

"Yes. Horse bucked him off. He went up so high the fashions had changed when he came down."

"So it was, George." And he chuckled over the memory.

"Where does Old Man Clarke walk to?" I asked; for the steps came scraping along again.

"Just around and around," said Henry. "He always would do things his own way. You can't change him. He has taken to talking to himself this year."

The door opened, and he looked in. "Hello, boys," said he.

"Hello yourself, Uncle Jerry," said Work. "Have a chair. Have a drink."

"Well, maybe I'll think it over." He shut the door, and the steps went shambling away.

"His voice sounds awful old," said Marshal. "Does he know the way his hair and beard look?"

"Buck Seabrook," mused Stirling. "I've not seen him for quite a while. Is he in the country now?"

Henry shook his head. "Buck is in no country anymore."

"Well, now, I hadn't heard of it. Well, well."

"Any of you remember Chet Sharston?" asked Marshal.

"Sure," said Stirling. "Did him and Buck have any trouble?"

"No, they never had any trouble," said Henry. "Not they."

"What was that Hat Six wrangler's name?" asked Work.

"He said it was Johnson," replied Henry.

Again the shambling steps approached. This time Old Man Clarke came in, and Henry invited him to join the game.

"No, boys," he said. "Thank you just the same. I'll sit over here for a while." He took a chair. "You boys just go on. Don't mind me." His pale, ancient eyes seemed to notice us less than they did the shifting pictures in his brain.

"Why don't you see the barber, Uncle Jerry?" asked Marshal.

"Nearest barber is in Casper. Maybe I'll think it over."

"Swan and Harp" said the man at the back of the room. "That's another."

"Not equal to Goat and Compasses," said Work.

"It don't make you expect a good meal like Goose and

Gridiron," said Henry. "I'll trim your hair tomorrow, Uncle Jerry, if you say so."

"Boys, none that tasted her flapjacks ever wanted another cook," said Old Man Clarke.

"Well, what do you think of Hoop and Grapes?"

"Nothing at all," said Henry. "Hoop and Grapes makes no appeal to me."

"You boys never knowed my wife," said Old Man Clarke in his corner. "Flapjacks. Biscuits. She was a buck-skinned son-of-a-bitch." His vague eyes swam, but the next moment his inconsequent cheerfulness returned. "Dance night and all the girls late," he said.

"A signboard outside a hotel or saloon," said Marshal, "should have something to do with what's done inside."

"That's so," said Henry.

"Take Last Chance and First Chance," Marshal continued. "Has England anything to beat that, I'd like to know? Did you see any to beat it?" he asked me.

"No, I never did."

"You come for fishing?" asked Old Man Clarke.

"I've brought my rod," I answered.

"No trout in this country anymore," said he.

"My creek is fished out. And the elk are gone. I've not jumped a blacktail deer these three years. Where are the antelope?" he frowned; his eyes seemed to be asking questions. "But I'll get ye some meat tomorro', boys," he declared in his threadbare, cheerful voice; and then it trailed off. "All at the bottom of Lake Champlain," he said.

"Have a drink, Uncle Jerry?" said Henry.

"Not now, and thank you just the same. Maybe I'll think it over."

"Buck Seabrook was fine to travel with," said Stirling.

"A fine upstanding cowpuncher," added Work. "Honest clean through. Never knew him to go back on his word or do a crooked action."

"Him and Chet Sharston traveled together pretty much," said Henry.

Stirling chuckled over a memory. "Chet he used to try

and beat Buck's flow of conversation. Wanted to converse some himself."

"Well, Chet could."

"Oh, he could some. But never equal to Buck."

"Here's a good one," said the man at the back of the room. "Bolt-in-Tun."

"How do they spell a thing like that?" demanded Marshal.

It was spelled for him.

"Well, that may make sense to an Englishman," said Henry.

"Doesn't it say where signboards started?" asked Work.

"Not yet." And the reader continued to pore over the syllables, which he followed slowly with moving lips.

"Buck was telling Chet," said Stirling, "of a mistake he made one night at the Southern Hotel in San Antone. Buck was going to his room fair late at night when a man came around the corner on his floor, and quick as he seen Buck, he put his hand back to his hip pocket. Well, Buck never lost any time. So when the man took a whirl and fell in a heap, Buck waited to see what he would do next. But the man didn't do anything more.

"So Buck goes to him and turns him over; and it isn't any stranger, it is a prospector Buck had met up with in Nevada; and the prospector had nothing worse than a flask in his pocket. He'd been aiming to offer Buck a drink. Buck sure felt sorry about making such a mistake, he said. And Chet, he waited, for he knowed very well that Buck hoped he would ask him what he did when he discovered the truth.

"After a while Buck couldn't wait; and so in disappointment he says to Chet very solemn, 'I carried out the wishes of the deceased.'

" 'I was lookin' over the transom when you drank his whiskey,' says Chet.

" 'Where's your memory? You were the man,' says Buck. Well, well, weren't they a nonsensical pair!"

"I remember," said Henry. "They were sitting right there." And he pointed to a table.

"They were playing cooncan," said Marshal. "I remember that night well. Buck was always Buck. Well, well! Why, didn't Buck learn you cooncan?"

"Yes, he did," said I. "It was that same night."

"Boys," said Old Man Clarke over in the corner, "I'll get ye some fresh meat tomorro'."

"That's you, Uncle Jerry!" said Henry heartily. "You get us a nice elk, or a blacktail, and I'll grubstake you for the winter."

"She's coming," said Old Man Clarke. "Winter's coming. I'll shoot any of ye a match with my new .45–90 at a hundred yards. Hit the ace of spades, five out of five."

"Sure you can, Uncle Jerry."

"Flapjacks. Biscuits. And she could look as pretty as a bride," said Old Man Clarke.

"Wasn't it Chet," said Work, "that told Toothpick Kid Doc Barker had fixed up Duke Gardiner's teeth for him?"

"Not Chet. It was Buck told him that."

Henry appealed to me. "What's your remembrance of it?"

"Why, I always thought it was Buck," I answered.

"Buck was always Buck," said Marshal. "Well, well!"

"Who did fix Duke's teeth?"

"It was a travelling dentist. He done a good job, too, on Duke. All gold. Hit Drybone when Duke was in the hospital, but he went north in two or three days on the stage for Buffalo. That's how the play come up."

"Chet could yarn as well as Buck now and then," said Stirling.

"Not often," said Henry. "Not very often."

"Well, but he could. There was that experience Chet claimed he had down in the tornado belt."

"I remember," said Henry. "Down in Texas."

"Chet mentioned it was in Kansas."

"San Saba, Texas," said Henry.

"You're right. San Saba. So it was. Chet worked for a gambler there who wanted to be owner of a house that you could go upstairs in."

"I didn't know Chet could deal a deck," said Marshal.

"He couldn't. Never could. He hired as a carpenter to the gambler."

"Chet was handy with tools," said Henry.

"A very neat worker. So the house was to be two stories. So Chet he said he'd help. Said he built the whole thing. Said it took him four months. Said he kep' asking the gambler for some money. The day he could open the front door of his house and walk in and sit down, the gambler told Chet, he'd pay him the total. So they walk out to it the day the job's complete and chairs ready for sitting in, and the gambler he takes hold of the doorknob and whang! a cyclone hits the house.

"The gambler saved the doorknob—didn't let go of it. Chet claimed he had fulfilled his part of the contract, but the gambler said a doorknob was not sufficient evidence that any house had been there. Wouldn't pay Chet a cent."

"They used to be a mean bunch in Texas," said Stirling.

"I was in this country before any of you boys were born," said Old Man Clarke.

"Sure you were, Uncle Jerry," said Henry. "Sure you were."

"I used to be hell and repeat."

"Sure thing, Uncle Jerry."

For a while there was little sound in the Last Chance Saloon save the light notes that Jed Goodland struck on his fiddle from time to time.

"How did that play come up, Henry?" asked Work.

"Which play?"

"Why, Doc Barker and Toothpick Kid."

"Why, wasn't you right there that day?"

"I was, but I don't seem to remember exactly how it started."

"Well," said Henry, "the Kid had to admit that Doc Barker put the kibosh on him after all. You're wrong about Buck. He didn't come into that." Henry's voice seemed to be waking up; his eyes were waking up.

"Sure he put the kibosh on him," Work agreed energetically.

"Wasn't it the day after they'd corraled that fello' up on the Dry Cheyenne?" asked Stirling.

"So it was!" said Marshal. He, too, was waking up. Life was coming into the talk of all. "That's where the boys corraled him."

"Well," said Stirling, "you couldn't leave a man as slick as he was, footloose, to go around and play such a game on the whole country."

"It was at the ranch gate Toothpick Kid saw those new gold teeth of Duke's," said Marshal.

"It wasn't a mile from the gate," said Stirling. "Not a mile. And Toothpick didn't wait to ask Duke the facts, or he'd have saved his money. Duke had happened to trail his rope over the carcasses of some stock. When he was roping a steer after that, his hand was caught between a twist of the rope and his saddle horn. So his hand got burned."

"Didn't Buck tell him he'd ought to get Doc Barker to put some stuff on it?"

"Buck did warn him, but Duke wouldn't listen. So Buck had to bring him into the Drybone hospital with an arm that they had to cut his shirt-sleeve for."

"I remember," said Henry. "Duke told me that Buck never said, 'I told you so' to him."

"Buck wouldn't. If ever there was a gentleman, it was Buck Seabrook. Doc Barker slashed his arm open from shoulder to elbow. And in twenty-four hours the arm wasn't so big. But it was still pretty big, and it looked like nothing at all, and Duke's brother saw it. They had sent for him. He rode into town, and when he saw the arm and the way it had been cut by Doc Barker, he figured he'd lay for Doc and kill him. Doc happened to be out at the C-Y on a case.

"The boys met him as he came back and warned him to keep out of the way till Duke's brother got sober, so Doc kep' out of the way. No use having trouble with a drunken man. Doc would have had to shoot Duke's brother or take the consequences. Well, next day the brother sobered up, and the boys persuaded him that Doc had saved Duke's life, and he was satisfied and changed his mind and there was no further hard feelings. And he got interested in the traveling dentist who had come into town to pick up business from the boys. He did good work. The brother got a couple of teeth plugged. They kept the dentist quite busy."

"I remember," said Marshal. "Chet and Buck both had work done."

"Do you remember the grass cook-fire Buck and Chet claimed they had to cook their supper with?" asked Work, with animation. Animation was warming each one, more and more. Their faces actually seemed to be growing younger.

"Out beyond Meteetsee you mean?"

"That was it."

"What was it?" asked Marshal.

"Did they never tell you that? Buck went around telling everybody."

"Grass cook-fire?" said Old Man Clarke in his withered voice. "Nobody ever cooked with grass. Grass don't burn half a minute. Rutherford B. Hayes was President when I came into this country. But Samuel J. Tilden was elected Yes, sir."

"Sure he was, Uncle Jerry," said Henry.

"Well, Buck and Chet had to camp one night where they found a water hole but no wood. No sagebrush, no buffalo chips, nothing except the grass, which was long. So Buck he filled the coffeepot and lighted the grass. The little flames were hot, but they burned out quick and ran on to the next grass. So Buck he ran after them holding his coffeepot over the flames as they traveled. So he said Chet lighted some more grass and held his frying pan over those flames and kep' a-following their trail like he was doing with the coffeepot. He said that his coffeepot boiled after a while and Chet's meat was fried after a while, but by that time they were ten miles apart. Walked around hunting for each other till sunrise and ate their supper for breakfast."

"What's that toon you're playing, Jed?" inquired Stirling.

"That's 'Sandy Land,'" replied the fiddler.

"Play it some more, Jed. Sounds plumb natural. Like old times."

"Yes, it does so," said Henry. "Like when the boys used to dance here."

"Dance!" said Old Man Clarke. "None of you never seen me dance."

"Better have a drink, Uncle Jerry."

"Thank you kindly. Just one. Put some water in. None of you never did, I guess."

"I'll bet you shook a fancy heel, Uncle."

"I always started with the earliest and kept going with the latest. I used to call for 'em, too. Salute your partners! Opposite the same! Swing your honey! That's the style I used to be. All at the bottom of Lake Champlain. None of you ever knowed her."

"Have another, Uncle Jerry. The nights are getting cold."

"Thank you kindly. I'll have one more. Winter's coming."

"Any of you see that Wolf Dance where Toothpick wore the buckskin pants?" asked Work. "Wasn't any of you to that?"

"Somebody played it on Toothpick, didn't they?" said Stirling.

"Buck did. Buck wasn't dancing. He was just looking on. Toothpick always said Buck was mad because the Indians adopted him into the tribe and wouldn't take Buck. They gave him a squaw, y'know. He lived with her on the reservation till he left for Alaska. He got her allotment of land with her, y'know. I saw him and her and their kids when I was there. I guess there were twelve kids. Probably twenty by the time he went to Alaska. She'd most always have twins."

"Here's a name for you," said the man at the back of the room. "What have you got to say about Whistling Oyster?"

"Whistling Oyster?" said Henry. "Well, if I had ever the misfortune to think of such a name, I'd not have mentioned it to anybody, and I'd have tried to forget it."

"Just like them English," said Marshal.

"Did Toothpick have any novelties in the way of teeth?" asked Stirling.

"If he did, he concealed them," said Work.

"But him and Doc Barker had no hard feelings," said Henry. "They both put the mistake on Duke Gardiner, and Duke said, well, they could leave it there if that made them feel happier."

"Doc was happy as he could be already."

"Well, a man would be after what came so near happening to him and what actually did happen."

"Did you say Buck was dead?" asked Marshal.

"Dead these fifteen years," said Henry. "Didn't you hear about it? Some skunk in Texas caught Buck with his wife. Buck had no time to jump for his gun."

"Well, there are worse ways to die. Poor Buck! D'you remember how he laid right down flat on his back when they told him about Doc and the Kid's teeth? The more the Kid said any man in his place would have acted the same, the flatter Buck laid in the sagebrush."

"I remember," said Stirling. "I was cutting calves by the corral."

"Duke was able to sit up in the hospital and have the dentist work on his cavities. And the dentist edged the spaces with gold, and he cleaned all the teeth till you could notice them whenever Duke laughed. So he got well and rode out to camp and praised Doc Barker for a sure good doctor. He meant his arm of course that Doc had slashed open when they expected he was dying and sent for his brother.

"Duke never thought to speak about the dentist that had come into Drybone and gone on to Buffalo, and the Kid naturally thought it was Doc Barker who had done the job on Duke's teeth. And Buck he said nothing. So Kid drops in to the hospital next time he's in town for a spree at the hog ranch, and invites the Doc to put a gold edging on his teeth for him.

" 'Not in my line,' says Doc. 'I'm a surgeon. And I've got no instruments for such a job.'

" 'You had 'em for Duke Gardiner,' says the Kid. 'Why not for me?'

" 'That was a dentist,' says Doc, 'while I was getting Duke's arm into shape.'

"So Toothpick he goes out. He feels offended at a difference being made between him and Duke, and he sits in the hog ranch thinking it over and comforting himself with some whisky. He doesn't believe in any dentist, and about four o'clock in the afternoon he returns to Doc's office and says he insists on having the job done. And Doc he gets hot and says he's not a dentist and he orders Toothpick out of the office. And Toothpick he goes back to the hog ranch feeling awful sore at the discrimination between him and the Duke.

"Well, about two o'clock A.M. Doc wakes up with a jump, and there's Toothpick. Toothpick thumps a big wad of bills down on the bureau—he'd been saving his time for a big spree, and he had the best part of four or five months' pay in his wad—and Doc saw right away Toothpick was drunk clear through. And Toothpick jams his gun against the Doc's stomach. 'You'll fix my teeth,' he says. 'You'll fix 'em right now. I'm just as good as Duke Gardiner or any other blankety-blank hobo in this country, and my money's just as good as Duke's, and I've just as much of it, and you'll do it now.' "

"I remember, I remember," said Marshal. "That's what the Kid told Doc." He beat his fist on the table and shook with enjoyment.

"Well, of course Doc Barker put on his pants at once. Doc could always make a quick decision. He takes the Kid out where he keeps his instruments and he lights his lamp; and he brings another lamp, and he lights two candles and explains that daylight would be better, but that he'll do the best he can. And he begins rummaging among his knives and scissors, which make a jingling, and Toothpick sits watching him with deeper and deeper interest. And Doc Barker he keeps rummaging, and Toothpick keeps sitting and watching, and Doc he brings out a horrible-looking saw and gives it a sort of a swing in the air.

" 'Are you going to use that thing on me?' inquires Toothpick.

" 'Open your mouth,' says Doc.

"Toothpick opens his mouth, but he shuts it again. 'Duke didn't mention it hurt him,' says he.

" 'It didn't, not to speak of,' says Doc. 'How can I know how much it will hurt you if you don't let me see your teeth?' So the Kid's mouth goes open and Doc takes a little microscope and sticks it in and looks right and looks left and up and down very slow and takes out the miscroscope. 'My, my, my,' he says, very serious.

" 'Is it going to hurt bad?' inquires Toothpick.

" 'I can do it,' says Doc, 'I can do it. But I'll have to charge for emergency and operating at night.'

" 'Will it take long?' says the Kid.

" 'I must have an hour, or I decline to be responsible,' says the Doc; 'the condition is complicated. Your friend Mr. Gardiner's teeth offered no such difficulties.' And Doc collects every instrument he can lay his hands on that comes anywhere near looking like what dentists have. 'My fee is usually two hundred dollars for emergency night operations,' says he, 'but that is for folks in town.'

"Toothpick brings out his wad and shoves it at Doc, and Doc he counts it and hands back twenty dollars. 'I'll accept a hundred and fifty,' he says, 'and I'll do my best for you.'

"By this time Toothpick's eyes are bulging away out of his head, but he had put up too much of a play to back down from it. 'Duke didn't mention a thing about its hurting him,' he repeats.

" 'I think I can manage,' says Doc. 'You tell me right off if the pain is too much for you. Where's my sponge?' So he gets the sponge, and he pours some ether on it and starts sponging the Kid's teeth.

"The Kid he's grabbing the chair till his knuckles are all white. Doc lets the sponge come near the candle, and puff! up it flares and Toothpick gives a jump.

" 'It's nothing,' says Doc. 'But a little more, and you and I and this room would have been blown up. That's why I am obliged to charge double for these night emergency operations. It's the gold edging that's the risk.'

" 'I hate to have you take any risk,' says Toothpick. 'Will it be risky to scrape my teeth, just to give them a little scrape, y'know, like you done for Duke?'

" 'Oh, no,' says Doc, 'that will not be risky.' So Doc Barker he takes an ear cleaner and he scrapes, while Toothpick holds his mouth open and grabs the chair. 'There,' says Doc. 'Come again.' And out flies Toothpick like Indians were after him. Forgets the hog ranch and his night of joy waiting for him there, jumps on his horse and makes camp shortly after sunrise. It was that same morning Buck heard about Toothpick and Doc Barker and laid flat down in the sagebrush.''

"Buck sure played it on the Kid at that Wolf Dance,'' said Work. ''Toothpick thought the ladies had stayed after the storm.''

Again Marshal beat his fist on the table. We had become a lively company.

"On the Crow reservation, wasn't it?'' said Henry.

"Right on that flat between the Agency and Fort Custer, along the river. The ladies were all there.''

"She always stayed as pretty as a bride,'' said Old Man Clarke.

"Have another drink, Uncle Jerry.''

"No more, no more, thank you just the same. I'm just a-sittin' here for a while.''

"The Kid had on his buckskin and admired himself to death. Admired his own dancing. You remembered how it started to pour. Of course the Kid's buckskin pants started to shrink on him. They got up to his knees. About that same time the ladies started to go home, not having brought umbrellas, and out runs Buck into the ring. He whispers to Kid: 'Your bare legs are scandalous. Look at the ladies. Go hide yourself. I'll let you know when you can come out.'

"Away runs Kid till he finds a big wet sagebrush and crawls into it deep. The sun came out pretty soon. But Toothpick sat in his wet sagebrush, waiting to be told the ladies had gone. Us boys stayed till the dance was over, and away runs Buck to the sagebrush.

" 'My,' says he, 'I'm sorry, Kid. The ladies went two hours ago. I'll have to get Doc Barker to fix up my memory.' "

"I used to be hell and repeat," said Old Man Clarke from his chair. "Play that again. Play that quadrille," he ordered peremptorily.

The fiddler smiled and humored him. We listened. There was silence for a while.

"Elephant and Castle" said the man at the back of the room. "Near London."

"That is senseless, too," said Henry. "We have more sensible signs in this country."

Jed Goodland played the quadrille quietly, like a memory, and as they made their bets, their boots tapped the floor to its rhythm.

"Swing your duckies," said Old Man Clarke. "Cage the queen. All shake your feet. Doe se doe and a doe doe doe. Sashay back. Git away, girls, git away fast. Gents in the center and four hands around. There you go to your seats."

"Give us 'Sandy Land' again," said Stirling. And Jed played "Sandy Land."

"Doc Barker became governor of Wyoming," said Work, "about 1890."

"What year did they abandon the stage route?" I asked.

"Later," said Henry. "We had the mail here till the Burlington road got to Sheridan."

"See here," said the man at the back of the room. "Here's something."

"Well, I hope it beats Elephant and Castle," said Henry.

"It's not a signboard, it's an old custom," said the man.

"Well, let's have your old custom."

The man referred to his magazine. "It says," he continued, "that many a flourishing inn which had been prosperous for two or three hundred years would go down for one reason or another till no travelers patronized it anymore. It says this happened to the old places where the coaches changed horses or stopped for meals going north and south every day, and along other important routes as well. Those routes were given up after the railroads began to spread.

"The railroad finally killed the coaches. So unless an inn was in some place that continued to be important, like a town where the railroads brought strangers same as the coaches used to, why, the inn's business would dry up. And that's where the custom comes in. When some inn had outlived its time, and it was known that trade had left it for good, they would take down the sign of that inn and bury it. It says that right here." He touched the page.

The quiet music of Jed Goodland ceased. He laid his fiddle in his lap. One by one, each player laid down his cards. Henry from habit turned to see the clock. The bullet holes were there, and the empty shelves. Henry looked at his watch.

"Quittin' so early?" asked Old Man Clarke. "What's your hurry?"

"Five minutes of twelve," said Henry. He went to the door and looked up at the sky.

"Cold," said Old Man Clarke. "Stars small and bright. Winter's a'coming, I tell you."

Standing at the open door, Henry looked out at the night for a while and then turned and faced his friends in their chairs round the table.

"What do you say, boys?"

Without a word they rose. The man at the back of the room had risen. Jed Goodland was standing. Still in his chair, remote and busy with his own half-dim thoughts, Old Man Clarke sat watching us almost without interest.

"Gilbert," said Henry to the man at the back of the room, "there's a ladder in the corner by the stairs. Jed, you'll find a spade in the shed outside the kitchen door."

"What's your hurry, boys?" asked Old Man Clarke. "Tomorro' I'll get ye a big elk."

But as they all passed him in silence, he rose and joined

them without curiosity, and followed without understanding.

The ladder was set up, and Henry mounted it and laid his hands upon the signboard. Presently it came loose, and he handed it down to James Work, who stood ready for it. It was a little large for one man to carry without awkwardness, and Marshal stepped forward and took two corners of it while Work held the others.

"You boys go first with it," said Henry. "Over there by the side of the creek. I'll walk next. Stirling, you take the spade."

Their conjured youth had fled from their faces, vanished from their voices.

"I've got the spade, Henry."

"Give it to Stirling, Jed. I'll want your fiddle along."

Moving very quietly, we followed Henry in silence, Old Man Clarke last of us, Work and Marshal leading with the signboard between them. And presently we reached the banks of Willow Creek.

"About here," said Henry.

They laid the signboard down, and we stood round it, while Stirling struck his spade into the earth. It did not take long.

"Jed," said Henry, "you might play now. Nothing will be said. Give us 'Sound the Dead March as Ye Bear Me Along.' "

In the night, the strains of that somber melody rose and fell, always quietly, as if Jed were whispering memories with his bow.

How they must have thanked the darkness that hid their faces from each other! But the darkness could not hide sound. None of us had been prepared for what the music would instantly do to us.

Somewhere near me I heard a man struggling to keep command of himself; then he walked away with his grief alone. A neighbor followed him, shaken with emotions out of control. And so, within a brief time, before the melody had reached its first cadence, none was left by the grave except Stirling with his spade and Jed with his fiddle, each now and again sweeping a hand over his eyes quickly, in furtive shame at himself. Only one of us withstood it. Old Man Clarke, puzzled, went wandering from one neighbor to the next, saying, "Boys, what's up with ye? Who's dead?"

Although it was to the days of their youth, not mine, that they were bidding this farewell, and I had only looked on when the beards were golden and the betting was high, they counted me as one of them tonight. I felt it—and I knew it when Henry moved nearer to me and touched me lightly with his elbow.

So the sign of the Last Chance was laid in its last place, and Stirling covered it and smoothed the earth while we got hold of ourselves, and Jed Goodland played the melody more and more quietly until it sank to the lightest breath and died away.

"That's all, I guess." said Henry. "Thank you, Jed. Thank you, boys. I guess we can go home now."

Yes, now we could go home. The requiem of the golden beards, their romance, their departed West, too good to live forever, was finished.

As we returned slowly in the stillness of the cold starlight, the voice of Old Man Clarke, shrill and withered, disembodied as an echo, startled me by its sudden outbreak.

"None of you knowed her, boys. She was a buckskin son-of-a-bitch. All at the bottom of Lake Champlain!"

"Take him, boys," said Henry. "Take Uncle Jerry to bed, please. I guess I'll stroll around for a while out here by myself. Good night, boys."

I found that I could not bid him good night, and the others seemed as little able to speak as I was. Old Man Clarke said nothing more. He followed along with us as he had come, more like some old dog, not aware of our errand or seeming to care to know, merely contented, his dim understanding remote within himself. He needed no attention when we came to the deserted stage office where he slept. He sat down on the bed and began to pull off his boots cheerfully. As we were shutting his door, he said,

"Boys, tomorro' I'll get ye a fat bull elk."

"Good night, Jed," said Marshal.

"Good night, Gilbert," said Stirling.

"Good night, all." The company dispersed along the silent street.

As we reentered the saloon—Work and I, who were both sleeping in the hotel—the deserted room seemed to be speaking to us; it halted us on the threshold. The cards lay on the table, the vacant chairs around it. There stood the empty bottles on the shelf. Above them were the bullet holes in the wall where the clock used to be. In the back of the room the magazine lay open on the table with a lamp burning. The other lamp stood on the bar, and one lamp hung over the card table. Work extinguished this one; the lamp by the magazine he brought to light us to our rooms where we could see to light our bedroom lamps. We left the one on the bar for Henry.

"Jed was always handy with his fiddle," said Work at the top of the stairs. "And his skill stays by him. Well, good night."

A long while afterward I heard a door closing below and knew that Henry had come in from his stroll.

During the first forty years of this century, Charles Alden
Seltzer (1875–1942) was one of the most popular writers
to follow in the broad footsteps of Owen Wister. His more
than fifty western novels include such well-received titles as
"Drag" Harlen, Channing Comes Through, Silverspurs,
and So Long, Sucker. "Love's International," which tells
the amusing tale of the British invasion of the American
cattle industry in the late 1800s, is among the best of his
shorter works about the Old West.

Love's International

Charles Alden Seltzer

"*I*n them days," remarked old Davey, as he nonchal-
antly kicked at a lizard that was regarding him with stony
gaze from the shadow of a rock, "they were heaps of lords
and dukes come a-fannin' out here to bust into the cattle
business." Age had brought an irritating garrulity to Davey, and I paid very little attention to his remark, being at
the moment more interested in the view—a great, vast
stretch of scorched and dusty plain broken here and there
by ridges, gullies, sand dunes, and draws, dotted with rock,
scraggly thickets, and brown, matted mesquite. Davey and
I were resting after a long ride; we were in a shade at the
brink of a grassy plateau; the rest was welcome, and I felt
more like dreaming than listening to Davey.

"They was hopin' to strike it rich, you see," went on
Davey, "an' they sure was a chanct in American cattle.
British lords flocked over here by the million, lookin' for
cash. Nowadays when a Britisher wants American dollars

he just grabs off a heiress or so an' hot-foots it back to his castle, turnin' his heiress over to the Lady-High-Some-thing-or-Other to be dressed down or up accordin' to the requirements of the nobility. After she's been made pre-sentable, she's introdooced to the queen, and the lord or duke—or whatever gits her—starts out to make his pile of American dollars look like a durty deuce in a pack of aces. They tell me that he gen'rally succeeds, but that ain't nei-ther here nor there. The point is—"

"How far would you say we are from the ranch?" I inquired at this juncture, hoping to divert Davey's thoughts.

"—the point is," resumed Davey, ignoring the interrup-tion, "that they wasn't so many heiresses then as they is now, an' your British lord had to make good in some other line. He took to cattle raisin' in preference to joinin' the army to fight the natives in Africa. Did you ever swap words with a real lord?"

One might as well have tried to harness Niagara with a shoestring, and so I gave up trying to divert Davey's mind from the British nobility and lay back with my hands clasped under my head and admired the clear blue of the New Mexican sky.

"Did you ever—" began Davey.

"Well, no," I returned; "that is, I never actually—"

"Well, I did!" declared Davey triumphantly. "An' you're from the East—sakes almighty! I hears they's scads of them lords around, lookin' up all the beef packers an' sausage makers an' so, to see whether they've got Ameri-can dollars enough to make a respectable figger in English pounds, an' so. An' you tell me you ain't never—well, I swan! But you don't need to feel bad about it; exceptin' in a thousand ways or so, British lords ain't no different than any other guy which c'n reel off English middlin' easy. This lord I was tellin' you about—or was I tellin' you?"

"I suppose it's all the same whether you were telling me or are going to tell," I began, feeling that I was in for it anyway.

"Skippin' over a lot at the start," went on Davey; "as I was about to say when you interrupted me, an' gettin' right down to the facts; the whole thing started when Sid Tucker, of the Lazy J, got word from his wife's brother—who had made four or seven million dollars in noiseless alarm clocks or rat traps or so, an' had a daughter which was dead set on takin' the eight or nine million to pay for the privilege of wearin' a cornet or a diagram—or some other musical instrument which the nobility sets on its head in place of a hat—that he was sendin' his daughter out West for a month or so. A British lord was comin' with her, and a maiden aunt for a chaperon. In the letter Tucker's brother-in-law asts if Tucker won't please do somethin' or other to break up the friendship between the lord an' his daughter.

"Well, that was a sure enough stunnin' combination to shove in front of an innocent cattleman. Tucker was plumb flabbergasted. 'Holy smoke!' he says when he could git his breath. 'I'm up ag'in it for fair! Whatinell will I do with a lord in this God-forsaken hole?'

"You never saw Webb Ball, did you?" suddenly demanded Davey. At my negative shake of the head pityingly: "Of co'se not—you didn't ever see him. You was just a kid when he was bossin' this here range."

"Bossing it?"

"That's what I said—bossin' it. An' nobody was questionin' his right to boss it. He was Tucker's foreman an' the fastest man on the draw an' the slickest bronc buster which ever forked a hoss. As I was tellin' you when you interrupted me: Webb Ball was a fine-lookin' man—a tall, upstandin', daredevil of a man which looked like one of them hero fellers which you see in the pitcher books. Of co'se he had a fault or so, but mostly he measured up to the size which has come to be considered the standard in these here parts. But I was tellin' you about the lord."

I reminded him that he had left Tucker facing a problem.

"Why, so I did!" he declared. " 'Whatinell will I do with a lord in this God-forsaken hole?' was what Tucker ast all of us. He had come down to the bunkhouse to tell us about the letter.

" 'What's he comin' out here for?' asts someone.

" 'He's comin' with a heiress,' said Tucker, 'which

heiress's father wants me to bust up the combination. Ben—that's my brother-in-law—says he'd rather have Evelyn—that's my niece—hooked up to a scrub cowpuncher. Whatinell will I do about it?'

" 'Turn him over to Ball,' says someone.

"I was lookin' at Ball an' I seen him sneer. 'Hell,' he says, lookin' straight at Tucker, 'I ain't figgerin' to be no lord's wet nurse!'

"Him an' Tucker kept lookin' at each other, an' I watched them pretty close. An' bimeby I thought I saw Tucker's eyewinkers flutterin' sorta peculiar.

" 'Webb,' he says sorta sorrowful like, 'it looks like a howlin' shame to have a bang-up American girl hooked up to a money-grubbin' member of the British nobility. It don't in no way fit in with my ideas of the speerut of American independence!'

"Webb didn't bat an eyewinker. 'It cert'nly ain't just the sort of thing which would make the eagle preen its feathers,' he said, sorta mild like. 'Still, they ain't no way of tellin' about a girl—mebbe she thinks her lord is holdin' a pretty good hand.'

" 'Mebbe,' admitted Tucker; 'they ain't no tellin'. But I reckon you've played poker some, Webb?'

" 'Some,' admitted Webb.

" 'Good hands don't always win at poker, Webb.'

" 'No, they don't,' agreed Webb.

" 'It all depends on who's holdin' the cards, Webb. I've seen a pair of jacks win a pot ag'in three aces an' a full house. I don't say it happens regular, but there's times when it does, Webb.'

" 'Yes,' agreed Webb, 'it does—sometimes. If you're thinkin' this game's goin' to be anything like poker, I'm willin' to take a hand.' "

Davey looked at me with a smile. "I reckon you git my meanin'?" he asked. "They was figgerin' to stack the cards ag'in the lord."

I nodded and Davey continued:

"I'm skippin' over a lot which followed—meetin's an' so between Tucker an' Ball, which I don't know nothin' about what happened at them, which I know was somethin'. Anyways, about a week after Tucker had took us into his confidence about the lord, Ball asts me to hook up the greys to the buckboard for a trip to Dry Bottom—me to do the drivin'. 'Goin' to git the lord an' Miss Evelyn,' he tells me, sorta grinnin'.

"When we git ready to start, I sees that he's ridin' Purgatory—which was the ornriest cayuse in his string, and which had killed two or three men, an' wouldn't allow he could be rid by anyone except Ball. 'What you doin' ridin' that devil?' I asts.

" 'Hush'' he says. 'Ain't we goin' to meet his lordship?'

"Sure enough we meets them, an' the maiden aunt. They wasn't nothin' about the maiden aunt to git excited over; she was just like one that I'd had myself back in the days when I was a kid—a fussy, suspicious ol' dame which had a good many eyes an' a mouth, or so. Anyways, she could talk! Hush! I've heard women which could—but shucks, what's the use? They're all that way, an' after lookin' Evelyn and the lord over, I didn't have much eyes left for the chaperon. Did I tell you how Evelyn looked? No, of co'se not—nobody could do that! I might git to her eyes an' her wavy hair, but that'd be about all. She had a way about her which I couldn't describe. The nearest I could come to it would be to say she was a thoroughbred—which will sorta give you an idee.

"British lords is a thing which I could never git no line on, bein' as I've never seen more'n one of them together in a corral at the same time. This here lord was the first one I'd seen, an' I allow I was some disappointed. I don't know just what I expected to see, but I'd got the idee that a lord must be some different than the rest of us, an' when I saw that he just about measured up with the average Eastern tenderfoot, I'm admittin' that I was some took back. But he was a clean-cut feller of about thirty, smooth-faced, with an inquirin' eye which could meet yourn pretty steady. He wasn't so tall as Ball, sorta blocky rather, but well put up.

"Soon's I saw the meetin' between Ball an' Miss Evelyn, I tumbled that Ball was dealin' the first hand in that game he'd talked about with Tucker. Ball wasn't nothin' like the Ball he'd been. He knowed the lord had a good hand, an' he was dependin' on bluffin' him from the start. Talk about puttin' it on! Laws almighty! When I saw him bowin' an' scrapin' to Miss Evelyn, I was sure some scared that he'd try to kiss her. His conduc' so got on my nerves that I was doin' the same thing to the ol' maid, bowin' and scrapin', I mean—lordy! How could any man kiss that!—when the lord—who'd been squintin' at me an' Ball sober like, up an' observes: 'By Jove, that's deucedly funny, don't yu' know!'

"I've thought since then that mebbe we did put it on a little too much, but if we did, it was Ball's fault, for I was playin' his hand. But I reckon Miss Evelyn didn't seen anythin' funny in it, for she was bowin' and scrapin' to Ball the same as he was to her, an' I don't know when I've seen a man bow any gracefuller than Ball did. I seen that he made a hit with Miss Evelyn, for a minute later when she was introdoocin' him to his lordship, I seen her lookin' at him sorta sideways, serious and appraisin' like. Ball had told her who he was while I'd been gassin' with his lordship.

"I could see that his lordship didn't like the way Ball had cottoned up to Miss Evelyn, for when she said to him, 'This is Mr. Webb Ball, my uncle's foreman; I am sure you'll like him,' his lordship soured up at Ball an' said in a tone of voice; 'I hope so, don't yu' know.' Which showed that he'd been doin' some tallyin' whilest I'd been gassin' to him.

"Pretty soon, whilest we was talkin', the ol' maid busts in with a question. How was we goin' to git to the ranch? Was we goin' to ride in 'that frail thing'?—pointin' to the buckboard.

"This give Ball just the chanct he was waitin' for. I seen his eyes sorta shine. But he says, casual like, 'The ladies will ride in the buckboard of co'se, an' his lordship. If his lordship was thinkin' of ridin' a hoss, he'll have to wait till we git to the ranch; there ain't nobody but an experienced rider c'n take liberties with my hoss.'

"I seen Miss Evelyn shoot a glance at his lordship from under her long eyewinkers, an' that glance sure did have a heap of significance in it. I'd have bet a month's wages right then that if she'd been a man, there wouldn't nobody ring in a bluff on her like that'n. But it went with his lordship all right. He sorta snickered an' said he'd not try ridin' till we got to the Lazy J. But Ball'd played the first card in the game, an' of co'se he'd wait now till his lordship got his cards all sorted out.

"Well, I hung onto the greys' heads till they got aboard. I was some disappointed to see the ol' maid climb into the front seat, for I'd been sorta figgerin' that it'd be much pleasanter ridin' beside Miss Evelyn. Ball hopped into the saddle an' we was off. Say! I've seen some swell riders, but I reckon I never seen any gracefuller ridin' than that which Webb Ball done that day. Miss Evelyn just couldn't keep her eyes offen him. Oncet I heard her say to his lordship; 'Isn't he perfectly lovely?' Which didn't seem to draw no reply from his lordship. I heard him sayin' somethin' about the dust an' the sun.

"But I reckon Miss Evelyn wasn't none interested in the dust nor the sun just then; she kept talkin' about Ball an' his ridin'. I could see that Ball's talk about his hoss had drawed her attention—which I knowed was Ball's game. I can't remember half what she said, but I heard her mention 'romance' in a trillin' sort of voice, an' somethin' about 'cowboy bravery'—which sorta made me swell up a little, though I ain't never met no brave cowpuncher, though I'm admittin' that I've seen them with nerve.

"Anyways, his lordship didn't seem to take kindly to Miss Evelyn's praise of Ball, an' after he'd stood it quite a while, he allowed that he could ride a hoss hisself. Followed some hounds, he said. I couldn't see nothin' excitin' about followin' dogs; I'd have been more interested if he'd said he'd followed a hoss thief, or so—I've had a plumb lovely time doin' it.

"But Miss Evelyn called him; you know how clever a

woman c'n do that. I sorta peeked back casual an' I seen her eyes dancin' with a plumb mischievous light. An' what she said to his lordship made me think I could see the feathers risin' on the back of our national bird.

" 'Yes,' she said in a sweet, Sunday-school-meetin' voice, 'followin' the hounds is an excitin' pastime, an' one must ride well. But that sort of thing ain't to be compared to the ridin' of the American cowboy.' Seemed as though what Ball had said had got to workin' on her, an' she was sorta darin' his lordship to measure up. An' his lordship riz to the bait.

" 'That's all jolly rot, don' yu' know, Miss Evelyn,' he sniffed. 'A rider is a rider whether he's a-top a steeple-chaser or one of them bally goats which our—ah-guide is ridin' oveh yondah.'

" 'Do you really think your lordship could ride one of them—er—goats?' said Miss Evelyn in a silky, insinuatin' voice.

"Of co'se that put it right up to his lordship. They wasn't no reniggin' after that, which his lordship must have knowed, for he up an' hollers to Ball—who's ridin' about fifty yards ahead.

" 'Hey, Ball—there's a good fellow. Stop a bit!' Which Ball pulled up an' waited whilest I druv up alongside him. 'If you don't mind,' says his lordship to Ball, 'I'm ridin' that bit of a goat which you've got between your knees!'

" 'Meanin' that you're wantin' to try an' ride my hoss?' asts Ball, squarin' around an' lookin' his lordship straight in the eyes.

"His lordship was already down an' walkin' toward Ball's horse, which as his lordship come near, snorted an' tried to back away. 'Did I understand you to say that you was thinkin' of *tryin'* to ride my hoss?' Ball asts him ag'in.

" 'You didn't hear me ast you that, don' yu' know,' says his lordship. 'What I did say to you was that I was *goin'* to ride him!'

"Ball grins—sorta pityin' like. Then he looks at Miss Evelyn sorta serious. Then he looks back at his lordship. 'I ain't in no ways desirin' to humble a member of the

British nobility,' he says—which I thought at the time was a right pretty speech—'but I'm tellin' you aforehand that this here hoss ain't never been rode by no lord, an' I'm some scared that he won't begin right now. But if you're dead set on tryin' to ride him,' he adds, winkin' at me, 'why of co'se that's your own funeral. But I'm callin' on the young lady to witness that I told you aforehand that he ain't never been rode by no lord.' Ball told me afterward that the game was to show Miss Evelyn the difference between a degenerated British lord and a simon-pure, dyed-in-the-wool, thirty-seven-carat American cowpuncher. Said he thought it'd create an impression in the young lady's mind

"Well, I ain't got no doubt that it did create an impression. Ball hung onto Purgatory's head whilest his lordship got into the saddle. 'Let go, my man,' says his lordship, an' Ball eased his hold of the bridle. Well, sir, things happened, as I knowed they would. Soon as Purgatory felt his lordship in the saddle, he looked sorta stunned like at Ball. I reckon it took him about ten seconds to kind of size up things, an' then without offerin' any apology, he made a plumb lovely jump about four or five feet straight up. Of co'se his lordship went up, too, but whilest he was up, Purgatory came down. An' of co'se his lordship came down, too, only he didn't come down at the same time, an' when he did, he run plumb into some New Mexican scenery, whilest Purgatory was sunfishin' sorta gleefully about a hundred yards away.

" 'I knowed it,' says Ball to Miss Evelyn, sorta dry like; 'that there hoss is forty-three-carat American, an' he won't let no british lord take no liberties with him. Mebbe you could coax his lordship to call it off?' he suggests, lookin' at her with a grin.

"I seen Miss Evelyn's chin go up a little. 'Indeed!' She tells Ball, lookin' him straight in the eye and reddenin' a little; 'His lordship isn't the man he ought to be if he allows himself to be coaxed *now*!' I could see that her American blood was up, an' if his lordship didn't ride Ball's hoss now, it was all day with him. She wouldn't want no lord which couldn't compare with an American cowboy. She watched sorta ca'm like whilest his lordship got untangled from the scenery an' stood there with his back to us, lookin' at Purgatory. An' there was a triflin' smile on her face when he turns to Ball an' says, 'By Jove, he sorta surprised me, don't yu' know, the bally brute. Do you think you could ketch him, my man?'

"Ball allowed he could an' he did. But when he led his hoss back to where his lordship was standin', he made the game strong. 'This here hoss,' he says, lookin' at his lordship an' not battin' an eyewinker, 'ain't hard to ride a'tall— if a man knows how to ride. More'n a million men has rode him, but mostly they wasn't lords.'

" 'It's a blasted country for exaggeration,' says his lordship, 'but I'm goin' to ride the bally goat or bust him!'

"Of co'se they wasn't no use of his lordship tryin' to ride Purgatory—nobody'd ever done that but Ball, an' they was some husky riders in that bunch of Lazy J boys. But his lordship made a good stab at it, an' things was plumb excitin' an' interestin' whilest they lasted. The trouble was that his lordship hadn't practiced ridin' volcanoes, an' Purgatory was sure a fifty-six-carat eruption. After he'd mussed up about half a mile of the landscape, his lordship was ready to give it up for a bad job. Say, he sure was a sight! I don't think I've ever looked at no mournfuler one. I sure did feel some sorry for him when he come back to the buckboard an' climbed in beside Miss Evelyn, sayin' nothin' an' Miss Evelyn settin' up awful straight an' tryin' to keep from laffin' in his lordship's face.

"They wasn't no more said till we'd got back to the Lazy J. They wasn't nothin' said then—by his lordship. Only Tucker ast him how he come to be so mussed up, an' he sorta grinned an' said he'd been ridin' Ball's hoss. But Miss Evelyn stiffened an' sniffed an' allowed that most of the time the hoss had been ridin' his lordship. The British nobility got a powerful setback there an' went into the house to git about a million yards of the landscape offen him.

"Well, his lordship wasn't exactly reclinin' in no bed of

roses after that. Miss Evelyn didn't seem to be interested
in him no more. Durin' the next two or three days, Tucker
had Ball gentlin' a hoss for her. That's about the only time
I ever seen Ball loafin'. Usual he'd gentle a hoss in two or
three hours at the most—or maul him around so's he'd
think he'd been playin' tag with a cyclone. But this here
hoss appeared to be unnatural hard to gentle. I seen Ball
leadin' him around by the bridle, Miss Evelyn settin' in
the saddle, takin' things easy like, an' smilin' at Ball an'
talkin' to him low. All this time his lordship was mopin'
around the ranchhouse. Seems as though he knowed he'd
got in bad by makin' a mess of ridin' Purgatory after he'd
yawped about that there animal bein' a goat.

"But whatever he thought, Ball had took the first pot,
an' I've allowed ever since that he'd played right up to the
limit. An' he kept right on—it was a clear case of stackin'
the cards. After Ball got Miss Evelyn's hoss gentled, nobody seen much of them durin' the day. Ridin' they was
mostly, I reckon, but I figger that Ball spent some of his
time tryin' to show Miss Evelyn that it would be more
patriotic for her to cotton up to a simon-pure, forty-seven-
carat American cowpuncher than to wear a cornet or a diagram.

"Well, sir, things sorta drifted along with Ball and Miss
Evelyn gittin' more an' more chummy, an' his lordship
mopin' more an' more. I could see that his lordship was
gittin' desperate, for one mornin, just after Ball an' Miss
Evelyn had gone off for a ride, I met him down by the gate
of the hoss corral, lookin' in kind of wistful at the hosses.
I didn't want to hurt his feelin's, an' so I just mentioned
Ball—casual like. Say! His lordship knowed what had come
off all right! I seen his eyes git sorta sharp an' chilly when
I spoke about Ball. But he wasn't no squealer.

" 'I rawther think you know hosses, my man,' he says
to me. I allowed that I'd had some experience with cayuses.

" 'Then I fawncy you know somethin' about that bally
beast 'Purgatory,' says his lordship, lookin' at me straight.

" 'More'n I'll ever find out ag'in by ridin' him,' says I,

thinkin' of how shameful I'd been treated when I'd tried to ride that hoss a year before.

"I begun to see that his lordship had figgered out that Ball'd been at the bottom of his troubles since comin' to the Lazy J. Of co'se some men would have tumbled to it sooner—but mebbe not.

" 'I fawncy nobody's rode him,' he says; 'neither no cowboys nor no lords.' An' I had to admit he was right.

"Well, after that his lordship didn't mope around no more. He got a hoss from Tucker which he could ride— an' he rode him. But he didn't look none graceful, seein' that he'd been used to a short stirrup—an' no cow pony is goin' to let nobody ride him with the stirrups up on his neck. An' so his lordship didn't cut no figger ridin'.

"The boys joshed him a heap; they pulled off tricks on him which they mostly kept in stock for tenderfeet. I ain't sayin' nothin' about how they went bear huntin' with him; how they rustled a bear an' got him to chasin' his lordship an' how the bear treed him, and how they roped the bear just when he was makin' things mighty interestin'. Nor I ain't sayin' anythin' about how they took him snipe huntin' an' had him holdin' the bag the biggest part of the night, settin' on a stump with a red lantern beside him so's the snipes could see to git into the bag. As I say, I ain't tellin' about them little things, though, take it all together, they succeeded in makin' things plumb interestin' an' excitin' for his lordship.

"But his lordship was game an' never squealed—takin' his medicine like a little man. Of co'se he didn't know nothin' about it, but mostly Tucker was behind the whole business. An' Ball wasn't so innocent as he appeared to be—though one day I heard him tellin' Miss Evelyn that lords was plumb ignorant an' couldn't be expected to measure up to American size.

"But I'm skippin' over a lot of preliminaries to git at the big pot. Of co'se after his lordship had been mauled around consid'able, he got wise to the fact that someone was makin' a fool of him. But that was after him an' Miss

Evelyn had been at the ranch for over three weeks an' was figgerin' on hittin' the breeze back East.

"Women is queer critters—now ain't they?" Davey suddenly questioned, looking at me with a defiant eye. "There was Miss Evelyn. She'd been actin' all along like she was plumb tickled that his lordship had been gittin' his in big doses. She'd been makin' things more onpleasant for him by cottonin' up to Ball. Well, you'd think that after his lordship had got his'n, she'd be satisfied. But that was where everybody was fooled, for what did she do but take to pityin' him—an' right out in public! She give Ball his Coupa Disgrace—as them dago duelists say—and rides off with his lordship—sayin' that she wasn't goin' to let no tribe of savages bully no member of the British nobility. She'd got wise, too.

"Well, that put a crimp in Ball an' the rest of us. I wish you could have seen Ball! He done mavericked for two whole days, an' nobody done seen him atall! But he shows up at the home ranch after a while, an' him an' Tucker does some more talkin' about poker an' bluffin'. Then him an' Tucker cooks up a deal.

" 'Somethin's got to be done,' allows Tucker; 'it won't do for me to send Miss Evelyn back thinkin' as much of that lord as she did when she come out here. We've got to the point where we'll have to git real busy. Women,' he says, 'like men which is heroes. There ain't no woman which can't be won by a hero. Pick up any storybook, read it frontways, sideways, backward, or upside down, an' you'll find there's always a hero an' that he wins the girl every time. Now what I'm figgerin' on is to make Ball a hero.'

" 'Not by a jugful,' says Ball, sneerin' like; 'don't you go for to try an' make no hero outen me. I won't stand for it!'

" 'Not a real, simon-pure, sixty-three carat hero,' says Tucker, gentle like; 'it would be unpossible to make ar real hero outen you. Real heroes is only for story-books. What I'm wantin' to make outen you is a phoney hero. That c'n be done easy. What I'm figgerin' on is this: Tomorrow one of the boys c'n ride over to Bill Parker's place in Dry Bottom an' buy about a million blank kattridges—which Bill got in a consignment about a year ago an' couldn't sell 'cause the boys'd ruther shoot the real thing on the fourth of July. Anyways, that ain't the point. One of you boys'll git the blanks. Then we-all load up with them.

" 'Tomorrow night we'll git Miss Evelyn an' his lordship to ride out on the other side of ol' Baldy'—which was a hill down the crick aways. 'We'll be in the brush, layin' for them an' when they come close we'll pop out an' make them think we're holdin' them up. There'll be a plumb lovely time—with the blank kattridges a-poppin' an' his lordship's eyes stickin' out. He'll be half-scared to death an' when things gits right warm, Ball c'n butt in an' run us all off an' save Miss Evelyn. I reckon she won't pity his lordship none after that, an' she'll be some stuck on Ball.'

"Well, all the boys was enthoosiastic. The next day Bud Hiller hits the breeze to Dry Bottom an' comes back loaded with the blank kattridges. We sorta laid low that day—given' his lordship an' Miss Evelyn plenty of room. An' that night it all come off.

"I don't know how Tucker fixed it up, but that night about nine o'clock when we was all layin' in the brush alongside of the trail around Ol'Baldy, Miss Evelyn an' his lordship come ridin' along, quiet an' easy as you please. As they got near us, we could hear his lordship talkin'. An' what do you 'spose he was sayin'? 'Bravery, don't yu' know, Miss Evelyn, isn't no local characteristic; we in England have been brave for thousands of years.' Wow! I reckon we all laid still just long enough for that there braggin' of his to git soaked in good an' proper, an' then we riz up out of the brush, hopped on our cayuses, an' went after his lordship.

"Talk about smokin' her up! I reckon that in the two or three minutes we was engaged with the enemy, we must have burned up about a million kattridges. The boys' sixes was a-sparkin' an' a-poppin' an' a-crackin', an' Miss Evelyn was screamin' an' hangin' onto her cayuse's neck, an' the smoke got so thick around that we had to brush it away with our hands so's we wouldn't be shootin' into one another's faces.

"Well, I allow we had some fun whilest it lasted. It appeared that his lordship was in pretty near as bad shape as Miss Evelyn at the start. Plumb scared out, we thought. But pretty soon, when the boys got kind of tired, I seen his lordship yank out a gun. Zam! It went handy enough. But I nearly fell offen my horse laffin' at him, for Tucker'd told us that he'd pulled all the ball kattridges outen his lordship's gun, an' of co'se he was shootin' blanks like the rest of us. Therefore it sorta surprised me when, after his lordship had let his gun go, I seen Bud Hiller holler an' fall ker-plunk outen his saddle. 'Ball kattridges, you fools!' he yells as he's layin' on the ground; 'the damn fool's got ball kattridges!'

'Well, that sorta stampeded the whole bunch; they wasn't none of us left around that there spot in about a jiffy. We backed away till we was out of range, an' just about that time—accordin' to the program—Ball busts out of the brush down the trail an' comes a tearin' toward Miss Evelyn an' his lordship.

"Surprised? Well, mebbe Ball wasn't. Anyways, when he git close enough, his lordship opens up ag'in. Down goes Ball's hoss, with Ball doin' a double sommerset all over the landscape. Ball wasn't hurt none, but I allow when he got up, he didn't have time to play hero, for his lordship kept poppin' away with his gun, an' Ball had plenty to do dodgin' an' hoppin' an' crawlin' to keep from gittin' perforated. But he got away without gittin' hit, an' we-all trailed back to the bunkhouse, feelin' kind of down in the mouth over the way things had turned out. The last we saw of his lordship, he was holdin' Miss Evelyn close to him an' strokin' her hair, an' she hangin' on to him like she was double clinchin' that diagram. The boys done a heap of cussin'."

"So his lordship wasn't a coward after all?" I suggested.

"Well," returned Davey, squintin' at me with a humorous eye, "mebbe not. It's some certain that Ball didn't look like no hero to Miss Evelyn, for the next day her an' his lordship took the train East. The worst of it was that Tucker sends me an' Ball to take them over to Dry Bottom. Neither me nor Ball done much talkin' on the way over; we spent most of our time listenin' to his lordship tellin' Miss Evelyn about the scrap. Miss Evelyn kept tellin' his lordship that she'd have quite a story to tell her friends about his lordship's bravery; how, single-handed, he'd licked about a million road agents. Once his lordship opined to me that it was 'extraordinary' how so large a gang of outlaws could roam the country like that. I didn't say nothin', not wantin' to give him a hint of the truth.

"Well, when the train come, his lordship helped Miss Evelyn on. He stayed on the back platform, talkin' to me an' Ball. His lordship done most of the talkin', as we couldn't find just the words we wanted to use.

"After a while the train started. His lordship grinned. 'I didn't ride your bally goat,' he says to Ball, with a wink, 'but I rawther think I showed you that shootin' blank kattridges wouldn't make a hero outen you.'

'I seen Ball's jaws saggin', an' my own felt like injy rubber with all the stiffenin' out of it. But of co'se Ball felt it more'n me, seein' that he was the one which had been on the inside track. 'Blank kattridges!' he says, snarlin' like a coyote. 'Whatinell do you know about them blank kattridges?'

"The train was goin' steady away. But his lordship laffs at Ball an' says, grinnin' all over his face: 'I was hidin' in the bunkhouse the night you-all cooked the blank kattridge deal. I'd have been plum chawmed if I'd have hit you instead of your bally goat—you sagebrush pirate!'

" 'I'll pirate you—you—' begins Ball, an' yanks his gun out an' begins shootin' at his lordship. But his lordship ain't none scared. He don't move out of his tracks whilest Ball's shootin'. But he laffs, sneerin' like.

" 'I drawed your gun before we left the ranchhouse, you blawsted idiot,' he says. 'You're still shootin' blank kattridges!' "

Davey hesitated. "Well?" I inquired, looking at him.

"Well," he returned, grinning. "It's about ten miles, if you want to know so bad."

"Ten miles to where?" I foolishly questioned.

"Ten miles to the ranchhouse," said Davey. "Didn't you ast me?"

Thomas Thompson has had two separate and highly successful careers involving the romance of the American West. As a fiction writer in the forties and fifties, he produced such outstanding novels as Gunman Brand, The Steel Web, *and* Bitter Water *and such expert short stories as "Blood on the Sun" and "Gun Job," which won consecutive Western Writers of America Spurs in 1953 and 1954. And in the sixties and early seventies, as both screenwriter and associate producer, he played a vital role in making* Bonanza *one of the most popular of all TV Western series. Thompson's fictional talents are nowhere more sharply honed than in "The Silver Dollar," the deceptively simple tale of a confrontation between a tough old cowman and a nester family—a story that says more about frontier life in 1,500 words than most stories do at much greater length.*

The Silver Dollar

Thomas Thompson

*B*y whipping Harold Calvert with his fists, Big Ben Lathrop found that this nester was different from most of the crew that came in broken wagons with mended tools, complaining of the heat, complaining of the cold, and never having the courage to admit that their discomforts were of their own making. Calvert hadn't asked for help as a permanent part of his existence; he hadn't tried to become a leech living on the abundant blood of the cattleman. He had been willing to fight for the land he was trying to own; and he had lost like a man.

But Calvert was one of them, and in time he built the

inevitable fence around his quarter section of land; and he put a timber-framed gate across the lane that led to the shack by the river. To add to that, he brought a boy with him to this unfenced land that Big Ben ruled—a towheaded twelve-year-old with a rag-bound toe and the level eye of an older man.

Ben Lathrop had little time for kids. He told the boy so the first time he caught Lonnie Calvert loping one of his father's mules, pretending to trail-drive four of Lathrop's cows across the alkali sink back of the butte. For answer the kid silently admired Ben's horse, and then without self-consciousness tried to imitate the easy slouch with which Big Ben sat his deep, brush-scarred saddle. It was an annoying thing.

Perhaps it was the boy that disturbed Big Ben now; perhaps it was something else. Whatever it was, the devil deserved his due, and Ben Lathrop was the first man to admit it. Calvert had fought well in an impossible fight, and he had won consideration if not victory. Admitting that, Ben Lathrop was bringing his own wagon to help the nester move, and he was bringing a silver dollar to salve any disappointment the kid might feel. What more could a man do?

The thing they didn't understand—none of them understood—was that a man had to earn his right to stay on a piece of land. Ben Lathrop himself hadn't always been big. He had had to grow, and it had been a slow process. Down there in the flat where the nester now had his shack, Ben had seen his mother killed by an Indian arrow. After that he had watched his father die too slowly of a broken heart. And once, when the old man was sick, Ben himself, twelve years old, had stood on this ground, holding a Sharps rifle in his hand, and convincing four riders he had a right to stay. A man didn't forget those things.

Still there was an uneasy concern on Ben Lathrop's broad face as he drove the wagon across the familiar undulations of the prairie toward the bottoms where Calvert and his son had settled. It wasn't that he expected further trouble from Calvert. The man had taken his beating and accepted it. It was just that he didn't want to be misunderstood, especially by the kid. It was why he had brought the silver dollar. There was no sense hurting the kid in a man's affair—

It was odd how in the few months the Calverts had been here, Lonnie had become a part of things. People had grown used to seeing him, in front of the barber shop in town usually, bareheaded and barefooted, watching with his serious eyes, his thumbs hooked in the suspenders of his faded bib overalls. Without knowing why, people knew that he was thinking of the day when he could have a mug in that shop, with his name in gold letters. It got so they spoke to him, and it was like a pleasant habit. He would answer them slowly, carefully, with a certain aloofness in his voice. It came to them gradually that he answered them much as Big Ben Lathrop might have answered them.

Ben himself hadn't noticed it much until the day Lonnie got his first pair of skintight waist overalls and the mail-order high-heel boots. He saw the boy that day standing in front of Millroy's staring intently at a cheap high-crown hat. Ben spoke to the boy before he thought.

"Good-looking hat."

Lonnie had turned, appraised Ben thoughtfully, hooked his thumbs in the beltless band of his overalls, and said, "It ain't too bad." It was an expression that Ben Lathrop always used.

He watched the boy more closely after that, and through him Ben became acutely conscious of mannerisms of his own that he had never noticed before. There was the habit of hooking his thumbs in his waistband and tilting back some on his heels before speaking. And the way he had of rolling his tongue against his cheek and pointing with his head when giving a simple direction. Ben realized finally that the kid was imitating him. The discovery was not entirely unpleasant.

The team strained up a roll of land, and Ben came to the place in the road where he could look down on the flats and see the shack there by the river. Some unidentifiable fragrance in the air brought a remembrance of yesterday. The sun lingered along the thin strands of new wire, and the posts of the framed gate duplicated themselves in dark shadows. Ben took a bandanna and gingerly wiped the dust and sweat from his still-bruised face. Calvert, the nester, had fixed the old place up quite a bit.

Ben had tried his best not to think of Lonnie, but now the pretense was useless. He felt in the pocket of his overalls, and the silver dollar was there—a new one with its mint shine and all the promise a dollar could have for a twelve-year-old boy.

He knew then that this was his compromise; this was the time he could not move a man from his land without giving something in return. He spoke to the team, and the wagon rolled down the incline toward the gate in the lane.

He was quite near before he saw the boy standing there in the shadow of the gatepost. At first it bothered him, then he relaxed, knowing it would be better this way. He could speak to the boy as if nothing were wrong, give him the dollar, and drive on to his house. By the time the boy knew what was going on, the wagon would be loaded and it would be over. The dollar would make everything all right—It wasn't until he drew his team up at the gate that he noticed the boy had a rifle.

It was an old gun, a short-barrel .30-30 carbine. The boy carried it leisurely in the crook of his arm, and when he looked at Ben, he shifted the weight of the rifle slightly.

"Can I do somethin' for you?" the boy asked.

Ben looked at him. He was wearing his waist overalls, his high-heel boots. He stood with his feet spread just enough, his head tilted to one side, the rifle resting easily across his arm. His eyes were a bright and unsmiling blue.

Ben said, "I wanted to talk to your dad." His hand closed around the silver dollar.

The boy ducked his head slightly and spit over his chin, much the way Big Ben might have done it. His left hand slid along the barrel of the rifle and his right hand gripped the stock near the trigger guard.

He said, "Dad's ailin' some today. You can talk to me."

Ben wrapped the lines around the brake and started to slide out of the seat. He stopped in that position, looking

down. He saw a boy, too thin, with an uncombed shock
of sun-faded hair and eyes that were too old for his face.
A wisp of breeze lifted a faint flag of dust and brushed it
against Ben's nostrils with a vague familiarity. Over by the
fence a meadowlark trilled once, an unchangeable song.
The nearly imperceptible scent of the river was in the air.

He had a strange feeling of being moved backward—
back to another time but not to another place. A little line
of perspiration formed on his forehead. He slid back into
the seat and slowly unwrapped the lines from around the
brake. The sun blistered across the land that had changed
little in forty years.

"Just happened to be going by," he said.

The boy said, "Right neighborly of you to stop. We'll
drop in on you some time."

"You do that," Ben said.

He turned the wagon and headed back down the road,
and there was no feeling of defeat in him. Rather it was
one of completeness. There for a second he had gotten a
glimpse of himself just as he had been at this boy's age.
He remembered how he had stood in a spot not far from
here with an old Sharps rifle in his hand. He would have
used that rifle that day if the need had arisen. He had bought
his right to stay here and grown because of that decision.

The dust of his own wagon wheels was pleasantly thick
as Big Ben Lathrop drove slowly back. The dryness of the
day touched his throat, and he decided that when he got
back to town he would buy a couple of drinks.

That was about all a dollar was good for anyway, when
you came right down to it.

A member of the first rank of popular Western writers for more than forty years, Frank Bonham began writing for the pulps in 1941, soon graduated to such slick magazines as The Saturday Evening Post *and* Liberty, *and turned to novels in 1948. Among the most notable of his Western novels are* Lost Stage Valley, Snaketrack, Hardrock, *and* Break for the Border. *In addition to his fiction, he contributed scripts to such Western TV shows of the fifties and sixties as* Tales of Wells Fargo *and* Death Valley Days. *Although "The Seventh Desert" is one of his early stories, it ranks with the best of the many he has written about cattlemen in the Southwest.*

The Seventh Desert

Frank Bonham

*W*hen they had put the fifth desert behind them, *Cole* Allan began to imagine he could smell California in the wind coming out of the West. Old-timers called the southern route to California the Trail of the Seven Deserts. Some turned back at the first desert, in Texas; some struggled on to succumb to the hot sands of New Mexico. And some reached California, but they were not many.

Cole Allan was traveling what you might call heavy. He had four hundred Texas steers, an aged cowpuncher, a spring wagon, and a new bride. Between the bride and the wagon it was a tossup as to which had lost more of its look of shining newness on that last scrape across New Mexico.

Partly on Elly's account, Cole had swung northwest across the mountains instead of southwest and around them;

and partly for himself, because no man hated heat and thirst much worse than Cole Allan, and there was nothing between Lordsburg and Tucson but sand and heat and whirlwinds.

Tonight they bedded the cattle on a little stream that ran through a pocket of rocky hills.

After the plains, this Arizona high-rolls country was cool and pleasant. The sunset was a glory of gold and purple. Elly stood a long time looking at it; Cole could see the tranquillity of the scene reflected in her face. It relieved him; he had worried about her lately. Only eighteen she was, still a girl in so many ways, and yet with a woman's quiet strength in her.

Elly said softly, "I could live here forever, Cole. The trees, and the water—the mountains . . ."

Cole's arm was about her waist. "It's nice," he admitted. "Of course it ain't California, but it looks good after the desert. You wait till we hit the coast!"

Elly had heard it all before, but he knew she was not listening to him now. Her eyes were dreaming. "Right in those trees I'd want the cabin."

Cole glanced at her. She had never talked of quitting; he hoped she was not going to do it now.

"I'd better drive the cattle out of the creek before they founder," he told her.

Elly said hesitantly, "Cole," and he turned back.

"Cole, dear, I think we're going to have to stop before we reach California. You see, we—we're going to have a family."

It hit Cole Allan between the eyes.

"I've known for quite a while," Elly told him. "I hated to tell you. I know how set you are on getting to California."

A mixture of gladness and disappointment filled Cole Allan. He said slowly, thinking his way, "Why, that's fine, Elly. Maybe it ain't like I'd have planned it, but we'll do the only thing we can. We'll throw up something temporary. In a year you and the baby will be fit to travel." He scanned her critically. "First thing," he said efficiently, "is to get you built up. I'll start weanin' Sudy's calf tomorrow. You'll need lots of milk."

Elly's eyes filled. "You're so kind, Cole," she said, "so understanding."

"No such thing," Cole declared. "You set yonder by the creek now while I get the dishes washed up."

Cole cut wild hay to blend with the adobe mud he and Shorty mixed for bricks. They built a one-room cabin with an adjoining lean-to. They laid out a stone corral. Looking the place over, Cole thought it wasn't so bad.

He tried to picture what it would be like around Los Angeles now. Cool, he bet; a refreshing shower every day that kept the grass green at all times. That was how the railroad pamphlets put it. Thousands of other folks were heading for California this summer of 1870. Cole didn't know how much land would be left after a year lost on the trail, but this California was a pretty big place.

One day, two weeks after they finished the cabin, four cowboys came through. They were pushing a bunch of steers down the ridge behind the cabin. Three of them stayed with the cattle while the fourth jogged down to where Cole was milking.

The stranger stood down beside his horse and looked the layout over with a slow, appraising eye. He said to Cole, offering his hand, "Pete Hubbell. Figure to stay on here, friend?"

"Might," Cole said. He reckoned the man's age at about forty-five. He was thick-limbed. He had black hair that curled up under his hat brim. In a reckless sort of way he was pleasant-looking.

"It's a good country," Hubbell said. "How much of it you claiming?"

Cole thought there was amusement in his eyes. He said, "Why, about all I can cover with my hat—in a day's riding."

Smiling, Hubbell began to tap the palm of his hand with two thick fingers. "There's just two things wrong with your plans," he told Cole. "In the first place, the Apaches like this stretch, too. They ain't always nice-mannered people. In the second place," he concluded, "this here range happens to belong to me—about sixty thousand acres of it."

Cole did not blink. "I thought it was government range," he said. "Appears to me there's enough room out here for all the cattlemen in Texas."

"It's the water, friend," said Hubbell. His eyes could grow unfriendly without seeming to affect the rest of his features. "I've filed on Peach Creek, do you see? You're welcome to stop here four-five days and rest your stock; but I don't allow no squatters."

Cole said, "My missus is expecting, Hubbell. I'm not taking her over the mountains until she and the baby are fit to travel. But I'll gladly pay you range lease. I don't see that you're running many cows hereabouts. Haven't passed ten head in a week."

Pete Hubbell said, "I'm mighty careful about overstocking." He turned the stirrup to his toe and mounted. He moistened a forefinger to register the direction of the wind. "Southwest," he said. "Means the desert is a-frying. Means the Apaches may visit you. But they won't misput you any, because you'll have moved on by then. I'll be back from Tucson in a few days; it'll be best if you ain't around."

Elly heard it all from the window of the cabin. When Cole turned, she was standing in the doorway.

"It was my fault, Cole," she said. "I shouldn't have made you stop. We'll go on a ways. I'll be all right."

Cole held her by the shoulders. "We'll stay right here," he declared. "Hubbell was just testing his wind. Two Texans are equal to a parcel of Arizonians any day of the week." He said, "You get back inside and rest. You look peaked."

Pete Hubbell did not reappear that week, nor the week thereafter. Cole Allan spaced his cattle around so that the graze would not be cut back in any one section. He meant to play square with Hubbell so that he would have no possible grievance.

He saw the cattle begin to put on tallow. Elly seemed pathetically eager to make him like the country. She picked berries and made jellies for him; she planted things around the cabin to give it a look of permanence.

Cole and Shorty were range-branding some late calves the day the man called California appeared.

He was a leathery little cowpuncher in his forties, riding a white-stockinged bay with a pack animal in tow. He watched the Texans wrestle a big coming-yearling.

At the moment Cole Allan was too engrossed in trying to flank the brute to pay much attention to the visitor. Suddenly the animal began to hump. Cole was deposited on his hunkers, while old Shorty, who was always more or less crippled up with rheumatism, swore ineffectively and threw a rock at the departing rump.

The stranger slipped his catch rope from the saddle, shook out a loop, and spilled the calf without running ten feet. This time Cole was sitting on the animal before it could rise.

Afterward, Cole said to the stranger, "You've worked cattle before, mister. Like to work them some more? Me and Shorty can't seem to be enough places at once."

The man looked up at the sky, as if the answer might be written in the weather. "I've got a little time," he said. "I'll see if I like it. You can call me California."

Cole's smile was as warm as his handshake. "There's nothing I'd rather call you," he said. "Matter of fact, I'm a-heading for the coast myself. But we're taking time out to have a family."

California shrugged. "Hope you like it," he said. "Some do." It wasn't quite clear to Cole whether he meant California or having a family.

As they rode in that night, Cole's conscience began to scrape. "Something I ought to tell you," he said. "I'm what you might call poaching here. The land belongs to a man named Hubbell. Until this baby is born, I don't aim to travel. There may be bad blood between us."

California gave a short hard laugh. "Pete Hubbell owns all of Arizona, to hear him tell it. If you weren't new here, you'd know about him. He steals cattle in the States and sells 'em in Mexico. Then he brings back a herd of wet cattle to sell here. Thing of it is, he don't want anybody on his favorite holding grounds to check up on him."

Cole Allan nodded. "I figured it might be like that," he remarked. "He mentioned Indians, too. What about them?"

"That's another story," said California. "Some tribes will bother you. Some won't. Mostly they keep to the reservations. Just assume that they're all after your scalp, and you'll get along best."

In his close-mouthed cynical way, California soon made himself indispensable around the ranch. A month after he arrived, he moved his blankets out of the lean-to that he shared with Shorty.

"I've got the crawlin' fidgets," he told Cole. "I'll sleep out a few nights."

The next morning the Indians came.

A single gunshot planted Cole bolt upright in the bed beside Elly. There was a great rustling in the grass, and then a soft thunder of unshod hoofs. There was another shot.

He laid the barrel of his rifle across the mud sill. In the ghostly half daylight he perceived a line of horses passing the window. But the moving file had no end—it was the rim of a wheel, the cabin was the hub.

Shorty's gun began to roar from the dark wedge of the lean-to. Cole shouted at Elly, "Get the carbine! Keep loading!"

He got into the rhythm of the spinning wheel. Fire between two horses and you would hit the second. The terror of his violent awakening had passed. He was proud, and a bit relieved, that he was able to live up to his own code of courage. He was proud of Elly quietly, hurriedly reloading the guns as he passed them to her.

Out there in the dark a lone rifle spoke from time to

time. It was California's .45-90 hacking holes in the line of riders.

Down in the bosque a flame broke out, flickered, and then flared brighter. Pitch fire, thought Cole; and the portent of it came upon him with a sense of horror that shamed his recent courage.

He watched the arrows arch across the corral and heard four solid thunks as they hit the roof. He looked at Elly. She was loading. She had not seen them. "Oh, God!" he murmured. He had meant to cover the riprapping of willow poles and cottonwood *vigas* with earth long ago.

He kept waiting for the heat. While he waited, he fought, and up in the rocks California was fighting. From the lean-to, Shorty's gun spoke with brash defiance. Suddenly Cole realized that there were quite a few Indians on the ground. The fabric of the noose was unraveling.

Elly said urgently, "Cole!" and tugged at his arm.

"I know," he said. "They did it with pitch-pine arrows. But they won't be around when we come out. They've about got their bellies full."

Elly obediently turned her back on the corner of the ceiling that was blackening, with tendrils of smoke leaking down and now and then a savage little lick of flame. She handed him the carbine.

Cole said, Keep it. Start shooting when I say."

Elly put the gun to her shoulder. Under the redoubled fire, the line of Indians swerved. California's rifle roared encouragement.

In the end, it was the thunder of his Sharps that convinced the Indians there was nothing in this small cabin worth dying for. They disappeared into the tall grass.

California kept guard while the others formed a bucket brigade from the horse trough. Luckily the roof timbers were still green. They burned reluctantly, finally subsiding into sullen steaming.

In the wreckage of her kitchen corner, Elly started to cook breakfast. Suddenly she sat down and covered her face with her hands. She cried, softly at first, then with terrible, convulsive sobs.

"It was my fault," she cried. "We might all have been killed. I'd have been to blame. Cole, I—I lied to you."

Cole said sharply. "No one's to blame. Get hold of yourself." Then curiosity crept into him. "What do you mean, you lied to me?"

Elly's fingers clenched whitely. "About the baby. I'm not going to have one, Cole! Only I couldn't cross another desert. Not then. I'm not a pioneer; I'm just a wife that wants to settle somewhere."

Her voice took on a small note of accusation. "I couldn't ask you to stop, because you'd say I was soft. You'd hate me. I thought I'd tell you later I'd been mistaken about the baby."

Cole got up. He stood in the doorway.

Elly said, "So now we can go on."

Cole would not look at her. "No," he said, "we're staying. Pete Hubbell is not going to brag to all Arizona that he scared a Texan. You got us into this, and you'll see it through with me."

Cole was angry and hurt; hurt because Elly hadn't trusted him with her feelings, angry because she did not possess the iron with which he had credited her. It troubled him because he knew a timid woman would be a stone around a man's neck out here.

At dinner that night Elly made her very last speech on the subject of pioneering.

"If some people wouldn't be so high-handed," she said, "it would be easier for a body to talk to them. I'd have let you know how I felt in New Mexico, excepting you were always taking about the weaklings that never made it to California." She sniffed. "How do you know this California is such a rose garden, anyway? With you, California is just a frame of mind."

Some deep-rooted wisdom cautioned Cole Allan to hold his tongue.

It was the weather which settled Cole's problem of whether to go or stay. In the air the next dawning there was the first taste of autumn. The heat would be going out of the lava-studded plains between Phoenix and the Colorado.

He said to Shorty and California, "I figure to pull out next week. By the time we get across the mountains, the desert will be fit to travel."

California licked a cigarette. "I'll help you across the mountains," he remarked, "but after that I draw my time. My compass points east."

They rode down Peach Creek to South Fork to start the strays moving in. There was a purplish haze over the land. It was a friendly sort of country, thought Cole.

They came onto a mesa and saw, below them, a train of five wagons at the ford. Four of them stood on the east bank, but the fifth was bed-deep in mud.

They rode down, watching the emigrants bend their strength to the wheels of the mired wagon. The wagon boss waded to the bank.

"Could shore use a pull, boys," he declared. "Don't want to take the mules out of harness again if I can help it." Like the rest of the men, and the women sitting on the wagons, he looked pinched, tired, brown and dry as the earth itself.

Cole noticed that the sideboards of the wagons were weathered; the mules were no more than racks of bone and hide.

They flipped ropes to the wagon and brought it out of the stream. The wagon boss wiped his forehead.

"That's number two hundred and sixty-five," he said. "This stretch has been the worst since Californy."

That the caravan was heading east struck Cole for the first time. He noticed a faded "California, By Heck!" painted on one of the canvas tilts. "What's the matter with California?" he challenged.

"Why, nothing much," said the other, "providing you like land sharks and deserts, and coolie labor on the land you thought you were going to work."

Cole stared at the man, condemning him. "If trouble rubs the polish off a man," he declared, "he ought to stay home."

The emigrant colored but not with shame. "I've seen my share of trouble," he retorted, "but I hadn't seen anything till I hit Californy. We're farming people. All the land except the deserts is owned by railroads and rich ranchers. They'll throw a squatter off before he can water his team. Some of the folks that went out there in '49 are still hunting a place to settle. The only free land is the deserts."

He stumped back to his wagon. Cole watched the caravan slowly lumber up the next hill. . . .

They found a few cattle on South Fork and got them drifting up the creek. But Cole was thinking of the face of the wagon boss—sour, pessimistic, defeated—and he was hating it. The man lied; his face lied. Cole Allan had seen the railroad tracts that told about good, cheap land in California; they wouldn't let them print stuff like that if it weren't true.

In the dusk they neared the cabin. Suddenly Cole said to California, "There's weak ones in any country. They make room for the strong." And for the first time he asked California about his name. "You ought to know California," he challenged, "being that you carry it for a name."

"Sure I know California. I lost an eye on the Mojave. Ran out of water, and there I laid till somebody found me. My hat covered one eye, but the sun did for the other."

"But the desert's only part of it!" Cole said desperately.

"California," said the cowpuncher, "is no better nor worse than a lot of places in the East. But the good land ain't free. And the free land ain't good. And to hell with the railroad and its pamphlets. Unless a man's well heeled, it's about twenty years late for pioneering."

Cole Allan had no answer. California was one man you couldn't call a weakling.

Gradually, as they rode, he took a good look around him. There were a lot of things he had been thinking about this country that weren't true. He liked its moods: the bright optimism of its mornings; the way the sun went down pensively at night, as if on a long sigh.

They pulled out of the bosque just below the cabin. And all in a moment fear caught Cole by the throat. Elly! Elly was alone, and there were horses before the cabin.

He rode the last hundred yards in a lope. When he realized that it was Pete Hubbell, he was both angry and lightheaded with relief. She'd be scared foolish.

But if she were frightened, she did not betray it. She stood blocking the door with one hand on her hip and the other holding her nutmeg mill by the crank. "These men," she told Cole, "think that they're going to set fire to our cabin. I think they've been drinking."

Pete Hubbell stared up at Cole Allan.

"You've had six weeks to get along," Hubbell charged. "Your cattle have stripped my graze down to bedrock. Now I'm telling you to pack and git."

If lying was the order, Cole thought, he could do his share. He told Hubbell, "I took the trouble to check up on your water rights. It seems like Peach Creek is still open. So I homesteaded my six hundred and forty and took a grazing lease on the rest."

"You're a liar," said Pete Hubbell levelly.

"What am I going to do?" asked Cole. "Swallow everything a cow-stealing borderhopper tells me? Cole Allan owns this land now, and you're saying *adios*."

Hubbell said shortly, "I'll be back tomorrow morning. If your cabin ain't empty by then, I'll empty it."

Cole glanced at California. "It's these comin' yearlin's that are hard to flank, ain't it?" he remarked.

California showed that he got it by slipping the thong that held his catchrope. Hubbell moved back.

It was one of the men behind him who blew the tension apart. His right hand dropped onto the butt of his gun and the barrel tipped up without leaving the holster. It was a swivel affair, a thing only a gunman would own.

The report of the revolver was a jolt of thunder that hit Cole solidly. His pony reared with a cry such as he had never heard from an animal before. Among all the other sounds, Elly's scream was a high, sustained note.

The yard was in uproar, men dodging for shelter and

horses beginning to fight their riders. Through his shock, Cole knew only that he must draw his gun. But even that he forgot when the pony went over on its back. He kicked out of the stirrups and threw himself sideways. He landed flat, pounding the wind out of his lungs.

Then he heard California yell. It was one of those ebullient cowboy shouts that defy translation but tell the world that somebody is about to do something. What California was doing was dropping a noose over Pete Hubbell's shoulders.

Cole found himself thinking: He can't do it this time. Hubbell will shoot him. . . .

He began to stare at Hubbell. What was the matter with him, anyway? Instead of pulling his Colt, he was rubbing his eyes! He was standing there like a fence post while the rope settled about his shoulders and California took his dallies and raked his pony with the spurs.

Hubbell's feet left the ground; he came down with a grunt and skidded along behind the running horse. He caromed off the man who had shot Cole's pony and knocked him rolling.

Cole Allan sat up to discover, with some amazement, that his gun was in his hand. Also he saw that where Pete Hubbell had stood, a small wooden box marked the spot, as if in memoriam. He recognized it as the drawer to Elly's nutmeg grater. Hubbell's eyes had been as full of freshly ground spice as Elly had been of wifely fury.

Pete Hubbell's men did not work well extemporaneously. The two who were still on their feet stood befuddled; they had not drawn their guns, and it occurred to Cole that an empty-handed gunman was no more dangerous than any other man without a weapon.

He said authoritatively, "Lie down on your faces with your arms out straight."

The gunmen sank to their knees, hypnotized by the blue ring of the Colt's muzzle. They went down on their faces, and Elly Allan hurried to disarm them.

Down in the willows they could hear California whooping as he pulled Hubbell through the shallows. When he came back, Hubbell lay limp as a wet hide at the end of the rope. ''Where did you want this strung up?'' California asked.

''I'll leave that to the boys,'' said Cole. ''There's a tree over yonder that could take care of four ropes and have a branch or two left over. Or there's plenty of trails leading out of here. It's their choice—this time.''

Pete Hubbell's men departed at a lope, with Hubbell tied across his horse and his head flopping.

Cole went in and watched Elly put plates on the table. He kept waiting for her to break, remembering that last time the tears had come after all the excitement was over. Well, if she held up until the danger was past, you couldn't say she was fearful. But to his surprise she didn't break down at all.

She confronted him abruptly. ''If anything had happened this time,'' she declared, ''it would have been your own fault. I told you I was ready for the next desert. And I still am.''

Cole Allan put his arms around his bride, and he saw her chin begin to tremble. ''Pete Hubbell was the last desert we'll ever cross, Elly,'' he told her. ''If so many people want this country, it must be worth having. Maybe California was just a frame of mind, after all.''

Elly answered like a good wife and a wise wife, her eyes on the second button of his shirt. ''Whatever you say, Cole. I think it's right nice of you to stay, if it's just on my account.''

''No such thing,'' Cole retorted. ''We'll just figure those first five deserts were put there to keep Arizona from getting overcrowded. As California was saying, it's a little late in the season for pioneering, anyway.''

*Now a best-selling crime novelist, Elmore Leonard began
his career by writing Western short stories and novels in
the late forties and fifties. Several of these have been made
into films of considerable merit, among them the novels
Hombre and Valdez Is Coming and the stories "3:10 to
Yuma" and "The Tall T." The cinematic quality of Leonard's writing is just one of its strengths; others include in-
depth characterization and a fine sense of mood and
place—attributes that are clearly evident in this story of
Willis Calender and Clare Conway, the rancher and his
lady.*

The Rancher's Lady

Elmore Leonard

*T*hey came to Anton Chico on the morning stage, Willis
Calender and his son, Jim; the man getting out of the coach
first, stretching the stiffness from his back and squaring the
curled-brim hat lower over his eyes, and then the boy,
hesitating, squinting, rubbing his eyes before jumping down
to stand close to his dad. It had been a long, all-night trip
from the Puerto de Luna station and a six-hour ride in the
wagon before that up from the Calender place in the Yeso
Creek country.

Willis Calender had come to Anton Chico to marry a
woman he'd never met except in letters. Three letters from
him—the first two to get acquainted, the third to ask her to
be his wife. She'd answered all of them, saying, yes, she
was interested in the marriage state, and finally she thought
living down on the Yeso would be just fine. Which was

65

exactly what the marriage broker said she would say. Her name was Clare Conway, and she was to come over from Tascosa and meet Willis.

He brought Jim along because Jim was eleven, old enough to make the trip without squirming and wanting to stop every second mile, and because he was anxious for Jim to meet this woman before she became his mother. Then, the trip back to Yeso Creek would give the boy time to get used to her. Just bringing her home suddenly and saying, well, Jim, here's your new ma walking in the door, would be expecting too much of the boy; like asking him to pretend everything was still the same. Jim had been good friends with his mother—though he didn't cry at the funeral with all the people around—and he had a picture of her in his mind as fresh as yesterday. Willis Calender knew it, and this was the only thing about remarrying that bothered him.

Little Molly was different. Molly was three when her mother died, and Willis wasn't sure if the little girl even remembered her still. The first few days with the new mother might be difficult, but it would only be a matter of time. It didn't require the kind of getting used to her that it did with Jim; so Molly had been left home with their three-mile-away neighbors, the Granbys. Molly was four now, though, and she needed a mother. She was the main reason Willis Calender had written to the Santa Fe marriage broker, who was said to have the confidence of every eligible woman from the Panhandle to the Sangre de Cristos.

The boy looked about the early-morning street and then to his dad, who was raising his arms to take the mail sack the driver was lowering. He saw the dark suit coat strain across the shoulders and half expected to hear it rip but hoped it wouldn't, because it was his father's only coat that make up a suit. Usually it was hanging with mothballs in the pockets because cattle aren't fussy about how a man looks. It was funny to see his dad wearing it. When was the last time? Then he remembered the bright, silent afternoon of the funeral.

Maybe she won't be here, the boy thought, watching the driver come down off the wheel and take the mail sack and go up the steps of the express office. A man in range clothes was standing there against a post, and as the boy looked that way, their eyes met. The man said, "Hello, Jimmy," his mouth forming a funny half smile in the beard stubble that covered his mouth and jaw.

As Calender looked up, surprise seemed to sadden his weathered face. He put his big hand being the boy's shoulder and moved him forward toward the steps and said, "Hello, Dick." Only that.

Dick Maddox was still against the post, his thumbs crooked in his belt. Another man in range clothes was on the other side of the post from him. Maddox nodded and said, "Will." Then added, "I'm surprised you brought your boy along."

"Why would that be?" Calender said.

"Well, it ain't many boys see their dad get married."

"How'd you know about that?"

"Things get around," Maddox said easily. "You know, I was surprised Clare didn't ask one of us fellas to give her away."

Calender looked at the man steadily, trying to hide his surprise, and hesitated so it wouldn't show in his voice. "You know Miss Conway?"

Maddox glanced at the man next to him. "He says do I know *Miss* Conway." Both of them grinned. "Well, I'd say anybody who's followed the Canadian to Tascosa knows *Miss* Conway, and that's just about everybody."

The words came like a slap in the face, but Calender thought, Hold on to yourself. And he kept his voice natural when he said, "What do you mean by that?"

Maddox straightened slightly against the post. "You're marrying her, you must've known she worked at at the Casa Grande."

Calender was suddenly conscious of his boy looking up at him. He said, "Come on, Jim." And glancing at Dick Maddox, "We've got to move along."

They started up the street toward the two-story hotel, and Maddox called, "What time's the wedding?" The man with him laughed. Calender heard them but he didn't look around.

When they were farther up the street, the boy said, "Who was that man?"

"Maddox is his name," Calender said. "He used to be old man Granby's herd boss. Now I guess he works around here."

They were silent, and then the boy said, "Why'd you get mad when he started talking about *her*?"

"Who got mad?"

"Well, it looked like it."

"Most of the time that man doesn't know what he's talking about," Will Calender said. "Maybe I looked mad because I had to stand there and be civil while he wasted air."

"All he said was other people knew her," the boy said.

"All right, let's not talk about it anymore."

"I didn't see anything wrong in that."

Calender didn't answer.

"Maybe he was good friends with her."

Calender turned on the boy suddenly, but his judgment held him, and after a moment he spoke quietly: "I said let's not talk about it anymore."

But it stayed in his mind, and now there was an urgency inside him, an impatience to meet this woman face-to-face and try to read there what her past had been. It was strange. From the letters he had never doubted she was anything but a good woman, but now—And with this uncertainty the fear began to grow, the fear that he'd see something on her face, some mark of an easy woman.

Damn Maddox! Why'd he have to say it in front of the boy! But he could be just talking, insinuating what isn't so, Calender thought. A man like that ought to have his tongue cut out. All he's good for is drink and talk. Ask old man Granby, he got his bellyful of Maddox and fired him.

They went into the hotel, into the quiet, dim lobby with

its high-beamed ceiling. Their eyes lifted to the second-floor balcony, which extended all the way around, except for the front side, so that all of the hotel's eleven rooms looked down on the lobby, where, around the balcony support posts, were cane-bottom Douglas chairs and cuspidors and here and there parts of newspapers. The room was empty, except for the man behind the desk, who watched them indifferently. His hair glistened flat on an angle over his forehead, and a matchstick barely showed in the corner of his mouth.

"Miss Conway," Will Calender said. The name was loud in the high-ceilinged room, and he felt embarrassed hearing himself say it.

"You're Mr. Calender?"

"That's right." Calender thought, How does he know my name? He stared at the room clerk closely. If he starts to grin, I'll hit him.

"Miss Conway is in Number five." The clerk nodded vaguely up to the balcony.

Calender hesitated. "Would she be—up yet?"

The clerk started to grin, and Calender thought, Watch yourself, boy. But the clerk just said, "Why don't you go up and knock on the door?"

The boy frowned, watching his father climb the stairs and move along the balcony. He was walking funny, like his feet hurt. Maybe she won't be there, the boy thought hopefully. Maybe she changed her mind. No, she'll be there. He pictured her coming down the stairs, then smiling and patting his cheek and saying. "So this is *Jimmy*." A smile that would be gone and suddenly come back again. "My, but Jimmy is a fine-looking young man. How old are you, Jimmy?" She'll be fat and smelly like Mrs. Granby and those other ladies down on Yeso Creek. How come all women get so fat? All except Ma. She wasn't fat and she smelled nice and she never called me Jimmy. He felt a funny feeling remembering his mother, the sound of her voice and the easy way she did things without complaining or getting excited. What did Molly have to have a mother for? She's gotten along for a year without one.

He saw the door open but caught only a glimpse of the woman. His father went inside then, but the door remained open.

The room clerk grinned and winked at the boy. "Now, if that was me, I think I'd close the door."

A moment later they came out of the room. The boy watched his father close the door and follow the woman along the balcony to the stairs and then down. The woman was younger than he'd imagined her, much younger, with a funny hat and blond hair fixed in a bun. And she wasn't fat; if anything, skinny. Her face was slender, the skin pale-clear, and her eyes seemed sad. The boy looked at her until she got close.

"This here is my son," Will Calender said. "We left Molly at the Granbys'. She's only four years old"—he smiled self-consciously—"like I told you in the letters."

The woman smiled back at him. She seemed ill at ease but she said, "How do you do?" to the boy, and her voice was calm and without the false enthusiasm of Will Calender's.

The boy said, "Ma'am," not looking at her face now but noticing her slender white hands holding the ends of the crocheted shawl in front of her.

A silence followed, and Will Calender suggested that they could get something to eat. He had intended mentioning Maddox's name up in the room, then watch her reaction, but there hadn't been time. She didn't look like the kind Maddox hinted she was, did she? Maybe Maddox was just talking. She was better-looking then he'd expected. Those eyes and that low, calm voice. Dick Maddox better watch his mouth.

They went to the café next door for breakfast. Calender and the boy ordered eggs and meat, but Clare Conway just took coffee, because she wasn't very hungry. Most of the time they ate in silence. Every now and then Will Calender could hear himself chewing, and he'd move his fork on the plate or stir at his coffee with the spoon scraping the bottom of the cup. Clare said the coffee was very good. And maybe a minute later, It's going to be a nice day. It's so dry out here you can stand the extra heat.

Then it was Will's turn. Where you from originally? New Orleans . . . I never been there but I hear it's a nice town . . . It's all right . . . Silence . . . How long'd you live in Tascosa? Five years. My husband was with one of the cattle companies . . . Oh . . . He died three years ago . . . Silence . . . That's right, you told me in your letter . . . That's right, I did . . . Silence . . . What've you been doing since then? . . . I took a position . . . Calender's jaw was set . . . At the Casa Grande? . . . Clare Conway blushed suddenly. She nodded and took a sip of coffee in the silence.

There were two men at a table near them, and Will Calender had the feeling one nudged the other, and they both grinned, looking over, then looked away quickly when Calender shot a glance toward them.

Calender passed the back of his hand across his mouth and cleared his throat. "Miss Conway, I planned on ordering some stores this morning, long as I was here. They're hauled down to Puerto de Luna, and I pick 'em up there. Some seed and flour"—he cleared his throat again—"and I have to speak to the justice yet." He looked quickly toward the front window, though it wasn't necessary because Clare's eyes were on her coffee cup.

"Jim, here, will stay with you." The boy looked at him with a plea in his eyes, and Will scowled. Then he rose and walked out without looking at the woman.

Standing in front of the hotel, Dick Maddox looked over toward the café as Calender came out, putting on his hat. Maddox glanced at the three men with him, and they grinned as he looked back toward Calender, who was coming toward them now.

"You married yet, Will?"

Calender glanced at Maddox's closed face, at the beard bristles and the cigarette and the eyes in the shadow of the hat brim. "Not yet," he said, and looked straight ahead again, not slowing his stride.

Maddox waited until he was looking at Calender's back.

He drew on the cigarette and exhaled and said slowly, "Some men will marry just about anything."

Calender's boots sounded on the planking one, two, three, then stopped. He came around. "Do you mean me, Dick?"

A smile touched the corner of Dick Maddox's mouth. "Old man Granby used to have a saying: If the shoe fits, wear it."

"You can talk plainer than that."

"How plain, Will?"

"Talk like a man for a change."

"Well, as a man, I'm wondering if you're going to go ahead and marry this—*Miss* Conway." One of the men behind him laughed but cut it off.

"What if I am?"

Maddox shrugged. "Every man to his own taste."

Calender stepped closer to him. "Dick, if I was married to that woman and you said what you have—you'd be dead right now."

"That's opinion, Will." Maddox smiled because he was sure he could take Will Calender, and he wanted to make sure the three men with him knew it.

Calender said, "The point is, I'm not married to her yet. Not yet. If you don't come out with what's on your mind now, you better not come out with it about two hours from now."

Maddox shook his head. "You're a warnin' man, Will."

"What did she do in Tascosa?" Calender said bluntly.

Maddox hesitated, grinning. "Worked at the Casa Grande."

"And that's what?"

"You never been to Tascosa?"

"I just never saw the place."

"Well, the Casa Grande's where a sweaty trail hand goes for his drink, gamblin', and girls." Maddox paused. "I could draw you a picture, Will."

"Dick, if you're pullin' a joke—"

"Ask anybody in town."

Calender looked at the hat brim shadow and the eyes, the eyes that held without wavering. Then he turned and went up the street.

From his office window, Hillpiper, the Anton Chico justice of the peace, watched Will Calender cross the street. The office was above the jail and offered a view of sun, dust, and adobe; there was nothing else to see in Anton Chico, unless you were looking down the streets east, then you'd see the Pecos.

Hillpiper sat down at his desk, hearing the boots on the stairs, and when the knock came he said, "Come in, Will."

"How'd you know it was me?"

"Sit down." Hillpiper smiled. "You had an appointment for this morning, and I've got a window." Hillpiper wore silver-rim spectacles for close work, but he looked over them to Calender sitting across the desk from him.

Calender said, "You know what everybody in town's saying?"

Hillpiper shook his head. "Not everybody."

"They're talking about this woman I'm to marry."

"I'll say it again. Not everybody."

Calender's rawboned face was tightening, and his voice was louder. "How can they know so much about her—and me, the man that's to marry her, not know anything?"

"It's happened before," Hillpiper said.

"You heard what they're saying?"

"I heard Maddox in the saloon last night. Is he the everybody you're talking about?"

"He's enough. But it's what she is!" Calender said savagely. "What she didn't tell in her letters!"

"Three letters," Hillpiper said mildly. Calender had told him about it when he made the arrangements and set the date: the marriage broker in Santa Fe writing to him, then writing to the woman. Hillpiper had told him it was all right as far as he was concerned, since he didn't see why two people had to love each other to get along. Love's something that might come, but if it didn't—look at all the marriages getting on without it. And Calender had said, that's right. I never thought of that. See, my little girl's the main reason.

"In three letters," Hillpiper went on, "a woman hardly has time to open up her heart."

"She could have told me what she did!"

"Just what does she do, Will?"

"You heard Maddox."

"I want to hear it from you."

"She worked at the Casa Grande!" Calender flared. "How do you want me to say it?"

Hillpiper put his palms on the desk and leaned forward. "All right, Will, she worked in a saloon. She danced with trail hands, maybe sang a little and smiled more than was natural to get the boys to buy the extra drink they'd a bought anyway. And that's all she's done, regardless of how Maddox makes a dozen words sound like a whole story. Why she did that kind of work, I don't know. Maybe she had to because there was nothing else for a girl to do and she still had to eat like anybody else. Maybe it killed her to do it. Or"—Hillpiper's voice was quieter and he shrugged—"maybe she liked doing it. Maybe she forgot where she carried her morals—assuming what she was doing is morally wrong. By most men's standards it is wrong for a female to work in a saloon, your standards, too, or you wouldn't be here with your face tied in a knot. But those same men have a hell of a good time with the females when they're at the Casa Grande."

Hillpiper smiled faintly. "You were always a little stricter than most men anyway, Will. Seems like most of your life you've been a hardworking, Bible-reading family man, with no time for places like the Casa Grande. You've sweated your ranch into something pretty nice, something most other men wouldn't have the patience or the guts to do. And I can see you not wanting to chance ruining all you've built—ranch or family. That's why I was a little surprised when you of all people came in with this mail-order romance idea. I suspect, now that I think about it, you had the idea if a girl wants to get married, she's the simon-pure family type and nothing else. You had a good woman before, Will; so you expected one just as good this time.''

Hillpiper leaned a little closer, his eyes on Calender's weathered face. ''Will,'' Hillpiper said. ''You might be shocked a little bit, but when you get to heaven, you're going to see a lot of faces you never expected to see. Folks who got up there on God's standards and not man's. For all you know, you're liable to even see Dick Maddox— though I suppose that would be stretching divine mercy a little thin.''

Anton Chico's justice of the peace leaned back in his swivel chair, his coat opening to show a gold watch chain across his vest. His hand came out of a side pocket with a cigar, and with a match from a vest pocket he lit it, puffing a cloud of smoke. When he looked up, Calender was standing.

''What've you decided, Will?''

''I've got my kids to think about.''

''It's your problem.'' Hillpiper said this in a kindly way, stating a fact. ''If you've decided not to go through with it, that's your business.''

Will Calender nodded. ''I suppose I should pay her stage fare back to Tascosa.''

''That would be nice, Will,'' Hillpiper said mildly.

Calender thanked him and went out, down the stairs and into the street. Crossing to the other side, he felt awkward and self-conscious. The suit coat held tight across the shoulders, and he could feel his big hands hanging too far out of the sleeves, and with nothing to hold onto.

It's gotten hot, he thought, pulling his hat lower. Maybe the dryness makes it easier on some people, but it's still hot. And then he thought: I'd better tell her before I buy the stage ticket.

Dick Maddox was still in front of the hotel, but now more men were there. It had gotten around that Maddox was having some fun with Will Calender, so they drifted over casually from here and there, the ones who knew Maddox standing closest to him, laughing at what he said. The rest were all along the hotel's shady ramada. One of the men saw Calender coming, and he nudged Maddox, who looked up, then pretended he wasn't concerned, until Calender was close to the hotel entrance.

"You change your mind, Will?"

Calender stopped and breathed out wearily, "If you showed as much concern for your own business, you'd be a well-to-do man."

"You can't take kiddin', can you?"

"Why should I have to?"

"You got a lot to learn, Will."

Calender shrugged, because he was tired of this, and went inside.

The boy was sitting alone, with his heels hooked in the wooden rungs of the chair. When he saw his father, he jumped up quickly.

Calender looked about to be certain the woman was not in the lobby.

"Where is she?" he asked the boy.

"She went upstairs. All of a sudden she just started crying and went upstairs."

"What?"

"It was when they started talking. We were sitting here, and then her chin started to shake—you know—and then she run upstairs."

"Who was talking? The men outside?" The boy nodded hurriedly, and Calender could see that he was frightened and trying to hide it and at the same time was not sure what it was all about.

"What did they say?"

"Just one of them, the rest were laughing most of the time. He was telling them"—the boy said it slowly as if he'd memorized it—"he said some women didn't know their place. They think they can live in the gutter then go out when they want and brush against people like nothing's coming off. He was talking loud so we could hear every word, and he said a man would be a fool to marry a woman like that and have her brushing against his kids with her gutter ways. It was like that, what he said. Then he spoke your name and he said he'd bet anybody five dollars American you'd changed your mind now about getting married. That's when she run upstairs.''

The boy frowned, looking at his father, watching his eyes go up to the room. ''Why'd he have to say things like that? We were sitting here talking—getting acquainted.''

Calender looked at the boy and saw that he was grinning.

''You know she never once asked me how old I was or if I knew my reader or things like that. She talked to me about affairs and interesting things like I was grown-up, like Ma used to do. And, Pa, she called me *Jim*! Can you imagine that? She called me *Jim*! If her hair was darker and her nose a little different, I'd swear she was Ma!''

''Don't say things like that!'' Calender was conscious of his voice, and he said quietly, ''There's the difference of night and day.''

''Well, her voice is different, too, and maybe she's a speck taller, though that could be the hat. I never seen Ma in a regular hat. But outside of that, they sure are alike.''

''You know what you're saying, comparing this woman with your mother?''

The boy looked at him questioningly, but the trace of a smile was still on his face. ''I'm just saying they're alike, that's all. Maybe they don't look so much alike, but they sure are alike.'' The boy smiled; he was sure his explanation was clear because he understood it so well himself.

Calender was looking at the boy closely now. ''What if she's done something bad?''

''Pa, little Molly's doing bad things all the time. That's just the way girls are. Most times they're not doing serious things, so they have more time to get theirselves into trouble.''

Calender's eyes remained on the boy. Calender asked, ''You think Molly will like her?''

''Couple of bad women like them will get along just fine.'' The boy grinned.

Calender left him abruptly, going up the stairs. In a few minutes he came back down, and in front of him was Clare Conway.

They walked across the lobby. Nearing the door, the woman hesitated and looked up at Will Calender. She was unsure and afraid. It was in her wide-open eyes, in the way her fingers held the ends of the crocheted shawl. Then she moved on again as if not under her own power—when Will touched her elbow and said to the boy, "Come on, Jim."

And when they were out on the ramada, the woman's eyes were looking down at her hands; she could feel Will Calender holding her elbow, she could feel the guiding pressure of his hand, and moved to the right along the ramada, along the line of silent men, hearing only her footsteps and the footsteps of the man at her side. The hand on her elbow tightened. She was being turned gently, and there was no longer the sound of footsteps and when she looked up a man was close in front of her, a man with heavy beard bristles.

"Miss Conway," Calender said. "This is Mr. Maddox. He's had such a keen interest in our business, I thought you might like to meet him."

"Now, Will—" Maddox said, looking at Calender strangely.

"And, Dick," Calender went on, "this is Miss Conway. Isn't there something you wanted to say to her?"

"Will—"

"Maybe you'd just like to tip your hat like a gentleman."

Maddox was staring at Calender almost dumbfounded, but slowly his face relaxed as he realized what Calender was doing in front of all these men, and he said mildly, grinning, "Now, Will, I don't know if I want to do that or not."

Calender's fist came around suddenly, unexpectedly, driving against Maddox's jaw, changing the smile to lopsided surprise and sending him back off the ramada into the street. Calender followed and hit him again, and this time Maddox went down, his hat falling off in front of him. Maddox started to rise, but Calender came for him again. Maddox hesitated, then eased down and sat in the street, looking up at Calender.

"One other thing, Dick," Will said. "I hear you're taking bets there isn't going to be a wedding today." He glanced back at the crowd of men in the shade. "Who's holding the stakes?"

There was a silence, then someone called, "Nobody'd bet him."

Calender beckoned to the man. "Come here." He brought a five-dollar gold piece out of his pants pocket and gave it to the man. "Dick Maddox'll give you one just like this. Now you add the two up and have that much ready for me when I get back."

He walked to the ramada. The tension was gone. Some of the men were whispering and talking, some just looking out at Maddox still sitting in the street.

The boy's face was beaming as he watched his father. Clare came toward him.

"You ripped the seam of your coat up the back," she said.

He felt her hand on his back pulling the cloth together. "Gives me a little more room," he said, conscious of the men watching him.

"It's your good coat, though," the woman said. "I'll mend it soon as we get home."

A former Navy combat correspondent during World War II, Bryce Walton began writing extensively for the mystery/ detective, science fiction, and Western pulps in the mid-forties. Since then he has published several hundred short stories in a wide variety of publications (one being The Saturday Evening Post) and seven novels, most of them juvenile adventure fiction; he has also contributed scripts to such TV shows as Alfred Hitchcock Presents. ''The Land Beyond'' is the larger-than-life, Bunyanesque tale of a Texas cattleman named Farnam and his impossible 670-mile Sacramento-to-Portland race against time and the steamboat Flora Belle.

The Land Beyond

Bryce Walton

*T*he local Sacramento agent for Logan-Meyers Express Company weighed out Farnam's gold as though it were cornmeal.

"Two thousand head of longhorns clear up from Texas," the agent said. "Prodigious feat, Mr. Farnam. And all so some fools with shovels in their hands and the god of gold in their hearts can eat beefsteak for a few days."

Farnam, a big, dusty, gaunt man with a stubborn jaw, squinted at the weighing and shuffled his boots. Those miners had paid him thirty dollars a head for beeves he'd brought in Texas for ten dollars. He could tolerate their hunger for beefsteak, but right now he was too beat-down tired to appreciate his considerable profit.

His son, Arch, clumped away from the window and the

painted women walking along the Sacramento river front. He didn't know what the gold meant, didn't care. Young and strong, he had plenty of good years left to make his pile.

When the agent asked what route Farnam had taken and was told that Farnam had taken the Southern, the agent exclaimed, "Good heavens, sir, that's Apache country! No one ever came up that way."

Blood specked Farnam's chapped lips as he grinned. "Our scalps set pretty loose."

"Hope you value your profit more than these gully-washing fools, Mr. Farnam. They think nothing of laying down six ounces of gold on the turn of a card. A fellow decided at a poker game that he needed more dust to see the last raise. He put the pile aside and said to his friend, 'Here, Jim, watch my pile till I go out and dig up enough to call him.' But they've already skimmed off the cream. Living in a fool's paradise."

Like my cowboys, Farnam thought, when I paid them off, rushing to the saloons, whiskey and women. They don't worry about tomorrow. It's the young who don't worry, and the old-timers who don't care anymore, never invested everything, or who don't have families.

Then Farnam signed the agent's receipt for 37,000 dollars folded it carefully, and put it in the pocket of his dusty buckskin jacket.

"You're wise depositing with us, Mr. Farnam. You might be tempted by the Goddess of Chance. Or more likely robbed and murdered before you got out of town."

Farnam knew a drover who started back south with over forty thousand in gold strapped to a mule's back. One night the mule walked away and was never found.

"Say hello to the Panhandle for me," the agent said and handed Farnam a shuck segar. "Fellow told me if he owned Texas and hell he'd rent out the first."

"Reckon he might," Farnam said, "if he knew the difference."

Farnam lay on the bed in a hotel room above the Golden Bar Saloon. Arch had dandied up and gone out on the town, but Farnam hadn't even taken off his boots. The gold was put away safe, but Farnam still couldn't unwind. The accumulated letters from Lucie lay about on the bed giving off a faint perfume, speaking from cruelly far away where she waited in their well-favored valley.

Their oldest boy, Isom, was handling the stock raising and farming well enough. Kell and Bart were growing taller than Sam Houston. Lucie missed him, of course, but there was no hint of doubt about him. But Lucie didn't know how long that trail had been, and that he wasn't the same man now that he had been when he left. He felt his age, weariness in his bones, a deep-down ache in his muscles. His straggly black hair had turned gray. Arch had become a man on that trail, for it allowed no one to stay young. That trail salted the desert with the bones of brave men.

An intangible loneliness possessed him, the kind that comes from knowing about important events lost behind in time, that can never alter or intrude within, and yet there is somebody there you know or love, but it's back of you and of all things the loneliest.

They had crossed the Rio Grande at Albuquerque, up the Little Colorado River, crossed part of Arizona under a killing sun before cutting into California and the Eastern escarpment of the Sierra Nevadas. Jolting endless miles. Apaches waiting. Sleepless nights waiting for the herd to spook from a lightning flash, a lighted match, a crackly twig. Blizzard, desert heat, swollen river, sudden storm, Indians. All of it howled, blistered, surged, crackled, and yelled in him.

But there was the sandstone fireplace cut stone by stone from the hill quarry. Lucie out there by the cream skimmer where the scales hung for the weighing of sausage meats, butter, sugar for the pound cakes. They had weighed the boys into the world on those scales, too, and she was looking at their weights and initials scratched into the metal.

There was Texas, going out for a thousand miles where a few trees grew only along the streams. Flat, bleak to the high tablelands—but clear. Open, wide, and clear so you could rest at ease, see what was coming . . .

"Pa wake up, wake up!"

Farnam sat up blinking a moment, staring up at the whale-oil lamp until he remembered where he was. He saw Arch's face the color of wet buckwheat, then the newspaper, an old copy of the St. Louis Dispatch, and the black sickening headlines:

> LOGAN-MEYERS EXPRESS CO BANKRUPT!
> RECEIVERS CLOSE OUT ALL BRANCHES!
> DEPOSITORS LOSE ALL!

"Just came off a boat," Arch said, then he backed away as Farnam ran out the door, figuring wildly that if the newspaper had just arrived, then he might beat the news to the Express Office. He seemed blind, running, fighting the street hub-deep in mud and surging traffic.

But the Express Office was locked, and three sheriffs, deputies with sawed-off shotguns, stood guard before a threatening crowd. Farnam stood numbly and watched a rock go through the window. A fat man recognized the cattleman and offered him a segar. "Got to celebrate," he yipped. "Who loses fortunes every day, even in Eldorado?" He struck sulphurous sparks from a locofoco match, set fire to his receipt from Logan-Myers, and lighted his segar.

Farnam jolted his way like a sleepwalker back to the Golden Bar.

Arch stood over by the wall. His face was full of fear and incomprehension, only suspecting or wondering how much it meant. He hadn't learned yet how heavy are the odds of the years when a trail is too long to face even one more time. All that Farnam and his wife had managed to rake and scrape together, and borrow, he had lost.

"Go fetch me a bottle of whiskey," Farnam said. Arch didn't move. "Fetch it now, and leave me be."

Arch backed away to the door not knowing what to do, knowing words wouldn't do it.

But the whiskey didn't even cut the fearsome edges off.

Farnam sat precariously balanced on the edge of the bed like a rock on the side of a hill. "Fetch me another bottle, boy."

Arch stared as if he'd never seen his old man before, didn't believe in what he was seeing, trying to stare it away. Arch seemed like a raw kid again, scared, bewildered, and lost. Then he turned, shamed, to the door.

All of life seemed frozen in this one loutish futile time and place. Farnam sitting here forever, Arch shuffling out to fetch another bottle of rye. It isn't right, it isn't right for Arch to see it this way. But then the door closed.

The sounds of winter spreeing from saloon row below faded further away. A few flaccid moments seemed to swell to swollen hours. And then he heard that voice again, the one from the crowd milling before the Express Office earlier. He'd forgotten it, but it came back now in sharp insistent whispers: "If we was only in Portland, Oregon, boys. The Flora Belle just steamed up north carrying the bad news. Until she gets there, that Logan-Myers office in Portland won't shut down."

Farnam lurched out the door and met Arch coming up the stairs and almost fell as he knocked the bottle from the lad's hand.

"They won't take us out, son." Farnam swayed dangerously over the bannister and looked down into the thick segar smoke of the barroom. "We're highland Cavaliers and our clan goes back five hundred years to Ulster. My Father was a flying whale, killed swamp Indians with a hand-axe, and he struck a blow like a falling tree."

Farnam swaggered downstairs, through muddy sawdust to the bar. The fat man was there, still handing out segars. "Well, well," the fat man said. "Drinks are on me, cowboy. Belly up."

"How far's Portland?" Farnam roared.

They laughed. The fat man said, "Figure to beat the Flora Belle up there? Can't be done. Fast steamer with a head start and ain't nothing can catch up to her."

"How far by horseback?" Farnam yelled and, catching

Arch's eye, laughed and slammed his hand down on the bar.

"Close to seven hundred miles overland," the fat man said.

Someone else hooted in derision. "You don't need a horse, mister. You got to sprout wings."

Farnam blinked at blurring faces. "Name's Farnam, from Kentucky by way of Texas, boys. And I can outride anything that flies, runs or rolls. Why, hell, I'm already half horse, and when I ride, I leave holes in the air for thunder to rush in."

"Give him a swig of panther juice," someone laughed. "Afore he talks up a nor'wester and lifts the roof."

Farnam laughed and stumbled all the way up the stairs.

Arch came up later, watched Farnam changing his socks. "They're still laughing down there, Pa."

"Little men invented laughter like that," Farnam said. He stood up and counted out two hundred dollars in gold and left it on the bureau for Arch, put the rest—three hundred in gold—in his saddlebag, and flung it over his thick shoulders. His haggard face, whipped to raw beef color by sun and wind, was shiny with sweat.

"That fellow had figures to prove it, Pa. Nobody can do it."

"Figures don't lie, just them that does the figuring. If a man paid attention to odds, he'd never dare get born."

Arch's lips quivered. He yelled out. "You're just drunk!"

Farnam roared. "Listen to me, not them." His voice quieted to a stubborn grit. "These who are laughing and sneering here will be staring later like owls in a thunderstorm. Listen now, and remember. There's times when you got nothing to fall back on but yourself. You got to throw away everything and stand up and risk dying. If you don't, then afterward you never will. And you'll be the same as dead anyway, long as you live."

After that he vaguely remembered telling Arch to wait, not to spend the money on gambling, whiskey, and women, then he was on a paddle-wheeler heading a few miles up river to a place called Bowstand's Landing, figuring that way to save a little time.

Farnam had never been tolerant of liquor, had avoided it, because it burned reason out of his head and filled it with red fire. He dimly remembered heavy gambling on the paddle-wheeler, which he couldn't afford and which he ignored. Drink was the dominating thought. The only indication of law and order was a notice warning that anyone entering the cabin with shoes or boots on would be fined a bottle of porter. The prohibition was silent as to dirty feet, or the cabin would have been empty or a source of fines. Farnam stayed topside, couldn't go below into that gamy pit even for a dish of beef and cabbage. Once he threatened to shoot out a star with a dueling pistol. And several times called attention to the fact that he was Steve Farnam and that he was independent as a hog on ice.

At Bowstand's Landing he bought a horse and a bottle of red-eye. He traded that horse at a freighter's station for another, and when that one dropped, quivering and foam-lathered, he swapped it for a hip-shot roan he ordinarily wouldn't have considered as crowbait. He watched the Big Dipper wheeling in the dark sky and knew he was heading north.

Whiskey drowned the tension in his chest, kept his throat wet enough to sing loudly and off-key

"Woke up one morning on the old cattle trail
Rope in my hand and a cow by the tail.
Feet in the stirrup and seat in the saddle.
I hung and rattled with them longhorn cattle. . . .

He swapped for another horse at a roadside tavern and pounded on and into the graying light of day

California, oh California . . .
Water, land, sky and sand, gold
    beneath the ground
Where Missourians meet and

sharpers cheat,
And nary a native is found . . . ."

A Conestoga wagon flapped ragged canvas in the dusky wind where two oxen stood hobbled in a hock-deep lake of fog. An old-timer crouched over a fire and whined petulantly at the cold. A child in a bad dream cried from under the canvas. The old-timer seemed glad to trade a stringy-legged sorrel for Farnam's blowing nag plus twenty golden eagles. Farnam changed saddles, stumbling, pawing; and swearing in the firelight. The sorrel humped and wheezed as the cinch tightened in. Then Farnam stood on wide-spread legs, weaving a little, a gaunt shadow in soaked buckskins spattered with mud and his eyes swollen and red-rimmed. His Stetson was gone, his wet hair plastered to his forehead.

The old-timer handed him a mug of coffee. The hot slash of it woke Farnam up. A loutish sickness, a weakness flowed down into his legs. All at once he was sober, cold sober. And he knew with awful clarity what he had said he would do and that nobody could do.

"Want to turn in," the old-timer said. "Spare buffalo robe 'neath the wagonbed."

"No, but much obliged," Farnam said hoarsely.

"Where you hurryin so all-fired to?"

Farnam looked down the wagon-rutted road. He felt a shudder that left his skin cold and grained. "North. I reckon. North—"

"Gold's down tother way. Diggin up a tin-cup a gold a day down there from Feather River to the Tuolumne in the South."

Farnam swallowed the sick taste of himself heavily, then raked spurs, and the sorrel found its stride and lined out down the trail.

No singing or laughing now, not even at himself. Laugh at a clown but not at a capering bluffing blowhard. He had made a good ringing speech back there for Arch's benefit. But Arch hadn't believed a word of it. Arch knew the dif-

ference between conviction and a man whistling in a grave-
yard of doubt. Between a man and a bluffer pouring green
whiskey down before a fight he knows he can't win.

Farnam swore and flung the whiskey away. He hadn't
been able to face up the big loss. So he'd made a big
grandstand play, an old rooster flapping and crowing thinking he screamed like an eagle. And now he couldn't go
back and eat crow.

The wind whistled through him the way it did through
the limbs of wintered trees. White bark from a stand of
quaking aspen shone white as death as he pounded by.

He could swap horses clear to British Columbia but not
his body or his brain. Couldn't trade in his heart for one
that was strong and young. But a man could ride on to
where he couldn't ride any longer, then stop. There's a
time to get sicker or get well, to live or die.

He rode with the thoughtless ease of a lifetime in the
saddle, but the trail got shorter fast. He swapped horses at
Marysville Buttes, Keller Springs, Rock Bluffs. He felt the
pain in his knees and thighs, his kidneys aching as if
pounded with a mallet.

Cold vapor breathed up at night among the buttressed
writhings of cypress trees. Squaw Ridge. Billingers Flat.
The increasing throbbing pain in his chest and back and
neck, the battered muscles and the protest of exhausted
bones.

The snowy twin peaks of Mt. Shasta appeared as the sun
burst over a wet land, where wind ploughed in the branches
of oak trees.

Valleys, ravines, rivers, mountains, forests, wastes went
on silent and awesome and empty save for Farnam, a speck,
an ant crawling where the miles seemed on the verge of
full fire.

Day broke over steep hills again, slashed down ravines,
revealed a sudden change to redwoods and singing winter
streams as Farnam raced with another morning's clouds
rolling north like a river. Forest thickened and wagon roads
dwindled to shadowed game trails and the haunted twisting
of Indian paths.

The trail would end anytime now, and Farnam kept riding because even a bad bluff was worth making good. He changed saddles again, pumped rein again until another horse stood foam-surfed and trembling, wringing wet by boulders blunted and damp as old bear's teeth. Another swap and another raking of spurs, not knowing where he was, not caring, knowing only that a trail is longer or shorter and that no man rides forever.

Thunder rolled down a narrow canyon and wore away to the west. A sunrise whitened bare hills where a drift of coyotes cried by a river for moonrise, and Farnam squeezed out another mile, another half, another quarter of a mile, and the ground turned to a brown feverish blue under his stirrups.

There was no longer any sensation of movement, or of pain, below his hips. Another horse trembled to a fumble-hoofed halt, and he was making another trade at an Indian trading post, a cross-trail cabin store, from a wagon train heading south, from a trapper, a trader, half-breed, a Vaquero.

"Keep an eye peeled when you hit the big timber," said the migrant preacher. "The Modoc Injuns on the warpath up there, and they're lifting a lot of hair."

He dozed off and on in the saddle with his hands rawhided to the horn. He might have put up a big bluff, but let no man say that Steve Farnam didn't make a damned good ride out of it—while it lasted.

Night and day blended into a solitude of exhaustion so profound it enveloped his spirit at last. Sensations washed through him in a filter of delirium. His horse sneezed, and the break was loud in its nostrils. It was limping, and Farnam started to lead it on north, but the grinding at the base of his brain turned like a dying mill wheel. He felt his strength of will going out, and he was powerless any longer to resist. Go as far as you can go, then stop. He saw a ghostly outline of fog fleeing down a canyon, tearing itself to pieces on giant spikes of redwoods.

Darkness rushed over his eyes and he sagged over his horse's mane. . . .

"Wake up, Steve, they're spooked!"

That seemed to be Shorty Myers standing by a tall spiny ocotilla, outlined by a flash of lightning. Dark clouds rushed over the moon. But it couldn't be him because Shorty Myers wasn't riding point again. Shorty Myers got an Apache arrow in his throat coming through Southern Arizona, and he was buried under a rock cairn.

"Wake up, Steve. Get up, dammit, get on your horse. You want to lose the whole herd?"

Farnam struggled to get free of the blankets like an animal in a net. The air crackled with electricity so heavy charged that he saw those ghostly luminous bulbs of levin lights dancing like swamp fire on the tips of the beasts' horns. The mass of saber-sharp horns, struggling bodies, churning hoofs roared around him. Cowboys lost in the melee. Thousands of hoofs drummed together. Hocks and horns clattered and clashed. The wild herd bawled and leaped in a single upsurge of motion to its feet and bounded into the blackness, thundering away in the lightning flashes. The gradually stampeding herd strung out as the fastest animals forged ahead.

"Steve, dammit, get to your horse. We'll lose 'em all!"

Only this time it wasn't Shorty. It was Hap Foley, only it couldn't be him either because Hap Foley was drowned in the Red River.

Farnam lunged up like a somnambulist torn out of sleep. His horse stood heaving and caked with muddied sweat. Farnam lay in the redwood shadows on a bed of damp leaves where he had fallen, but his hand still held to the stirrup. He dragged himself back up into the saddle. His heavy features hung slack, mouth open, lower lip drooping, and he breathed with a regular panting rhythm.

He gave a hoarse whispered yell as he raked his spurs up the bloody flanks.

Then a wickiup appeared through the leaves. A long splinter of a man in a hickory shirt and high homespun breeches was washing his bearded face out of a barrel. Beaver peltry hung on willow racks. An Indian woman moved like a shadow from under the canvas into speckled sunlight and gazed without expression at a swaying apparition covered with foam and half-dried mud.

"Looks like you're riding through hell," the trapper said.

"Need another horse."

"I only own one beast, a good mare. You wouldn't be leaving me much."

It was a good mare, Farnam saw, maybe fifteen and a half hands high and with perhaps a strain of Kentucky blood. Too bad—because he hated to break down a good horse. "No time for horse trading," he whispered. "I'll give you this bay and twenty golden eagles."

The trapper started to say no, then looked into Farnam's face drawn back so that the cheekbones stood out and his nose was beaklike and his pupils a painful green in the reddened ovals of his eyes. He shrugged. "Take my beast. A man's got to outride the devil."

Farnam changed saddles. The Indian woman brought him a thunder mug of meal, a slab of salt meat, some pemmican hard as nails. The trapper added a small wooden keg of whiskey. "May want a last swig to take some extra fire into hell."

The trapper told Farnam he was ten miles south of the Klamath River, wherever that was. He also told him what day it was, and that didn't mean much either, except that Farnam had been riding four days. Four days, four years, the trail was thinning down.

He rode the sun down. Skittery deer leaped without a sound. Coyotes yipped from hills where stars began lighting up. But even the best horse has to stop somewhere. Farnam slid down the long slope of the saddle and stretched out blissfully in cool yama grass . . .

Arch was looking down at him, shame and disbelief on his face.

"You ain't asleep. But you ain't never going to get up. You're just drunk."

He climbed blindly into the saddle, and a wet shine of

rock drew his blurred gaze downward. There was a rock cairn by the turn of the trail.

Oregon, the letters on the rock cairn said. The Oregon line.

At a mining camp near Jacksonville, he swapped for a single-footed bay, then rode into the deeper shadows of the Oregon woods. When he stopped to let the bay drink from a creek, he sank down into the earth. It was warm, soft, a downy bed. Even a fool knows when he's beat. . . .

"Wake up, son."

He lay in the attic, scared, listening to wintry wind against log chinks, shivering and sleepless with Indian fear. His father stood over him wearing his bearskin coat, his coonskin cap, carrying his squirrel rifle, and looking bigger than an oak tree. "Get up, son. We're taking a walk in the woods. You can't go on running scared. Get up and get dressed."

The boy's teeth chattered as they edged away into the marshy woods where ghosts with tomahawks gibbered and hooted, then fled before them and became whispering wind. They walked far away from the cabin squatting in wet ground, its squared logs dark with night's rain, the dogs sniffing at corners. Ever since he'd seen those butchered migrants, their bodies charred between the wheels of a corn train, their scalps hanging, he'd been scared of Indians. There was always an Indian scare. Nothing was worse than when an Indian scare got going through the woods and around the hills. An Indian was seen slipping along through the brush and everyone locked the doors and waited with primed muskets. But Steve Farnam never feared Indians after that.

"Wake up, son."

He opened his eyes and lay there on his belly, his face near the water of the creek. His horse stood a few feet away, its breath loud in its nostrils. Farnam didn't move. He listened to the wind whispering in the deep forest shadows, and he felt a tingling on the backs of his hands. The wolf howled again, but it didn't sound right. His upper lip glistened with sweat as he dared his body by inches slowly to its feet, then he stood looming a solid shadow among shadows.

He worked his eyes slowly over the walls of quivering leaves. Sweat ran down his face. All the water in his body seemed to rush to the surface. His throat tightened as he stared across the creek. And he remembered that one faint show of cowardice to an Indian and the game is done.

A lighter brown shifted against muddy light, and three of them slipped out of the leaves and glided to the edge of the creek ten feet away. Their dark faces watched, speculated, turned to either side looking and listening to see if Farnam was alone. Their eyes narrowed under coarse braided hair. The wind brought him the smoke-grease smell of their skins, the smell that comes from rubbing themselves with fat. A raggle-taggle crew of Rogues in bits of cast-off clothes of white and savage, with bows, knives, a lance, and two battered muskets. Two of them made sudden stomps at the water, made stabbing motions with knives, testing him to see if he jumped or ran. He slid his jacket back to show off the butt of his old Walker Colt. He moved toward them slowly, down to the creek's edge and faced them, mouth pressed thin by the powerful clamp of his jaws.

He returned their steady stares. Their scared bare hides gleamed, the leather breeches were dirty and the ears with shells in them, and the bright eyes dark and flitting over him, eyes that never told what they were going to do until they did it. They jumped suddenly, hooked their knives, leveled their guns, and crouched in the water on quivering legs. Two of them let out sudden frightening yells. They always tested a man, enjoyed doing it; they could go on doing it for hours to see how much a white man could take. Their respect for a man always determined what they would do, how they would do it, and when.

They leaped in closer, stomping and shrieking. If he flinched once, he was their supper. He drew the elk-horn-handled bowie knife and snapped it open and held it blade-up in his left hand. He drew the Walker and held it in his right hand. The rogues stood frozen. Dark eyes brightened with scheming and wonder and the stain of warpaint washing off with the day's sweat and melting grease.

He kept walking, and they slipped out of sight without a sound into the leaves. Indians don't want to die either, and they had known that he could get one of them for sure, maybe two, maybe three. One white man's hair wasn't worth it.

He stumbled back and reached for the saddle horn, got onto his horse, and rode on, bewildered that he was still going on as a cold rainy drift began hissing through the leaves.

His mind drifted off into fevered blankness. There was a sour memory of stealing horses when no one would trade or sell, and crossing the Rogue River on a pioneer ferry, and wheedling another trade at a log and canvas settlement called Winchester near the Umpqua.

He was riding through a dense fog, letting the horse pick its way at a gallop. It lurched sickeningly and rolled as Farnam covered his head with his arms and smashed into the rocks. The horse's pitiful wheezing guided him to it where it lay with a broken foreleg. Its eyes watched him forlornly as he shot it in the head.

He lay for a long time beside the dead horse, looking into the fog; then he got up and started walking, feeling like an infant as his legs folded under him and he sat blank on his things.

So this was it, in a lost valley of fog, smack-dab in the middle of nowhere, but then one place was much like another when you weren't going any further. . . .

"Steve," she said again. "You awake, Steve?"

Lucie? He felt about for her body warmth beside him in the bed, but the bed was cold as if she had never been there. But she had always been there, beside him all the way, the best a man could have, in all ways, long ago all the way from Kentucky down the Mississippi on a flatboat in '46, all the way across Texas deserts by oxwagon past bleached skull markers, and always brave, always willing to go on. So much a part of him always that lying without her, he knew he wasn't even a whole man anymore. Cold wind outside the cabin walls. The tallow candle smoked in its cup on the cupboard, shone on her embroidered pillow-cases, the log cabin quilt, the bullet molds, and the ladle for melting lead, the pack saddle in the corner back of the door. Then he saw Lucie in the rocker he'd made from cottonwood and laced with rawhide, looking out the window and singing. But she always sang glad, and this song was all of melancholy:

> "When roses blow in winter snow,
>   Then will my love return to me. . . ."

"You don't want me to take that trail herd north, do you, Lucie?"

She touched his lips with her small strong hands. "If you weren't the kind of man who would do this, I wouldn't have married you."

"Then what's wrong?" he asked.

"It's just that I don't want it to mean too much, Steve. It's us together that comes first. You and I and the boys. The family together. I know you need to do it, something big, Steve. Something so big maybe you can't put a word to it or set it out in thought. But maybe there isn't anything bigger than us here together. One little old room in a cabin's big enough when we're together. Just don't let the gold mean too much, or the biggest spread in the Southwest. Just make sure you bring yourself back to us. Any fool can get gold, but it's the land beyond that counts."

He tried to open his eyes as if suddenly she were gone and the wind was getting higher.

"Lucie?"

"Steve, are you awake, Steve. . . ."

Then he was walking knee-deep in fog that seemed thick as mud, down the Valley of the Yoncalla, his feet dragging like stumps of firewood. A digger Indian gave him a ribby mustang in exchange for a thick thumb-pinch of gold and the bowie knife. He rode on north toward Eugene, where a man who led a bear on a chain told him he was about 200 miles from Portland.

He stole two more horses, swapped them for two more, and on the sixth day took a ferry across the Willamette. Reflected in the water he saw the face of a man hell wouldn't take as a down payment on the whole human race, but the filthy, matted image grinned back at him. For he knew it was still in him, had always been there, that he hadn't lost it, a violent shred of life that would sustain to the end. He felt the sudden increase of force and life in his mind, like a transfusion of strong red blood. They were with him always, them and a few words of courage and hope they had given him on the way. And their actions that were deeper than words moved in him, part of his own blood. And he knew why he had rode north, and why he would make it to Portland. Because Arch had heard the words but hadn't believed them. He had to make those words true for Arch because someday Arch would need them, need to know they were true. For when the time would come when Arch had nothing to all back on but himself and he had to throw away everything and stand up and risk dying, then there would have to be that someone, that voice in his past to back him up, make the words deep and true.

The hardcased Yankee trader sat in his sod hut and haggled up chunks of beef from a greasy pasty with his bowie knife. "Like I said, cracked. That's a California mustang with Moorish blood, a quarter horse with barb blood speed in her. She's two hundred, take or leave. Ain't no skin off my tail."

"That's why I want that horse, Yankee. I said I'd give you what I got, seventy-five dollars. I'll pay the rest when—"

"Two hundred, take or leave."

Farnam threw the saddlebag in the moldy straw. "That's yours. I'm taking that horse. I'm making a six-hour run into Portland, and I need a good horse."

The trader looked up past a piece of speared beef, then he sprang over the wooden crate and snicked at the air with his bowie, and his black-bearded face grinned as he circled. "You steal my horse, cracker, you get your brisket sliced."

Farnam's trembling breath quieted. He drew a long, shaky sigh as a drunken man will do when fighting for control, then with a vicious lunge he stomped his boot out and down on the trader's moccasined instep. The man fell to one knee, and Farnam kicked him under the chin. The trader came up bleeding and howling and Farnam jammed the old Walker Colt in his belly.

"Don't stick your topknot out," Farnam said, backing toward the door, "or I'll fire it off." He grabbed up a jar of molasses from a shelf as he went out. To cut down weight, he didn't use the round-skirted saddle but smeared molasses on the mustang's sides to help him stick to her. Instead of the usual bridle, he used a simple rope hackamore. The animal's muscles sprang together, stretched and heaved into the wind of the ride. . . .

Five hours later the mustang pounded down the main riverfront street of Portland, hock-deep in mud, flying lather, fiery hot and quivering with strain in its stride. Farnam pulled up before a false-fronted building on which a board sign swung in the freezing wind:

LOGAN-MYERS
EXPRESS COMPANY

He dismounted and stumbled, half-blind and reeling, across the boardwalk. As he opened the door, he turned and saw the steamer anchoring in the river. It was the *Flora Belle*. He had beaten her by a few yards, a few minutes, and later he learned that he wouldn't have done it except that she had stopped over a few extra hours at Humboldt Bay.

Farnam's knees started to give way as he got inside and leaned on the counter and dug out the Logan-Myers receipt from his money belt.

"You want this cashed," the Portland agent asked, staring at Farnam's mud-caked figure and the burning, red-rimmed eyes. Farnam nodded. "I want it all in gold," he whispered.

"Seems in order, sir. There's a one and a half percent charge for cashing—"

"That's fine," Farnam interrupted. "That's all right."

Farnam put over a hundred pounds of gold in the saddlebags and staggered out of the Logan-Myers Express Office and down the riverfront street to a hotel two blocks away before he finally quit.

A Ranger is said to have once ridden 110 miles in 23 hours. Steve Farnam rode 670 miles in six days. As far as anyone knows, Farnam's ride to Portland town has never been matched, but hardly anyone ever knew about it. Farnam didn't bother telling it, suspecting that no one would believe it anyway. He was not, by nature, a man of brag.

As he sat there looking at the *Flora Belle*, it was enough that when he got back to Sacramento, Arch would know that his words had been true. He closed his eyes and thought of Lucie, and went to sleep.

———

Steve Frazee's excellent Western stories have appeared in a number of anthologies (including two previous Best of the West volumes, The Lawmen *and* The Outlaws) *and in two collections,* The Gunthrowers *and* The Best Western Stories of Steve Frazee. *He is also the author of such well-crafted novels as* Cry Coyote, High Cage, Rendezvous, *and* A Gun for Bragg's Woman. *"The Big Die-Up" is the suspenseful account of a group of ranchers struggling to survive "the hardest winter the Great Park country (of Colorado) had ever known."*

The Big Die-Up

Steve Frazee

W*ith the warmth of the fireplace pressing against his* back, Jim Heister looked east along the snow fields and saw them coming. They rode through the drifts like men with defeat upon them, and that could make them savage. Six of them. There might have been twelve, but some of the Great Park ranchers were too full of pride and some of them hated Heister too much to come begging.

He was a lean, tall man with a look of hard-sharp assurance on his snow-burned features. He stood in the warmth of what was his and watched the snow trail away in streamers from the legs of the laboring horses that were carrying men to Whispering Pines on a futile mission.

His pistol hung in its holster on a peg near the door. He glanced at it, and he looked again at the stubborn way the ranchers came on, with their heads lowered against the wind, with the white breath of the horses whipping away.

99

This had been the hardest winter the Great Park country had ever known, and no man could guess when spring would arrive.

Beckett came from the kitchen, an old man bumping along on run-over heels. His full lower lip made a red streak against gray beard stubble. His face was rutted, his eyes reserved. He had wanted little from life, and that was what he had got, a horse, a saddle, a good pistol, and a place to work. It was hard to understand a man like that; but Heister was glad now that he had not put on his pistol.

Beckett said, "Company coming."

"I'm looking at them."

"Yeah." Beckett spat into the fireplace. "So you are." He turned around and started back to the kitchen. His brief presence and his leaving spoke of a complete understanding and a great gulf.

Nettled, Heister said, "Fred, you think I'm wrong, don't you?"

Beckett looked across his shoulder. His lower lip might have been a pout if his seamed, brown face had not been so cold. "I know you are." He clumped on out of the room.

Heister glanced again at his pistol, and then he looked at the riders struggling through the drifts. He couldn't question Beckett's loyalty. The man thought one thing and was blunt in saying so, and yet he would stand solidly beside Heister if there was need.

There was a disturbing edge in the thought, just as there was something mildly painful in watching men fighting cold and wind while Heister stood in warmth. He wanted them to be here quickly, to have it done and settled. But the riders came on slowly; they could not hurry.

Heister walked out on the porch. His woodpile was still as large as some ranchers had laid in for the entire winter. You expected the worst and prepared for it. If you got less, that was a dividend. The long sheds in the west field were full of cattle. The sides of Heister's haystacks showed dark against the land. Some on those snow-rounded stacks had been there three winters, when there was no need for them. As usual, Heister had cleaned out in the fall, selling stuff that other ranchers carried over until the next summer. His herd now numbered less than one quarter of the number owned by the smallest rancher in the park.

The difference was, when spring came, if it ever did, there would be no winter loss at Whispering Pines.

They came into the yard, the horses stamping at the velvety whiteness, blowing past the rime around their muzzles. Several of the ranchers were wearing skullcaps under their hats. Walter Sexton had a woolen shawl wrapped over his hat and knotted under his chin. His big red nose, with a drop of moisture on the tip, jutted out fiercely.

He looked like a frozen monk.

"Run your horses in the barn and come inside, boys."

"Maybe later." Sexton said. The ranchers looked to him; he was the spokesman. He was a genial man, brawny, wasteful of effort in his work, but he had plenty of stamina to give. He was always the loudest man, the stoutest worker at a house raising. Now his face was set with cold and he was not happy in his role.

"We got it from Dinnie Myers that you don't care to sell any of your hay," Sexton said.

"That's right." Heister said it, and then he watched the cold run deeper into Sexton's face and he wondered how Alinor Sexton would have taken his answer; but that was a problem he would have to meet later.

Some of the ranchers looked out at Heister's stacks and then they looked at each other. Brent Fulgham said, "You know what's happening to us, don't you?" It was an accusation and a challenge.

"I don't control the weather, Brent."

"By God, Heister—" Fulgham's temper was at once as brittle as the cold, but Sexton cut him off with a wave of his hand and quick words.

"We ain't here to argue." Sexton removed one of his ragged woolen gloves and thrust his hand under the edge of the saddle blanket. "We got to have hay and you know it, Heister. You've got stacks out there three years old. You can't feed it up before spring.''

"You think I can't? When is spring anyway? Two more months of this and I'll be scraping my stack yards.''

"You know damned well we won't get two more months of winter!'' Fulgham said.

"Winter wasn't supposed to start in September.'' Heister felt the needles of the cold spiking through his heavy shirt and underwear. "Come inside.''

Sexton started to answer, but Fulgham cut in. "All right, you want to hold us up. What's your price?''

Heister shook his head. "It's not money. I'm taking care of myself. When the weather starts to break, you can have hay.''

"Not money, huh?'' Fulgham's eyes narrowed.

The sides of Frank Eggleston's neck were red from rubbing against the crusted edges of his sheepskin collar. His broad face bulged with anger. "We can't wait for a break in the weather, Heister. A chinook right now wouldn't be soon enough. How much for your hay?''

"It's more than that,'' Fulgham said. "By God, he's figuring to get land cheap by starving us out!''

"Now, now, Brent,'' Sexton said. He stared at Heister, troubled, trying mightily to summon reason and fairness.

"I don't want your land.'' Heister said. "And I don't want your money. When the weather breaks, you can have all the hay you need at ten dollars a ton.''

"You know that'll be too late.'' Sexton's doubt was hardening.

Cold and angry they bore their weight in silence against the man on the porch. The wind whisked snow around the corner of the house.

"Too late,'' Sexton said. "We need hay now.'' He looked toward the stacks.

"I'm taking care of my cattle first.''

"Of all the stinking, lousy squeeze plays!'' Fulgham pulled off his right mitten. He began to unbutton his mackinaw. "If you was wearing a pistol, Heister—''

"I can get one."

"You damned fools!" Sexton yelled. "Stop that kind of talk right now!"

For the first time the desperation of the ranchers struck Heister with full force. He saw their bitterness. He saw the willingness of at least half of them to spin this moment into him. The knowledge angered him unreasonably. They thought he was deliberately trying to wreck them. They were improvident. They had taken long chances when he took the short, safe way. Now they were willing to drag him into ruin with them because they had been short-sighted.

He laid his anger on all of them. "Not one of you here has as little meadowland as me. Every one of you has made four times the money I have. For years we've had open winters when you laughed at me for selling short and adding to my haystacks. Now you've got your tails in a crack and you want me to risk everything I've got to help you out."

"You like that, don't you? You're damned well pleased about it." Fulgham's voice had a ragged, grating sound.

Heister liked the situation no more than they did and they should have known it. He said, "I didn't order the weather, boys. I've told you the best I can do."

Brent Fulgham drew a pistol from under his mackinaw. He cocked with trembling fingers.

"Put that away!" Sexton cried.

Fulgham swung his horse close in to the porch. "By God, we're going to have an understanding, Heister!"

"You've already had it, Fulgham." Beckett was at the corner of the house with a rifle resting on a log. His weathered face was deadly with blankness.

Heister looked steadily at Fulgham and he saw the wildness seep from the man's expression, leaving only desperation; and then that, too, faded away and left the marks of bitter defeat. Fulgham put his pistol away. He turned his tired horse and started the long ride back on a trail where the tracks were already nearly drifted over.

In a curiously puzzled voice Sexton said, "I know you don't *want* to see us ruined, Jim, but—"

"I can't take care of the whole park."

"Yeah." Eggleston looked bleakly at the haystacks, at the low sheds.

"I've got to think of myself," Heister said.

"Yeah," Eggleston said heavily. "We see that." Snow crust had cut the legs of his buckskin gelding on the way here. Now the bright blood was frozen in beads on the pale hair. He turned the horse and started after Fulgham.

"You don't really mean . . ." Sexton, like any easygoing man, could summon terrible, short-lived anger on occasions. He seemed to be headed that way now. There was a white frost spot on his cheek. He probed against the numbness for a moment, staring at Heister, and then he rode away.

Neighbors, Heister thought bitterly. *Neighbors, friends until a real test came, and then they got sore because he refused to be dragged under with them.*

He went inside. Beckett was dumping wood into the box behind the kitchen range. He banged the stove lids. Heister heard him grinding coffee. Chilled and shaking from cold that seemed to have settled in his spine, Heister stood with his back to the fireplace. The riders were going slowly. The wind had veered, and now it was coming against their right flank, rolling scud across the snowfields. It was six miles to Sexton's place, the nearest shelter.

The stubborn fools could have warmed themselves and eaten before they left. After a while Heister said, "How's the coffee coming, Fred?"

"All right."

They sat at the oilcloth-covered table. Beckett was silent, looking at the curves of snow caught in the corners of the windowpanes, a grizzled man making his disapproval heavy.

At last Heister said irritably, "You could have let him shoot."

"Yeah, I could have." Beckett's glance was hard, direct.

"I haven't got the hay to save the whole park."

"No," Beckett said.

"To save even enough breeding stuff to start their herds again might use enough of my hay to put me under with the rest of them."

"Yeah, it just might."

"When do you figure the weather will break, Fred?"

"A man's a damn fool to guess." Beckett got out a deck of cards and began to play solitaire.

The air was still crackling when they fed the cattle the next morning after breakfast, forking the long, crisp native hay along the trampled places near the low sheds. Afterward Heister looked at his stacks, sparkling with the wind-driven frost, and then he looked across the long land where there were no fences.

They went back to the house. There was nothing to do until late afternoon when they would have to break ice in the creek again. The warmth of the house and Beckett's silence made Heister irritable. He was on the verge of telling Beckett that he didn't have to stay here if he didn't like it.

But Beckett was a good man. He got along with the summer crew better than Heister. Besides, he was an old man and had no place to go. Then, how could he have so much pride, a sure pride, too, not the touchiness of an attitude falsely held. He had nothing and he didn't care, and yet he was a man respected. It was damned odd.

Beckett sprawled in a chair by the fireplace, reading a soiled magazine. Whatever satisfaction he had taken from life would not suffice for Heister. Fred Beckett was a living example of what Jim Heister did not want to be at sixty. A few fool deals like listening to Sexton and the others would fix a man so that he would wind up with nothing.

Heister kept studying the old man until he hated the sight of him.

"I think I'll go to town, Fred. What do we need?"

"Nothing."

Heister's sorrel humped when the blanket touched its back. It bucked down the yard and all the way to the first deep drift. After that it settled down. The sounds of hungry cattle came a long way across the snow from the Sexton place. Heister saw that Sexton had put boards on top of the wire around his last haystack. Five hundred cattle were milling there, bawling their hunger, pawing down through the layers of crust to the frozen earth.

In Sexton's east fields was more than enough hay to have carried them through, but it was all uncut and under three feet of snow now. Heister rode into the yard. He knew he was not welcome and so he sat his horse and called out. Sexton came out of the barn, kicking away the snow that piled up in front of the door when he tried to close it.

"What do you want, Heister?"

"I want to talk to you about that hay."

After a time Sexton said, "Put your horse in here." He opened the door of the barn. It was warm inside, or so it seemed once the wind was cut off. "Let's go to the house," Sexton said.

"In a minute." Heister walked past the stalls and looked outside at the corrals. There was a whiteface bull in one and ten heifers in another. "That all you figure you can save of the new stuff you bought last fall?"

"About," Sexton said glumly.

"I can give you the hay to save your Herefords, at least."

Sexton nodded. "Uh-huh."

"Don't you want it?"

"Let's go to the house."

There were six girls in the family. Alinor was the oldest, tall and dark, with a direct way of sizing up the thoughts behind a man's words. The cool civility of her greeting was a sharp change from the last time she and Heister had been together. All the girls but she left the kitchen when Mrs. Sexton nodded them out.

Mrs. Sexton poured coffee. "A steak, Jim?" she asked.

"That's one thing we're like to have plenty of before the winter's over." She gave him a speculative look.

Heister shook his head, aware that the sounds of the hungry cattle had never ceased. He said, "I think I've got the hay to save your Herefords, Sexton."

Sexton sipped his coffee. His expression lightened instantly and then the trouble clouded into his eyes again. "That would be a big help. Anyway you figure it, all of us are going to lose so heavy that it will be like starting over again when summer comes."

Alinor stood by the stove, her expression grave, considering. She acted, Heister thought, like both he and Sexton were on trial.

"Of course, if I could save the new stuff I bought last fall, or even a good part of it . . ." Sexton was musing without any sureness in his voice. He looked at his wife and stopped, swinging his gaze then to Alinor.

"We're all neighbors in this park," the girl said.

"I can't take care of everybody," Heister realized that he was suddenly on the defensive.

"You could try. You could make it a little easier," Alinor said.

"I could ruin myself, too." His next words were for Sexton, but he kept looking at the girl. "Shall we figure to try to save as many of your Herefords as we can?"

Sexton pushed his coffee away. His wife was watching him. His daughter was weighing him. He spoke slowly. "I guess maybe I'll just ride along with the others, Heister, but I'm obliged to you for the offer."

"You're in deep with that new stock, Sexton."

"Yeah." Sexton nodded. All at once he was no longer doubtful or troubled. "I guess I am, but there will be summer again. The land will be here, and we all will know things we didn't allow before. I reckon I'll pray for a chinook. If we don't get it, I'll still see greenup time with just as much, or maybe more, than before."

Heister heard the bawling cattle. He heard the wind rasping dry snow across the roof. He pictured the situation in the entire park and he knew how far he stood apart from men at the moment. There was a solidarity in this room now, a wall set against him.

Mrs. Sexton smiled and touched her husband's shoulder lightly as she passed him on her way into the living room. Sexton rose. "I guess we'll make it, one way or another," he said, as cheerfully as if the range were not snow-locked. "I'll see you, Jim." He put on his coat and went out.

In the living room Mrs. Sexton and her daughters began to talk of new spring dresses. The mournful voices of the starving brutes in the field went on and on. There was something here as strange and difficult to understand as old Fred Beckett.

Heister looked hard at Alinor. "When I was a kid my father ran a little store. He gave everyone credit. He went broke, still bragging about how honest people were. They would pay up if they could, he always said. He took up a little ranch and he tried to help everyone that came along. He would up with nothing. I said I'd never do that, Alinor, and I won't."

Alinor watched him thoughtfully. "More coffee, Jim?"

"He didn't have anything. I can't forget that."

"Was he a happy man?"

"Why, I suppose he was, but he wasn't practical."

Alinor nodded. "The world is full of practical men." She began to gather up the cups and saucers.

Sexton was harnessing a team when Heister went to get his sorrel. "You're foolish if you don't take up my offer, Sexton."

"I guess so, Jim. I was about ready to jump at it until Alinor said we're all neighbors here. I'm like most men, I suppose, wanting to win when everybody else wins and silly enough to want to lose when everybody else loses." Sexton grinned. "Just one of the herd, Jim."

When Heister rode away from the shelter of the buildings, Sexton's two hands were going toward the creek with shovels. They would try to dig down where the wind had thinned the snow in pockets, grubbing for frozen grasses. The bawling of the cattle was a death dirge. Drags and shovels and a hundred men could not do now what should have been done last fall.

Heister turned toward home, but after a hundred yards he knew he was in no mood to face Beckett's silence.

He went instead toward Park City, with the wind in his face. When the noise of Sexton's herd died away, the same sounds came down the wind from Frank Eggleston's place. Eggleston was worse off than Sexton because he had more cattle. The fences were down around his stackyards and the snow had blown over them. His cattle were on the ice of the creek, fighting to get the overhanging grasses along the banks. Some of them were already white-covered lumps on the ice.

Heister rode on past. The buildings had a lonely, deserted appearance, but smoke was coming from the stovepipes, laying down the wind in gray streamers.

Far away against the hills where the forage was still plentiful beneath the snow, the buildings at Brent Fulgham's place were huddled together in the ghostly distance.

They were idiots, all of the ranchers. They could have had hay to burn this winter, but they had been taken in by long years of mild weather, laughing at Heister's caution. Security. That was the rule by which Heister lived. If he had had too much of anything, he had always been nagged by a fear that extraordinary circumstances could snatch everything from him in an instant.

The trough at the end of the livery stable was a block of ice. The pump was frozen, its spout choked with a blue icicle. Heister hailed the place. It took him and Dinnie Myers, one inside and one outside, to slide the door open against the wind that bound the rollers in their guides.

"I was going to Arizona, I said." Myers removed Heister's saddle and shook the snow from it. "I said it, but here I am." He was a rangy young blond man, a daring rider, a careless man who had never wanted much of anything except Alinor Sexton, and that had been broken up a year ago when Heister got into the running.

Heister stamped his feet and rolled his shoulders. "We

both should have gone to Arizona.'' He like Dinnie Myers better than any man he had ever known, in spite of the fact that he deplored the man's lack of ambition. Five years younger than Heister, Dinnie could have owned a small ranch in the park if he had set his will toward it; but here he was working in a livery stable, waiting for spring.

Together they took care of the sorrel. It was a relief to Heister to be away from hostility and with a friend. "How about a drink or two and some grub, Dinnie?"

"That suits me. Business ain't rushing by no means."

They were going toward the Golden Eagle, thrusting their shoulders against the wind, when Myers asked. "What sort of deal did you work out with the others over the hay?"

"None at all. I told you last month how I felt about that."

"That was last month."

"I haven't changed my mind," Heister said.

"You can't afford not to change your mind. The park is in a hell of a fix."

"I don't control the weather."

"No, but you control the hay."

"You're putting the wrong twist on things, Dinnie. I've had enough hay talk for one day."

They broke into the stifling heat of the saloon. Some of the townsmen were playing checkers near the stove. Brad Edwards, the owner, was behind the bar. "Well! The wind can blow in anything these days!"

"What do you mean by that?" Heister asked, and he knew that he was bristling over nothing.

Edwards gave him a sharp look. "Forget it."

Myers fiddled around with his glass and then he took the drink at a gulp. "How did Sexton take it?"

"You mean Alinor?"

"All right, Alinor then." Myers's gaze was as tough as Heister's.

"I offered Walt hay to tide over his Herefords. He was about to take me up on it, and then Alinor changed his mind."

"Good for her."

Heister put his glass down slowly. "What's sticking in your craw, Dinnie?"

"Hay." Everything between them was changed by the simple word.

"How many cows do you own, Dinnie?"

"How many friends do you have now?"

"You talk mighty funny for a man who never lit anywhere for more than a few months at a time.

Myers said, "You mean for a man who ain't cornered all the hay in the country. Sure, Jim, I'm a rider for somebody else. Maybe I like it. No responsibility, no worries. But if I ever got around to being a rancher, I'd be one. I'd take on the obligations that go with the name."

"So?" Heister poured himself another drink. "You'd give your hay away, is that it?"

"No. I'd give my friendship. You can call it hay if you want to. It's a funny thing—you've never been small and mean in any little thing, so I can't understand how you'd be that way when the chips are all in the middle of the table."

Heister's anger was the slow-burning kind that had been mounting steadily since yesterday. He said carefully. "A man with no chips in the game can always tell someone else how to play."

Myers was an even-tempered man and the two of them were friends. Myers could have shrugged it off or blunted it with a quip, but he looked at Heister for a long moment and said, "When you made an offer to Sexton that you refused everybody else, you were trying to buy Alinor. What kind of woman did you think she was, Jim?"

It was a cold-blooded thrust that struck home. "Anything else?" Heister asked.

"Yes," Myers said. He poured a drink. "This." He threw the whiskey in Heister's face. Somewhere from beyond the red-streaked agony of blindness, Myers's voice came coolly. "I'll get a pistol, Jim. I'll meet you in the street outside in a half hour."

The wind played in the street, piling curving slopes

against doorways. A few men passed quickly, with their heads pulled low into their coat collars. There were three or four more men in the Golden Eagle now, silent, waiting. The word was around. Heister waited at the end of the bar. He did not want to go ahead, and he could not back out. The world had gone to hell all of a sudden.

Oddly, it was the quick loss of Myers's friendship that was the sharpest bite of all. Beckett and Sexton and Myers had been his friends. They held something in common now that was lost to him. It was Heister's loss alone and he knew it. What had been all-important an hour before was submerged now under the realization that he must go into the street in a few minutes and try to kill his best friend.

He watched the street. The silence of the men at his back kept pushing him.

A large part of Myers's hasty action must be because of Alinor; and some of it because friendship had turned to disgust. A man who had no material stake in any of the park had set himself up to act for the whole country. Heister kept asking himself why.

He guessed that the answer must be that Beckett and Myers, owning nothing, were more a part of the land than he was, with the roots of their thinking twisted deep into the customs of the country. They were neighbors. They were men reaching their friendship toward each other, even with nothing else to give.

All this could be true, but it did not alter the fact that Heister must go into the street soon to face Dinnie Myers. That, too, was a custom of the country. A half hour passed. Myers was not afraid; he would show up. Looking back, Heister could not justify any part of the causes that had led to this.

Another ten minutes ground away, and by then everyone in the saloon was at the windows. Heister pulled his hat on tight and stepped out. At once the cold dug hard into him. There was cold like this over every inch of the park, and dying cattle, and worried men. He was alone in the street. He was alone in the world.

After a while he kicked through the snow and went to the side door of the livery stable. He touched the butt of his pistol. He kicked against the door. "Dinnie!" No answer came. He pushed the door open and stepped into the gloom, sliding quickly to one side, "Dinnie!"

"Yeah?" Myers's voice came from the dimness halfway down the building, and after a time Heister saw him standing there leaning on a pitchfork.

"You weren't—You didn't intend to—" Heister said.

"Of course not, you damned fool. Don't you know a man's hands would stick to a pistol outside in this weather? Besides, I sold my pistol two months ago."

Heister's relief was like a stabbing pain that ends suddenly. He walked down to Myers. The man had taken a long, wild gamble, basing everything on an understanding of Heister that the latter was just now realizing of himself. Without faith, without friendship, there was nothing.

"I—I've changed my mind about the hay," Heister said. "We'll gamble it against a break in the weather inside of three weeks. If we miss . . ." He shrugged. For the first time in months he felt truly satisfied.

"It's no gamble," Myers said. "It's the thing you had to do. I knew you would if you got jarred a little."

Two abreast the cattle came through the drifts, following the trail broken by horses. There were brands from every ranch in the park. The long line was only about fifteen percent of the stuff from twelve outfits. By agreement of everyone, that was all there was a chance to save, and maybe most of that would go.

But there was hope and there was a oneness in the effort. With their faces blue from cold, the riders pushed the herd along until the brutes broke on ahead of their own accord, running toward the hay Fred Beckett had spread near the sheds in Heister's west field.

Fulgham rode up beside Heister. "I was out of my head that day, Jim."

"So was I." There was no security, Heister thought,

unless it was the security of all. Neighbors. There was a powerful word when you came to appreciate it.

Fred Beckett was coming toward a stackyard with a hayrack. His Scotch cap was turned down over his ears. His full underlip was a streak in his gray beard stubble. He looked at the blowing snow and rubbed his dripping nose on the sleeve of his coat. His face was expressionless, almost, when he looked at Heister. "Ain't this a beautiful day?"

Heister nodded. "Never expect to see a better one, Fred."

This memorable tale of cattle ranching in Wyoming in the 1880s is typical of the work of T. V. Olsen, whose thirty novels over the same number of years have earned him recognition as one of the most accomplished of contemporary Western writers. Eminent among his novels are The Stalking Moon (which became a successful motion picture), Arrow in the Sun (which was also filmed, under the title Soldier Blue), Eye of the Wolf, and Lazlo's Strike. The best of his too-few short stories can be found in the 1976 collection Westward They Rode.

They Walked Tall

T. V. Olsen

"*W*alk with your head up," my Pa used to say. "Walk tall. Never look down. Good sense to be afraid only so long as a man don't show it. Man who don't look down never backs down."

Pa was built to see other men from that perspective. In a country of big men he stood bigger than most. He was six-four in his sock feet, broad as a beam, and hickory-hard. Not that he misused his size, not by his own standards. He was a pioneer, a builder, not a destroyer. Most always his eyes had the look of far blue horizons. And there were other times, warning times, when they flashed small lightnings.

Pa had been a captain of cavalry in the Army of Northern Virginia. "Then damn Rec'nstructers and carpetbag politicos wouldn't let a Southern man hold up his head on his native ground," he used to growl. "Man's got to keep

115

a tight fist around his pride, or he's nothing." He'd settled into Wyoming as the first flush of gold seekers were drifting out and the cow barons were on the rise.

It was natural that Pa go into cattle, building his Sickle spread from a shoestring. He built sturdy, built to last. He worked from sunup till dusk, bossing his three-man crew. When he married my Ma, he threw up a tight stone house under the Absaroka peaks, cool in summer and warm in winter. It fitted the country like a hand in a glove; it was a good place, a good life. Pa didn't overset his sights, but he built with an eye to permanence. He ran his small herd on open range and forced respect even from Hugh Buckhorn.

Old Buckhorn owned the huge Chainlink outfit that sprawled over all the eastern half of our valley except for the mountain-backed pocket where our Sickle was nested. This Buckhorn was an old-time settler who'd grown to a purse-proud son. While Pa stabilized his holdings, Buckhorn got the fever of expansion. He claimed up to and around our Sickle proper, moseying over our open range some but not over the patented line, you can bet. Buckhorn was mean and tough. Pa was only tough, but that was enough.

The other little ranchers kept over on the west side of the valley; they were careful about that, except at roundup time.

Funny thing how Pa's mettle was never really tried until this nester man come, first of his kind in the valley. Joe Lynch was a hardscrabble sort who set out to crop his quarter section astride Tie Creek, a horseshoe stream that enclosed Sickle. It was the unspoken boundary betwixt us and Buckhorn, as far as open range went. This Lynch took over an old Chainlink line shack longtime abandoned by the outfit and moved in with his tired drudge of a wife and their towheaded brood of five. Joe Lynch was a worker. He fixed up the shack and made most of his homestead improvements inside of a couple weeks.

Pa glowered and muttered some, but generally he stood by the law. Anyway—and he sounded positive—this wasn't farm country. Few nesters might come and stick a year or so till the land licked 'em and move on, leaving the valley flats to grass and cattle as the Lord meant them to be.

I make it the real trouble came when Joe Lynch brought in barbed wire, what the old, free-ranging cowmen hated most—and maybe feared—for it was the end of a time.

I was twelve that early summer of '88. It comes back like yesterday how on a certain sunny morning I came in for breakfast from doing the first chores. Ours was a warm little household, and I smelled out right off that something wasn't right.

Here was the old man sitting and putting away corn bread, bacon, and coffee with his ordinary appetite, and Ma, as usual, bustling back and forth between stove and table. Only the stubborn blue of Pa's eyes was flicking little lightnings, and Ma's back had a stiff angry set and her round, strong face was flushed with more than oven heat. I edged over to the woodbox and eased down my armload of wood so as not to bust up all this quiet and took my place across from Pa.

The old man cleaned up his plate and lighted his pipe. I knowed he was waiting on me, so I ate fast, so fast that Ma scolded, "Tim, for heaven's sake."

Soon's I'd gulped the last mouthful, Pa said quietly, "Boy, you leave the rest of them chores. You ride with me today."

Ma swung around from the stove, quick and sharp. "Jud Tasker, you'll not take the boy with you. It's bad enough having this un-Christian thing in your head without it taking in him."

Pa acted like he didn't hear. That was his way. He just went ahead and never wasted a breath. "You know why, Timmy, eh?"

"We taking the crew?"

In those days range gossip was a wildfire kind of thing—kids, parents, the old ones—they all knew when something was up. I expect I sounded eager as any cub, because Pa smiled a little. "No, boy. This here's between me and Joe Lynch."

The grin faded as he looked at Ma, like he wanted to make her understand. "Martha, now I told the boy never to back water. Words got an empty sound without a body takes to their meaning."

Ma wouldn't look at him.

He sighed and shoved back his chair and walked to the east wall. He took down the Spencer .54 repeater carbine he had taken off a dead Yankee trooper twenty-four years ago. It had been converted to take metal-jacketed cartridges. He broke out a fresh box of shells and loaded her up. I had seen him do as much aplenty, loading for varmint, but this bright morning those smooth metal noises made my scalp prickle.

Pa lifted off his hat from a wall peg and didn't look back when he walked out, me close on his heels. We saddled up down at the corral, Pa cinching his rig on his rangy lineback dun and waiting while I threw a hull across the whey-bellied old mare.

We cut west over the rolling, grass-grown flats to Tie Creek. I kept off behind the old man where I could see only the gnarled-oak set of his big back and one hard edge of black-bearded jaw. I was some squirrelly, I tell you, but also fair to split for wanting to see Pa give that damn' nester what for.

Pa only said one thing the whole ride, "You mark your Ma, boy. Got a heart big as all outdoors. Just don't understand these things. Mostly a woman don't. Ain't to say your Ma don't know aplenty in her own right, you mind me?"

I minded, all right, but there wasn't a lot of sense to it. It doesn't mean much at twelve that a man's got his ways, a woman hers. What sense I made was that Pa meant there would be no disrespect to Ma on this account. If I showed any, his broad leather belt would come off fast. I cleared my throat and said, "Yes, sir," making it as respectful as I knew how.

In an hour we came in sight of Tie Creek winding between its low banks like a sparkling snake. Pa turned upstream toward Lynch's homestead. We'd gone maybe a half mile when we came on this line of new peeled posts lined by three tight strands, barbed and shiny. It was kind of a wall, and I felt Pa's temper crackle inside my own head. He rode up to one post and leaned from his saddle and grabbed it. He gave a hard tug, but it was ground-braced, solid against his big muscles. He said something under his breath, heeled the lineback around, and headed up the line of posts at a fast trot.

We came up on a grassy knoll and saw the nester's wagon pulled up below. The bed was piled high with fresh-cut cedar posts; a couple rolls of new wire were under the seat. This Joe Lynch was on the ground working with wire stretchers and pliers, putting all his stringy muscle into pulling that damn' wire drum tight. He was too intent to see us as we came on down the slope.

Pa's voice froze the nester as he bent over to fetch up a staple from the keg by his feet. He came up slow, trying to straighten his shoulders. They were thin and work-stooped. He wiped his hands on his pants.

"Morning, Mr. Tasker," Lynch said. I don't know that he was so scared, but he sounded on a caution for sure.

Pa never wasted time. He didn't now. He looked at the posts, nodding as if to himself. "These here'll have to come down. When it turns cold, my cattle'll drift with the winds and pile against 'em. First'll be cut to ribbons, rest'll pile three, four deep, freeze that way."

Pa was making reference to a couple years past when the Great Blizzard of '86 hit the high plains. That had been no ordinary time; even I knew as much. The amount of wire around Joe Lynch's little homestead might catch a few far-drifting beeves, no more.

Lynch, he thumb-nudged the slouch hat back on his lean towhead, being uncertain about it all. "Well, that could be so, Mr. Tasker. Me and mine are fresh out of Ohio, you know."

Pa swelled a little. "I reckon. No cattle of mine been grazing this way, no call for all this. Man, are you meaning to wave a red flag under my nose?"

"Why no, sir." Lynch licked his lips and shuffled his

feet around. "Now, I don't say it was apurpose, you mind, but Mr. Buckhorn's riders whooped it up t'other side of the crick where I had the land new seeded. Drove some cows through and trampled it all up and ruint my seeding. I'm not meaning to prod anyone, but I got to pertect myself. You see how it is."

Pa didn't, for a fact. "You wire your side borders on Buckhorn's range first off?"

"Well, no," Joe Lynch said helplessly. "Not yet. You see—"

"I see right enough. You figured to wire off my side first, try me out before you brave Buckhorn." The blood was high in the old man's face, and he was madder than I'd seen him. "That was your big mistake. No one pushes Jud Tasker. No one!"

He lifted the coiled rope from his pommel and shook it out. He dabbed off a short loop and snaked it over the nearest post. "Your rope!" he snapped at me. My fingers were shaking as I followed up.

We dallied and heeled off to take up the slack. As the horses leaned into it, little mounds of earth broke up around the base of the post. Finally it came free and sagged over.

Quick as a flash Pa turned his horse. Joe Lynch had sidled over by his wagon and was fumbling under the seat. Pa rode against him, and the linebacker's shoulder smashed Lynch in the chest and bowled him butt over tea kettle in the dust.

Pa reached under the seat and came up with an old Sharps buffalo gun. He opened the breech and pulled out the four-inch fifty-caliber shell and tossed the gun back in the wagon.

Pa's eyes were the color of ice. "If you ain't a man, you hadn't better go armed like one."

Joe Lynch crawled to his feet and didn't look up, wiping his hand across his mouth.

"Hear me good. I make you a yellow back-sneaking dog. You are pulling that fence down now, mister, hear?"

"Yes, sir." Lynch said it soft, his shoulders slumped.

"I find it up again, I'll shoot you on sight. Make me out clear, nester?"

"Yes, sir." Lynch's voice came thin, with a quiver to it.

We coiled and slung our ropes. Pa swung off and I followed. He didn't look back, so neither did I. My belly felt a mite snakey. More than once I had got my boy's pride flattened by the weight of Pa's hand, and I thought of the crushed look in Joe Lynch's mild eyes. He was a bent, scrawny one for certain, but he was a man—or had been before he became a lousy nester.

With that I pushed the notion out of mind. As Pa said later on that day, show these damn' hoegrubbers a soft side one time, and they would get mean and snotty.

Next day was Saturday and that meant town day. Pa hitched up the spring wagon and we went in, Ma beside him on the seat and me in the back end hanging my heels over the letdown tailgate.

Pima Flats wasn't much in these days—one dusty street and dirt sidewalks, a general merchandise store, feed company, blacksmith shop, stable, professional building, and a couple of saloons.

The tie rails were already lined with rigs and saddle horses. Pa set our wagon between two others in front of Marsh Whalen's general merchandise store and then got to the ground and helped Mother down. They hadn't spoke much since the day before. Pa tramped stiff-backed around the wagon and headed for the Shorthorn Saloon across the way to find a rancher crony or two. I skipped along behind Ma, going into Whalen's store.

It was a favored place of mine, old Marsh's. It was cool and smelled of far-off places, of spices and new leather and kerosene. Flocks of women were clucking around between the counters; Ma joined a covey of them. There were some little kids hanging on their mas' skirts but none near my own age, so I made to ignore the lot, going over to where the stick candy was. Usually did Marsh give me a free piece if I hung over the counter a spell.

I was eating it up with my eyes and didn't look around till I heard a man say something to old Marsh. It was Joe Lynch with his wife and the five towheads. Mrs. Lynch was a timid kind of soul with a washed-out look. The kids—two boys and three girls—were all runty for their ages, shy as mice, and they had a scary-eyed look except for the oldest one.

Now with this whole towhead brood standing a yard off, I got up my hackles and put a stare on that oldest Lynch kid. I'd never seen him close before. His name was Marty, and I guess he was my age but maybe a half a head shorter and mostly bone and skin and tow-colored hair. Me, I was already running to Pa's beef. Pretty soon his eyes, like pale moons in his thin face, dropped away from mine. Which made me rooster my chest out some.

Meantime old Marsh Whalen, a kindly rabbit of a gent, was talking low with the kid's old man. "Don't know as I should stretch your credit one cent more, Mr. Lynch. Folks're already down on me for selling you them bales of barbed wire."

"Sure." Joe Lynch sounded like he was past caring much.

"Allowing folks are dependent on me to freight in their supplies, I can't afford losing a lot of good will."

"Sure. Ain't asking for no more wire, Mr. Whalen. I need to have grub, though. Some more seed, too."

"Well, now," said Marsh.

He broke off and some tight lines pinched up his old face. He was looking at the doorway. I faced around and saw Hugh Buckhorn standing there, a squarish big block of a man who looked like he was wedged in his black broadcloth suit. The trousers were stuffed into bench-made Justins, and a white Stetson rode his handsome crop of pure white hair. His face looked like it had been chipped from the side of a mountain. He fingered an inch of ash off his palm-held cigar and didn't say anything. Just looked at poor Marsh.

Off behind him, but in plain sight, stood Bourke Claypool, a long, lean elegant sort who wore neat range clothes and was no cowhand. There was a black-butted Colt's in a beautifully tooled holster along his thigh. Bourke had a generally bad name, and of course all us kids looked up to him in an inside-out way. Gaming sometimes, we used to bloody noses over whose wooden gun would be Bourke Claypool's. There was Bourke and there was General Custer. You had your pick how you wanted to be killed.

Old Marsh, he swallowed spit a couple times and allowed he couldn't sell Lynch a thing. Sorry. Hugh Buckhorn and his shadow moved out of the doorway and walked on. Joe Lynch stared down at his scuffed thick shoes and didn't say anything.

I saw Ma walk off from the other women, over to Addie Lynch. She said something quiet and nice, and Mrs. Lynch give a timid smile. A few other ladies came over and joined them. The rest sniffed and took a well-I-never expressions.

Joe Lynch got warm under the collar. "Come on."

"I'll stay a little while, please, Joe."

Joe Lynch flung out, "Have it your way," and walked from the store, his steps long and angry. He didn't like his wife taking charity friendship, and I wasn't het on Ma giving it. In those days there was only one brace of pants to a family, and Pa wore 'em. Here was Ma going flat against him, taking up friendly with these nesters. I expect I puffed my crop a bit, because Ma's mouth tightened up.

She looked at the oldest Lynch kid scuffing his bare feet on the planks and said, "Tim, why don't you take Marty and find some of the other boys?"

She flattened my glare with one of her own, and I went out muttering. The Lynch kid tagged along. I got off a ways and turned on him. "Don't want you tagging me, kid."

I stood in front of him and above him and planted my hands on my hips. He looked more over sober and careful. "Why not?"

"Taskers don't have truck with no 'count poor trash."

The kid's pale eyes flared and he tucked his chin "You better take that back."

"What you gonna do about it?" I put all the sneer in it I could. "Bet you're as yella as your old man."

Right off, I expected he would bluster some. Boys used to brag up to a fight and maybe set a chip on their shoulder and toe a line or two in the dirt. But this runty squirt didn't waste a word. He just lit into me, his skinny arms wind-milling.

Next I knew, I was flat on my back with this Lynch runt standing over me and his fists doubled. A thin laugh sounded. I twisted a look around. There was Bourke Clay-pool, lounging by the tie rail a couple yards away. Bourke's black eyes were dancing, and his grin was mocking and lazy.

"Drag out them spurs, rooster. You ain't letting a chicken-livered hoegrubber stomp you now, are you?"

I crawled up and went after the Lynch kid, swinging wild. He was pretty fast. He stepped off from my first couple swings; then I caught him flush on the jaw and put him down in the dust. I straddled him and pinned his el-bows with my knees and began punching his face. Some woman let out a screech. I was crazy mad, and I kept hitting till a big hand clamped around my neck and set me on my feet.

"Lordy, boy," Pa said very quiet. "Lordy, boy. You're half again his size."

Bourke Claypool's thin laugh echoed again. I looked around, breathing hard, seeing the shame in Pa's face, and a kind of protest boiled up in my throat. *What about Lynch, Pa? What about him?*

I left it unsaid. Ma stood in the store doorway, looking a little white around the mouth. Mrs. Lynch was on her knees by Marty and crying and wiping his bloody face on her faded skirt. There and then all the rage was drained out of me, and I stood there with a foolish and belly-down feel.

Joe Lynch came out of the blacksmith shop now and crossed the street at a tired, shuffling run. He shook his wife by the shoulder, asking her the question, and when she answered, he faced around. His eyes targeted me first, but I don't think he really saw me. He looked at Pa then, like he was looking through him, and Pa pulled his glance away.

"If you're through here, Martha," Pa's deep voice was none too steady, "we'll be going home."

There was no talk on the ride back or during the noon meal, nor afterward. There was work to do, but none of us stirred ourselves. I moped in a corner. Pa sat at the table, puffing his pipe like mad. Ma stared at the untouched food on her plate and made no move to clear the table.

Finally, Ma said, very quiet, not looking up. "We should all be very proud of ourselves. Are you proud, Tim?"

"No'm," I muttered.

"Why not ask me, Martha?" Pa didn't sound angry, just tired and a little baffled, like he was trying to study things out.

"Jud." Her voice was very gentle. "Jud, you're the master in this house, and that's as it should be. I can't make your decisions. I should have known that. I tried to push you before, and that was a mistake. I won't make it again."

Pa motioned with his pipe. "Say it anyhow. There's a thing working in me, and I don't know how to put it."

Ma leaned toward him with a kind of glow in her face. "Jud, your self-respect is the root of your life. It has been since I first knew you. And now the root is being torn out, and that isn't right. It's just that you never saw how other people have lives to live, too, and a pride that keeps them going. They have a right to that pride."

Pa sighed, long and deep. "Yes, that's it. Martha, I don't know that I can feel the right of anything anymore. I used my strength yesterday to smash a weaker man down. Why, yesterday I'd of skinned Tim alive for mauling a lad half his size. Lord! how do you blame a boy for following his Pa?" He puffed hard on his pipe, like he did when downwind of a strong thought, and he said, "Martha, a man can't take back a mistake that bad. But he can grow with it and live better for it."

"Why, Jud, you've said it all yourself!" Ma said, real proud.

I suppose up to that moment Pa was God to me. Seeing him as just a big man, capable of big mistakes, of big regrets, twisted hard in me. Growing up is not a sudden thing, and reaching a foot or so toward manhood in one day can make for some tall hurting. You have been choking down too much in favor of a clay-footed idol; you flounder and you hurt. Still . . .

Pa was no god, but it took a mighty big man to change the set of his ways when youth was far behind him. I was the lucky one, and I knew it. I ran over to him and he held me tight for a minute, and Ma looked on, not tearful but a little misty.

"Come on." Pa was gruff again. "We got a thing to do, you and me."

The two of use left the house and got our horses. I didn't have to ask. I knew where we was headed.

Around midafternoon we came to the Lynch homestead on the east bank of Tie Creek. We stopped up on a rise west of the layout. It didn't take an Injun eye to study out something was wrong. Down along the creek bank a cluster of mounted men was gathered around one of the huge old trees we called an ironwood.

Pa, he socked in steel and boiled down that rise, me a horse's nose behind him.

Mrs. Lynch stood in the door of the shack, her scared towheads grabbing ahold of her skirt. Her face was white as plum blossoms, and she had a wild eye. We went off on past 'em, over to that ironwood.

The horsemen broke apart as we came up, and Joe Lynch was sitting one of his spavined plow horses, wearing a rope jerked up so tight his head was angled sideways and he was fighting for breath. The rope was flung over a big old limb, and a Chainlink hand was tying down the free end.

Pa halted a few yards off and made a motion I was to rein away from him. I did so, feeling a knot of trouble doubling up in my craw. I was sure there was going to be trouble when Hugh Buckhorn cantered out from the group on his fine special-gaited sorrel. Bourke Claypool edged up, too, making it casual. The four Chainlink crewmen, just workaday hands, stayed by the tree. These were times for touching off the mean in a man's soul, and the good, and these fellows were not sure which way they were going. They looked uneasy, even shamefaced.

Hugh Buckhorn crossed his heavy scarred hands on his pommel, his voice a-crackle with authority. "I'm hanging him, Jud. I trust you got no objection?"

Pa said, slow and easy, "That's pendin' you say why."

"Why? An hour ago we caught this damn' cocky sodbuster stringing his wire on my west range."

"Along the boundary of his homestead?" Pa suggested, very dry.

Well, it was that plain. First off Lynch had been timid enough to feel out just us with his wire stringing. After what happened that morning, he'd found it in him to tackle the big dog, Buckhorn.

Hugh Buckhorn's meaty face was sweating, but it was from the heat. His times hadn't bred the fearing strain, and when they did crop up, they didn't last long. This Buckhorn was of a breed that handled their own problems, shot their own dogs, and it had turned old Hugh hard as flint.

"I ain't bandying that point, Tasker. There's a limit to what a man can take."

"Why, Hugh, I'd say so. Run your cattle through his new-seeded fields, didn't you?"

"Hell fire, man! Don't give me a scripture reading. Lynch said you made him tear down a length of wire he strung on your side yesterday. Says he's sorry he let you buffalo him, says he's glad to take on the lot of us." Saddle leather creaked to his shifting weight. "I ain't liking this much, but it's the frying pan or the fire. A man takes his choice."

"He docs," Pa says softly. "I come to apologize to Joe Lynch."

Bourke Claypool gave a short ugly snicker. "Mr. Tasker, you better make it fast."

"Why bring him back here to string him up? Why make his wife and young 'uns watch it?''

"An object lesson to future nesters. I want this told around. It will head off a lot of future trouble. Now you ride out, dammit, Jud. I want no trouble with you.''

You didn't argue it. He was an old man who had out-lived two wives and three sons, and the days he'd known had burned out the humanity in him. So Pa half reined his horse around as if to go. Then his hand, hid to Buckhorn's view, snaked down to the saddle scabbard and tugged out his carbine and brought it up sharp and swift, left forearm bracing the barrel, right hand levering the weapon light-ning-fast, then ready to the trigger.

"You ain't hanging Lynch. Tell that hand to cut the rope. Now."

Buckhorn's eyes glittered snake-cold, and I knew how it would be, knew in the split second before he mouthed the flat word "Bourke!"

Bourke Claypool moved faster than I'd of reckoned a gunman could, straddling leather. The hair-triggered gun blurred from its black sheath. Pa gave his lineback one spur and sent it careening in a half circle while Claypool's shot smashed down the hot silence. He scored a clean miss.

Pa reined in the lineback with an iron hand, at the same time bringing the carbine to bear level. It was like an in-visible fist hit Bourke Claypool and wiped him off his sad-dle. He hit the ground and rolled and lit on his back with a sightless stare fixing the sky.

Pa levered the carbine, the sound making my nerves jerk like the shots hadn't. He dead-centered the sights on old Hugh Buckhorn's broad chest. "Say how it'll be, Hugh. Now, for I won't wait."

Buckhorn's long white hair plumed in the wind; his granite face didn't twitch by a muscle. "You goddamn nester-loving fool," he said, very stony and clear. "I never give a damn what you or any man thought. Cut him loose, Calem."

He spoke true enough; he was a man looking into the hot muzzle of death and knowing it and shaping his action to the size of the stakes. The Buckhorn legend might sit shakier after today, but a dead man would never care. Silently one of the crewmen cut away the rope around Joe Lynch's neck. Another freed the nester's hands. The other two walked to Claypool and lifted his body across his saddle. Mounting, they rode away, tight-bunched.

The near-scrape hadn't touched the crazy and dogged something in Joe Lynch's face as he tramped past us, past his family, into his shack. He come out with the old Sharps gun in his right fist. This, I knew then, was another man, a man grown tall.

"I want to know now and for good, is the trouble done between us?"

"I apologize to you, for me, for my boy." Pa scowled and swallowed with the words, for a prideful man doesn't change. "It's done all right, Joe."

"The fence," Joe Lynch went on, then hesitated. "Say we leave it down for now, see how things go."

Pa nodded and touched his hat to Mrs. Lynch and reined around and away. I started around, too, but then reined back. Making my apology was my place, not Pa's.

I looked at Marty Lynch. "You want to come over some time?"

"Maybe."

The kid sounded pretty stiff, and I reckoned he was taking after his old man, too. It would take a spell, but I judged he would come. And he did.

A professional writer for more than forty years, Talmage Powell has better than five hundred short stories, sixteen novels, and several television scripts to his credit. In the forties and fifties he was a frequent contributor to such top-of-the-line Western pulps as Dime Western, 15 Western Tales, *and* Western Story. *His only Western novel,* The Cage, *the powerfully offbeat account of a manhunt across a southwestern desert, was filmed in France. Equally unusual is "The Day the Earth Burned," in which a wild grass fire forces an uneasy alliance between homesteaders and a hard-bitten old cattle baron.*

The Day the Earth Burned

Talmage Powell

*P*hil Hyder noticed the smoke pall in the east Tuesday morning. The haze hung along the entire rim of the horizon.

He'd ridden a mile toward the fire when he saw a pair of riders a couple hundred yards south of him. He angled to intercept them. They were Sam Hoskins and young Tim Archer.

"Looks like all hell's busted loose in the high grass," Hoskins said.

Phil Hyder nodded agreement. He had seen one such grass fire in his twenty-eight years. A red demon swallowing everything in its path, leaping, prancing, crackling as if with glee. This was virgin land where grass had died over the centuries to feed other grass. Now the old grass burned, too, the very earth itself burning, smoldering hotter than a smithy's coals to a depth of two feet or better in places.

"We'll lose everything we got," young Archer said, wiping his pale face.

"If this wind don't change," Hyder said.

As they rode forward, they were joined by others from the east bank of the river, Epstein, MacIntosh, and Ledbetter.

The group of homesteaders neared the fury of the fire in midafternoon. Hyder dismounted to give the tired and jittery mare a rest. Better than a hundred yards from the fire the heat slapped him across the face. He saw tongues of flame shoot skyward as brush and trees were devoured.

He looked north and south. There seemed no end to the fire. There certainly was no way a few puny creatures like men could stop it.

The group pulled back and rode again westward toward their homes along the river.

The group halted in early darkness near Sam Hoskins's place.

"We'd never outflank the fire," Hyder said. "Too big, moving too fast."

"If the wind hasn't changed by morning," Sam Hoskins said, "we'll have to load all we can on wagons, drive in our livestock, and cross the river."

"Into Corliss Mather's territory, onto the Iron Triangle?" Tim Archer said. The question drew looks from the others, but it was a question, Phil Hyder thought, that no one else had been willing to voice.

"It's been three months since her husband was found shot to death on this side of the river," old man Ledbetter said. "Three months since she vowed none of us would ever set foot on the west bank of the river long as Jethro Mather's killer is free. But shorely she won't stick to that vow in the face of a thing like this fire."

"She'd better not," Hoskins said. "With the fire pinning us here in the bend of the river, ain't but one way we can go—across, onto the Triangle.''

Hyder slept fitfully, that night, snapping awake between troubled dreams, unable to get Corliss Mather off his mind.

He had worked for the Triangle and he knew the iron that was in the woman. It was not surprising that the death of Jethro had brought an unwomanlike reaction from her.

It had taken a Jethro and Corliss Mather to carve an outfit like the Triangle out of this land. Long a law unto himself, Jethro Mather had bossed a territory that counted itself in square miles and its cattle in herds. The years had not slowed the activity of the man or dampened his zest for life or taken the edge from his tempestuousness. It had taken a bullet from an unknown man three months ago on this side of the river to do that.

After the sheriff from the raw, young town of Fardeen had failed to find Jethro's killer, the countryside had crackled with the expectancy that Corliss would send a strong force across the river to drive the few settlers away.

Instead she had delivered her pronouncement: ''I'll never set foot east of the river, on land besmirched by my husband's blood. As long as his murderer goes free, no living soul from over there shall touch Triangle soil.''

Phil Hyder got out of his bunk at daybreak. He opened the cabin door. Outside, the new day was tainted with the smell of smoke. And the breeze had freshened.

By ten o'clock he had a loaded wagon and his few head of livestock moving toward the river.

He stopped a low rise and came in sight of the river bend. Wagons, livestock, and people were gathered there. His knuckles tightened on the reins. Nobody seemed to have made a crossing. Looking across the broad yellow river, he saw the reason. Armed riders, possibly two-score strong, were patrolling the west bank.

An infuriated Sam Hoskins confirmed what Hyder's eyes and logic had told him.

''The crazy old she-bear ain't breaking her word,'' Hoskins said as Hyder swung from the wagon seat and watched his own cows drift in with the other livestock.

Hyder turned to find that the men had drifted up to form a semicircle about him.

Hoskins said, "You got any ideas, Hyder?"

"I don't propose to defend Corliss Mather's action. . . ."

"You damn well better not," Hoskins said. "Not to me, leastways!"

Hyder looked at Hoskins steadily. When Hoskins had paused to stand sweating and breathing shallowly, he said, "Corliss is embittered, carrying a deep, raw wound of the mind. But I'm going to try to find reason left in her."

As Hyder moved toward his mare, Hoskins said, "Just see that you come back, Phil."

"We can't afford burring among ourselves," Hyder said, unable to keep heat from his voice. "But I'll expect explaining of that when I get back."

"I can explain it now. I know who's crossed the river from the Triangle more times than one."

Hyder stared at the short, solidly built, weathered man and said in a low voice, "It will pay you, Hoskins, to keep Faith Mather out of this." His gaze swept the others. "You can depend on me not to take a one-way ride across the river."

"You'd best make it brief, then," Hoskins said. "Or we're going to cross."

As Phil Hyder edged the mare into the lazy current of the river, his eyes swept the west bank for the slender, trim figure of Faith Mather. He didn't see her.

When the mare reached the middle of the river, water swirling about her withers, a man on the west bank yelled, "That's far enough, Hyder!"

Hyder relaxed a little. He'd expected a closely placed shot to be his first warning.

"Randall?"

"Yeah?"

"I want to see Corliss. I'm unarmed."

"If you come, you'll be floated back," Jake Randall said. "Her orders. You've made yourself one of them.

You're not to walk on Triangle soil. Ride a quarter mile downstream to white water. We'll talk to you there.''

Hyder rode downriver to the fringes of white water, the mare stepping gingerly.

His wait was a short one. Presently, Corliss and the two Randall brothers rode down the west bank and into the water.

Wearing leather breeches, flannel shirt, and a flat-crowned hat, Corliss was an amazonian woman of the outdoors who had retained the firm, well-proportioned lines of her youth. She sat her saddle with easy grace and handled the reins deftly.

She was flanked by Jake and Tyne Randall. Jake was foreman of the Triangle, a heavyset, middle-aged man with an almost melancholy face, a quiet man who did his job well. His brother, Tyne, was a slim, wiry youth, quick with temper, a man who liked to work until his jeans jingled with coin and then ramble off for a laugh, a drink, the company of a pretty girl until the results of his toil were expended. It was as if ancestral qualities had been sharply divided between the two brothers, gravity going to Jake, levity to Tyne.

Corliss Mather drew rein a dozen feet from Phil. "Well, Phil, you seem to have reaped a lot of trouble on the wrong side of the river. Appears even the powers of heaven and earth don't like the cry of spilled blood.''

Her eyes were bright, hot. Her husband's death had affected her even more deeply than Phil Hyder had imagined, and he suddenly knew this parley would fail.

"I don't figure the powers had much to do with it,'' Hyder said. "Unless you class among them a chance lightning bolt, or sunlight pinpointing through a chunk of quartz, or a lazy camper's fire somewhere in the east.''

"The trouble is no less real,'' Corliss said shortly. She regarded Hyder for a moment. "You could have come back to the west bank as recently as three months ago, if you'd so chosen.''

He didn't speak, because to answer her would have offended her or forced him to speak dishonestly. He could never have gone back while Jethro Mather lived, except with his hat in his hands and an apology and a promise on his lips. The final scene between him and the old man had been too violent. *You're a drifter, you got nothing, Hyder, you're a forty-a-month-and-found cowhand, and you're not paid to come to the parlor of the main house and court my daughter.*

East of the river there had been land for the homesteading where a man could build a house and bring a woman after the crops of a season or two were in. Such had been his intent.

Hyder said slowly, "I'd choose to cross the river now, under any terms, if I could bring the rest of the people with me, Corliss."

"Including the murderer of my husband?"

"It appeared he wasn't murdered," Phil Hyder said. "He wasn't shot in the back. He fell with his own gun near his hand, fired once."

"No man east of the river could have outdrawed Jethro Mather fairly," Corliss said in a blunt tone that echoed a closed mind. " 'Twould be easy to fire the gun of a dead man and leave it near his hand."

She pulled herself rigid in the saddle and looked eastward, to the heavy smoke pall. There is my sign, Phil. Consuming fire. Cleansing fire. However you feel about it, it has brought my husband's killer to bay. He's on the east bank, among you. I said that as long as he's free, no one shall cross this river. Now let him step forward—bring the man who killed my husband to me, and you shall all cross the river."

She turned her dappled gray quickly. Phil Hyder watched the stiff arch of her back as she rode out of the river. Young Tyne Randall rode out behind her. Jake Randall hung back. "Phil," he said quietly, "I've worked on her, reminded her of the women and children over there. I'll keep trying."

Hyder looked at Randall's tired, melancholy face. "Thanks, Jake. But it appears to be a real opportunity for her to get what she wants. I don't think she'll give in easy— but I wish you luck, and I appreciate it."

Randall seemed on the point of saying something more; then he turned his horse and followed his brother and Corliss out of the river.

Phil Hyder studied the faces of the east bank men when he delivered Corliss's ultimatum. Here a facial muscle twitched, there an eyelid flickered, but only anger and fear were apparent. No pair of lips parted to speak the story of a gunfight with Jethro Mather.

The silence lengthened, minute by minute. The rising breeze flapped canvas on wagons and brought a stronger smell of smoke.

"The old she-wolf," Hoskins burst out. "Has she reckoned Jethro might have died at the hand of a townsman or even a passing stranger?"

"She's reckoning only revenge," Archer said. He was the youngest of the bunch. He had a sweet young wife and two babies born within thirteen months of each other. He turned away suddenly to hide tears in his eyes.

The silence returned, remained until it was a hateful thing. Hyder knew what it was doing to each man. He could feel the mistrust of each for his neighbor rising.

Old man Ledbetter cleared his throat finally. "Would appear there's an unworthy man among us. But we have no way of naming him. . . ."

The knowledge of what had to be done came to Phil Hyder. He said, "One among us is going over the river. Directly over. To Corliss Mather."

Young Archer was the first to fathom his meaning. "For her to hang?"

"Or deliver to a court of law."

"You think she'd do that, Hyder?" Hoskins said.

"I don't know. She's not herself right now. I don't know for sure what she'd do. But one thing I do know for sure— our hours here are numbered."

He watched them shrink involuntarily from his words.

"We do this," Hoskins said, "even if the guilty man ain't among us?"

"Can you think of any other way?"

Hoskins sank to a hunkered position, facing across the river. "How do we decide which man goes? Draw lots?"

"That would be fair."

"All right," Hoskins said. "I for one will chance it. We've got to get our women and kids across." He rose and dusted the seat of his jeans with his hands. "I got a deck of cards in my wagon. Hyder can shuffle. Epstein will cut. MacIntosh will cut again and set the deck on the ground. Each man will step forward to take one card. High card crosses the river."

Hyder watched Hoskins move to his wagon and return. Hoskins handed him the cards. He shuffled and passed them to Epstein.

Ledbetter stepped forward and drew first. "Ten of diamonds," he said.

Tim Archer stood with his wife clinging to him. Hyder watched the boy. With a bolting motion, Archer pulled free of his wife and almost flung himself at the cards. He drew one and an uncontrollable laugh ripped from his throat. "Three of spades!"

MacIntosh and Epstein drew. Ledbetter's card remained high.

"After you," Hoskins said.

Phil Hyder walked to the deck and pulled the top card. He turned it face up and saw that it was the king of spades. He sensed before Hoskins drew that he would remain high man.

He watched the suddenly unreal form of Hoskins move to the cards.

"Jack of clubs," Hoskins said quietly.

Hyder let the card fall from his nerveless fingers. He turned toward his mare. He was glad that they watched him in silence. He sensed their relief. He felt the unspoken thought they shared, that if a man had to go, it was better that it be the one single man among them.

He felt as if he were among strangers. Then a woman sobbed, and a man touched his hand, and another man said, "We'll never forget, Hyder. She'll pay for this one day."

Astride the nervous mare, Hyder had reached the middle

of the river when Jake Randall called from the west bank, "Who's out there?"

"Phil Hyder."

"You've come far enough."

"I'm coming all the way. I've got a message for Corliss."

"Speak it out, then," Corliss's voice came to him.

"We've accepted your proposition. We want a trial by jury, not the taking of the law into your hands."

The mare was almost at the west bank now. Phil Hyder could clearly make out the shadows of men and horses drawn up to await him.

"Who is the man?" Corliss said.

For answer, Hyder spurred the mare forward, forcing her to haunch herself on the west bank. She came out of the water with head tossing and tail switching.

Hyder rose onto the flat and drew rein facing Corliss and Jake and Tyne Randall.

"Now," he said, "let the others cross."

"I'm not much of a mind to believe you, Phil Hyder," Corliss said. "You think that because of Faith and because I grew fond of you when you worked here . . ."

"Go back, Phil," Jake Randall said. "Corliss is right. You wouldn't have killed Jethro."

Jake Randall shifted his bulk in the saddle, turning his melancholy face to the woman who ordered his hours and tasks and depended on him. "Corliss, for the final time, let me plead with you to realize what you're doing."

"Hush, Jake," Corliss said without looking at him.

"Let's have an end to this talk," Phil Hyder said, fighting the desperation and fear that beat at him. "You've got what you want—now let the others cross."

"That's all you have to say, Phil?" Corliss asked.

He took off his hat and wiped his forehead with the back of his hand. "Yes."

Then he was aware of sound and movement and looked up to see Faith Mather riding out of the shadows. She was young and the most beautiful thing Hyder had ever seen in the moonlight. She rode with a rifle across her saddle and stopped her horse at Hyder's side.

"Faith," Corliss said in a thick, low voice, "I gave you orders to . . ."

"Stay away from the river," Faith said. "I know. But I'm here, and your madness has gone far enough. I'm standing between you and Phil, and you'll not take him."

"Girl, I've given my bounden word to bring justice to the man who killed Jethro."

"And you're all forcing my hand," Jake Randall said in a bitter voice.

Hyder looked at the Triangle foreman. Jake Randall had drawn his sidearm and was resting the pistol on his saddle horn.

"I'm sorry, Tyne," he said with a pleading in his voice. "I've played the string to its end, first hoping that time would make Jethro's death a memory, then when the fire put the people over there in a helpless spot, believing I could talk Corliss into letting them across."

His voice broke. When he resumed speaking, it was to Corliss. "The boy never meant it to happen, Corliss. You remember he was working line camp. He had a cold and was drinking to sweat it out. But Jethro misunderstood and didn't give Tyne a chance to explain."

"Jake . . ." Tyne said, bunching in his saddle.

"It's got to come out, boy. We were wrong. You can't live with a thing like this without the poison of it, the hiding of it hurting other people more than they deserve. Corliss, Jethro cursed and struck the boy and found a temper to match his own. Before the boy knew what he was doing, he had struck back, said words of his own, and got himself too far out on a limb to return. It was one of those quick, hot things that happen out here in this country sometimes—and Jethro was dead. I was going up to the line camp to see how Tyne was feeling and saw him taking the body across the river where he left it."

"Jake," Corliss said, "you've been with me, and Jethro, for more than twenty years. You've helped make the Triangle. You're part of it. And now . . ."

"Now, Corliss," Jake Randall said, "I'll be in Fardeen until after Tyne's trial. Maybe things will seem a little different then. But there's no use talking more now."

Phil Hyder watched Jake Randall make a gesture with his hand. Tyne hesitated, then turned his horse and rode out across the flat, Jake following him.

Corliss sat in her saddle like an image graven of the very soil and stone of the Triangle. Then Hyder saw her bring her hands up to cover her face. A single moan escaped her before she turned the horse and rode off slowly.

Phil Hyder turned his gaze from a torment that was too vivid, too private to watch. Much as she is suffering, he thought, good will come from it. Good must come from it.

He reached toward Faith Mather. Their hands met; their fingers locked.

"We must show her," Phil Hyder said, "that she's not really alone."

Those bygone days in which "everybody [was] pouring cattle into Montana" are vividly evoked in this exciting novella by a celebrated Western writer of the forties and fifties. Among the thirty-three novels Norman A. Fox (1911–1960) authored between 1941 and 1962 are such standouts as The Thirsty Land, Tall Man Riding, Broken Wagon, Rope the Wind, *and* The Trembling Hills. *Other examples of his short story art can be found in the collections* The Valiant Ones *and* They Rode the Shining Hills, *and in the previous Best of the West anthology,* The Steamboaters.

The Longhorn Legion

Norman A. Fox

*T*hey came upon the valley's rim in midafternoon, Tod Kirby riding far ahead of point position and having the first look; and when Canaan spread before him, lush in the sunlight, something grew in his throat that was bitter to the taste, something made of hope and fear and fulfilment's nearness. For a while he merely sat his saddle gazing at the shouldering hills, pine-stippled and forbidding, gazing at the tawny floor, so far below, and the distant rooftops of Beulah town. *She's grown some,* he decided and was surprised that so ordinary a thought should come to him at such a moment. He had waited twelve years to look again upon Canaan.

Behind him the longhorns surged out of the south from far Texas, a blunt arrowhead of beef spilling across the levels; and their bawling filled his ears and brought him back to the full realization of this day and this hour. The herd was a brown, seething sea, gaunted by all the miles to Montana; the herd was an invading army. He looked at it fondly. Then he raised his hat in signal to Big Sam Block; and Block, riding point, answered in kind, and made the sweeping circular motion that told Hashknife's crew to mill the herd.

Block left this task to the others and came riding up, a squat brown man looking almost deformed in the saddle. He drew rein abreast of Tod and gazed down into the valley, his broad face taking on a look of intent interest, for he, too, had waited for this moment.

Tod flung out his arm. "There's Hashknife's new home, Sam."

He expected Block's approval, and when it was slow in coming, a youngster's impatience grew in Tod, and he was two men in one: Hashknife's segundo who'd found new graze for its longhorn legion, and Sam Block's foster son, who'd drag the stars from the sky for Block's casual nod. Tod had led the way for Hashknife; but now Big Sam Block only said, frowning, "Those damn' hills make a prison out of it."

"That's what Caleb Trumbull figured when he settled his colony here," Tod said. "A prison in reverse—one that would keep out the rest of the world. But those hills will shelter your cows when the winter winds blow, and there's grass down yonder, and water. It's rich, Sam! Where did we see anything like it in the Nations or Colorado or Wyoming? And if Trumbull's been keeping the gate closed to outsiders, the land's probably still open for entry."

Block drew his tufted eyebrows together. He was, Tod knew, a slow-thinking man and an unimaginative one, but his world was cows, and in all his fifty-odd years, he'd thought always as a cattleman: he would surely be pleased. Block crooked one leg around the saddle horn, drew out his tobacco sack, and fashioned up a cigarette, then passed the makings to Tod. Exhaled smoke wreathed about Block's face and made him look like a Chinese idol, bland and graven and unreadable.

"I know how you hate him, kid," Block said then. "I'm not blaming you for that. But were you finding me the best graze? Or were you making yourself a chance to hit back at Trumbull?"

Tod said impatiently, "Have you seen anything better since we crossed the Yellowstone? Timber to build your house and barn and corrals. Hills to hold your herd and save you the trouble of fencing. Man, we're lucky to get here first! You've heard the talk in Texas and on the trail. Everybody's pouring cattle into Montana. Pilgrim stuff out of Wisconsin, Minnesota, and Michigan. Cows from Washington, Oregon, and Idaho. And with Texas graze growing thin, they're piling up out of the south. How many herds did we count after we left Dodge? Another five years and this kind of range will all be preempted. I tell you we'll never find a better spot than Canaan Valley."

Still Block's face revealed nothing. He looked down the timbered slope where the hills pinched together at this south end of Canaan. "How do we get there?"

Jubilation rose in Tod. "You can't see the road, but it's yonder. It's narrow and full of switchbacks, as I remember it, but we can move the herd down it." His lips drew tight; he was a lean youngster, dark-haired and dark-eyed, who sometimes looked older than he was. "It's the same road Owen climbed that winter to get to Nugget. That old mining camp was west of here. I've heard it's nothing but a ghost town now. Owen had quite a job with snow higher than a horse's head. But he made it out, and he made it back, and he was leading three pack horses loaded with provisions on the return trip. That trip killed him, really."

"Snow . . . ?" Big Sam Block mused, and suspicion's glint came into his eyes. "We'll be needing hay for five thousand longhorns, eh? It's way too late in the season to be putting any up."

"I've told you the snow never really gets deep on the levels," Tod said in exasperation. "Not unless there's an awful bad winter. Trumbull's colony ran short of food for the people, but such stock as they had wintered through fine. My God, Sam, do you think I owe you so little that

I'd sell Hashknife short just to get my chance at Trumbull?''

Big Sam's face softened. "No, Tod," he said. "It's just that you've got that one twist in you about Trumbull that muddles your thinking. I saw it in your eyes that night in Dodge City when I found you there, trying to keep Owen alive. That's all of eight years ago, but you've never lost that look. From the moment I decided to sell out in Texas, you've talked of nothing but Canaan Valley. And I've kept remembering what it is you really want here.''

"Sam," Tod said, "you made a cattleman out of me, didn't you?''

Block nodded. "I made a cattleman out of you.''

"Then I'm talking like a cattleman now. This is the place for Hashknife. It's the rainbow's end. If I'm wrong, I'll eat the dust of the drag from here to anywhere on the map!''

Block squinted at the sun, and his face turned speculative. "We've got a good six hours of daylight left. We'll have Hashknife's herd bedded down on Canaan's grass tonight.''

Tod said, "Sam, that wasn't the bargain.''

Block said, "I know. You still want to go in ahead and tell him we're taking over the south end of the valley. But there's only one thing I need to know, and I'll find that out soon enough: Will Trumbull fight?''

"Not when I've palavered with him. Not after I've told him how big a crew we've got.''

Block said, "What will it get you, son? Your notion doesn't make sense. The smart ones move up on an enemy. They don't go in ahead giving him his chance to get ready. Hell, I fought through a war once.''

Tod said grimly, "The deal was that if I led the way to this place, I was to have my hour with him. We understood that in Texas, you and I. I want to see Caleb Trumbull's face when he recognizes me. I want to see how he looks when he realizes his hold here is broken, his little kingdom turned upside down. I have to do that for Owen's sake. And that's why I'm going in first, Sam.''

Block grunted. "You drove the bargain. But I'm taking the chuck wagon and most of the crew down there. I'll leave a few to hold the herd, but I want my guns where they can defend the graze. I'm not going to have a fight my way downhill tomorrow. Look at that timber! Trumbull's men could make Injun warfare on us and keep us out forever."

"Have it your way," Tod said. "Just so long as I get that talk with him."

"Sure," Block said, and dropped his leg to the stirrup and wheeled his horse about. Tod watched the man ride back to where the herd had been milled into one vast pool of cattle; he watched Block ride here and there bellowing orders, his voice carrying back to Tod in fragments. He had gained his victory over Block, and he was satisfied. He thought of Caleb Trumbull and a man dead in Dodge City, a man named Owen Kirby, and his lips thinned down again. Soon now a long circle would be finished.

The chuck wagon came rumbling forward, pocketed by a score of riders, Big Sam Block leading them; and when they were almost upon Tod, he neck-reined his own horse down into the timber and found the road and began following it. At his heels came Hashknife's crew, and he led them along the switchbacks, along that tunnel of a trail where sometimes the timber pressed so close as to scrape the canvas of the chuck wagon and sometimes the way was barred by deadfall trees that had to be snagged aside by the lariats of Hashknife's riders.

This road was little more than a game trail, but ruts had been driven deep into it; there were more signs of passage than Tod had expected. Seeing these, he wondered how much change had come to Canaan and was fainty alarmed. He wanted the valley as inviolate as it had been; he wanted Caleb Trumbull as secure as of yore before he snatched that security from him.

Big Sam Block said, "A helluva road!"

"It will likely discourage other outfits, Sam, and keep them from crowding your graze."

But Block was a man used to the treeless llanos of Texas;

and this crowding timber put a shadow on him, making him surly, making him uncertain. The shadow lay also on the bearded faces of the others. They had dared the Nations and the beef-hungry treaty tribes who took toll of the passing herds; they had dared all the wild rivers of the north trail; but those had been known dangers. Now they were a silent group, with even the cook, a salty and vociferous man, awed. They toiled on downward, the chuck wagon lurching and groaning; and then suddenly the timber was behind them and they were on the valley's floor, openness spreading before them, a sea of grass broken by intermittent clumps of trees, a lush land spreading northward to where Beulah town lay lost to their gaze by the undulating sweep of country.

Block looked about him and his eyes came alive. "God!" he breathed and was a man transfixed in his saddle.

Tod Kirby said, "It's everything I told you it was. Can you see why Caleb Trumbull has kept it to himself?"

Block said, "Him and his damned colony! All this wasted on a bunch of stubble-jumpers and small-fry cattlemen!"

"Not anymore," Tod said. "Not anymore."

Block motioned to his waiting men. "We camp here."

Tod said, "I'll be riding." He glanced at the lowering sun; it had taken them well over an hour to make the descent. "I can still reach Beulah by daylight. I should be back long before midnight."

Block said, "You're a fool to do it. If you've got to ride in, why not ride with twenty of us along?"

"Because it's my deal, and mine alone, Sam. Because I've waited too long."

"I've waited, too," Block said. "I've waited all the way from Texas to look on Hashknife's new graze. You get back fast, Tod. Because when the sun comes up tomorrow morning, my boys are spilling those longhorns down the slope." He raised himself in his stirrups, his gaze sweeping the valley. He was a man reaching out to grasp a dream in his hand. "I'll build my house on this very spot, and it will be the biggest house north of the Yellowstone. I'll range my cattle farther than the eye can see. Our work's cut out for us, Tod."

"Sure," Tod Kirby said, but this was the moment when he knew his first doubt. He looked upon Big Sam Block with the same fondness a son gives a father; but this was not the Sam Block he had known, not this man with avarice in his eyes and a lust for grass naked upon his face. There was a feeling then in Tod Kirby that he had unleashed a force upon Canaan that would brook no interference, and he had a brief regret that he had done so. Then he thought of Caleb Trumbull and that man dead in Dodge, and this thought was the crowding, surging one, for now his hour of fulfilment was near.

He lifted his hand to Big Sam Block. "Be seeing you soon," he said and headed his horse to the north at a high gallop.

II

Once, not so many years before, there had been a war, a long, bitter, bloody war, in which men with a common tongue and a common heritage had pitted themselves against each other, and the names of sleepy villages and river landings and tired old hills had taken on new significance. Shiloh . . . Gettysburg . . . Lookout Mountain . . . Appomattox . . . These were remembered milestones on the long, long road. . . .

Tod Kirby had known that war, but only as a child who'd waited; for the fighting had been done by men—men like Big Sam Block, who had ridden with Jeb Stuart; and Owen Kirby, who'd been in on the defense of Vicksburg; and Caleb Trumbull, who'd known the bloodiest warfare of all, the guerrilla forays of that border state Missouri. And remembering this as he rode across the fair, bright face of Canaan in Indian summer's golden glory, Tod supposed that each man had brought with him from the war a different set of pain-blighted pictures and a different tempering of his individual soul.

Trumbull, for instance. he had been an oak of a man, silver-haired and bearded when Tod had known him; and Trumbull had seen not one war but two, for he had stormed Chapultepec at an earlier day. A giant with hands made horny by the plow, he had come home from that second war sickened, finding his farm in ashes and all of an old life destroyed. He had gathered other men about him, linsey-garbed men like himself who had seen the border laid waste by ebb and flow of conquest. They had turned their faces westward, not with the restlessness that had made the hearth too tame for some who'd known the sword but with a dream in their eyes, the dream of a peaceful place where the wars of the world might pass them by.

And so they had come to Canaan and given the valley its name; and Tod supposed that one day they, too, must have looked from the south rim, even as he and Sam Block had looked today, and looking, had seen a dream's fulfilment. And so they had founded a colony, and Trumbull had given that colony its law and its leadership. They had come with their tattered wagons and their footsore stock and built a town and called it Beulah, choosing a name from a people who had also sought a Promised Land; and that was the beginning.

They would be a world unto themselves, allowing no outsiders and depending upon no one. They would till the ground and tend their herds, growing their food and spinning their cloth; and they would hold this sanctuary inviolate by a rigorous adherence to a rule: no dealings with the outside world. Caleb Trumbull had laid down that rule, and Tod Kirby had known it full well; for he'd faced Trumbull with his father that first fall after the founding of the colony, and he'd heard Trumbull speak.

"You are a gambler," Trumbull had judged; for Owen Kirby's soft, quick hands must have told him as much.

"An ex-gambler, Mr. Trumbull."

"There could be a place for you here. I am no Bible-quoting fanatic who frowns at even the simpler sins. We shall have a saloon in Beulah, but the whiskey will be of our own making. Among my men are those who'd grow restless if they were denied the kind of pleasures they've known. When restlessness comes, then, too, comes the end of all our planning. What brought you here, Mr. Kirby?''

"An accident to my wagon on the downgrade into this valley. I looked about me then and liked what I saw. That's why I'm staying."

"And what is it you are fleeing?"

"Myself, Mr. Trumbull."

"So? There is the flavor of a scholar to your speech and to your thinking. I, too, am a scholar of sorts, Mr. Kirby. That surprises you when you look at me, eh? I read my books by lamplight when my day's work was done. We shall talk often, the two of us. You may stay if you abide by the rule. No man leaves this valley without my permission. Not if he expects to return. This is your son?''

"My son. Twelve years old, and made half an orphan by the cholera.''

"We need the young ones; they will carry forward the dream when we are gone. You are welcome here, both of you. If you wish the rural life, I will allot land to you in the north of the valley. We have decided to concentrate there. If you prefer town life, you will find Beulah marked off in lots. Pick one and build your cabin. Your neighbors will be eager to help. In turn, you will help them. You are the first outsiders we have permitted. Be sure to remember that you've been privileged.''

"I thank you," Owen Kirby had said gravely.

But he'd not been a gregarious man; so he'd built his cabin in the south end of the valley, the only man of the colony to do so, and he'd asked no one's permission. Caleb Trumbull had ridden down once, a giant astride a mule, to look at the cabin and had frowned, saying nothing. But he hadn't come for those bookish talks, and the Kirbys had lived alone. For a couple of months that fall Tod had gone to the community schoolhouse, but he'd found himself apart from the colonists, and there had been several fights. Tod recalled a certain Lou Bodeen, an older boy who'd trounced him more than once. After that, Owen Kirby had taken over his son's education.

All this Tod was remembering today, the forgotten pictures and the forgotten voices coming back to him, distilled from his looking again upon the familiar land, his coming to the end of the long waiting. He recognized landmarks as he rode along—a familiar grove of trees, the creek that wound up out of the south—and when he flushed a family of quail from a brushy thicket, it was as though this precise thing had happened at this precise spot long ago. Nostalgia softened him, and out of nostalgia came a hunger to see the cabin. Thus he veered his horse from the straight course that would have taken him to Beulah and sought out the sheltered coulee of Owen Kirby's choice and rode down into it and found the cabin there.

Memories rose up and choked him but only for a minute; for surprise came then, and anger.

The hard-packed yard was the same, and the cabin squatted as of yore, safe from the blustering winds; but the surprise was that the door did not sag on its leather hinges as he'd supposed it would, and the oiled deerskin panes, the frontiersman's substitute for glass, were intact. The years had not ravaged this cabin. Anger came because a girl stood in the doorway.

She was young and lithe and altogether beautiful, a tall, slim girl with black hair that fell to her shoulders; and she had a wildling look to her in this first moment as her lips pursed with surprise. She wore a buckskin riding skirt and a woolen shirt and a man's hat, and Tod supposed that she lived here and was about to go riding. He came off his horse, letting the reins drop to anchor the mount. He was too choked for words; he had not supposed that anyone from the colony would usurp the cabin.

The girl looked at him wordlessly, and recognition came into her eyes, and she said, "Tod! You *are* Tod Kirby, aren't you? Don't you remember me?"

"No," he said. "I don't."

"I'm Nan—Nan Trumbull."

She'd been one of those who'd gone to the community school, but it was only her name that carried significance to him; he could tie her to no real memory. Not at first.

He said, "His granddaughter! So he gave the place to his own kin."

She smiled. "No one lives here."

Frowning, he strode forward and shouldered past her and came through the doorway and stood in the single room. The stove was here, the one Owen Kirby had fetched in the wagon that had broken down; the stove was brightly polished. The hand-hewn table was intact, and so was the bunk. There were fresh blankets on the bunk. Owen Kirby's books stood on a shelf, the books from which he'd taught his boy; Tod stepped to them and touched them reverently with his fingertips, and no dust stirred. He crossed the room and swept away the burlap curtain to the lean-to and peered into the semidarkness. Cases were here, wooden cases, still nailed tightly shut. There had been flour sacks, too, but these were gone; he supposed that the rats had been at them long ago.

He turned, more bewildered than angered. He said, "It's exactly as we left it. Why is that?"

She had come inside and put her back to a wall. She had the look of one deeply moved. She said, 'It was kept this way. You see, we knew that some day you would come back."

This made him more puzzled. "How could you know that?"

"Because every man looks for Canaan, and one who'd once found it would remember and return. Your father, Tod? Is he coming, too?"

"Owen's dead."

She closed her eyes. "I'm sorry," she said.

He was beginning to remember her now; she had changed greatly in the twelve years; she had been a child and now she was a woman; but the remembered things were little things, the cant of her head, a way of speaking. She had been kinder to him than anyone else in Canaan; and he was remembering that, too, and was sorry for his first anger. He asked, "Do you come here often?"

She nodded, opening her eyes again; and he saw that she was pleased. "You've come back," she said, "and that proves we were not wrong. Your place is here for you, Tod; there is even kindling laid in the stove.''

He said, ''I didn't come alone.''

''You have a wife?''

''I came with a man. His name is Sam Block, and he is a Texas rancher. I'm his foreman.''

''I see,'' she said. ''That accounts for the lean look of you and the clothes you wear and the gun at your hip. What brought this Sam Block along with you?''

''Five thousand longhorn cattle. They're on the south rim right now, and Big Sam Block is in the valley. We've needed new graze. Starting tomorrow, this is Hashknife's range.''

He might have struck her. She reeled on her feet, then braced herself, raising a hand to her cheek. Despair showed in her eyes. ''You brought them here?''

''All the way from Texas.''

''Why, Tod? Why?''

''To put an end to the hold Caleb Trumbull's got here. To bust up the little scheme that keeps him king over Canaan.''

She shook her head; she was like a child overwhelmed by a reality beyond her understanding, yet there was a mature gravity to her. ''You must have been bitter when you left, Tod. I can understand that. But you've had time for thinking since. You wouldn't be here to destroy what has taken years to build!''

''You're his kin,'' he said. ''You think like him.''

''No, Tod! Sometimes he's been a despot, stubborn and wrong. But there's been some great good in his idea; he has taught people to live together and work together and share the fruits of that work. I know he was crazy to think he could shut us off from the world. He knows it, too. He's let in a lot of people in these last few years, poor people looking for a place to settle. But nothing can be saved from his idea, not even the best of it, if the valley is to be overrun by one man with a lot of cattle.''

Tod said, ''Just the same, that's the way it's going to be.''

She looked desperate; she looked older than anyone of her years should look. He thought: *She's taking this hard,* and he wondered why his announcement should affect her so, but he supposed her thinking had been shaped by living always in the grim shadow of Caleb Trumbull. He said in a softer voice, "Sooner or later this was bound to happen. If it wasn't Hashknife, it would be some other brand. Your granddad thought he could stop the clock. It can't be done."

"What are you to this Sam Block?"

"What a son is to a father. I was lucky, Nan. I lost Owen and found Sam."

"Then you carry weight with him?"

"Enough."

She moved from the wall and came close to him, placing her hands on his shoulders. Her lips were slightly parted; the fragrance of her hair was strong in his nostrils. She said, very intently, "There's a lot of graze to be had. Persuade him to take his herd someplace else."

"Why should I?"

"I knew you long ago, Tod. I watched you on the school ground, a thin boy with eyes that were too big and bright. I knew you were different; somehow I supposed you were made of better stuff than the rest of us. Did we hurt you so badly that nothing will do now but to ruin all of us? Look around you, Tod! I think you owe me something for believing you were big enough to come back here with peace in your heart. That was why the cabin was kept as it was."

He said, "And if I don't see it your way—?"

"Then I shall have to fight you as best I can. And I shall not budge from here until you've promised you'll take Sam Block and his cattle away."

"Oh, hell!" he said.

"I can be stubborn," she said. "It's the only weapon I've got, but you can't use your gun or your fists against it. You can't drive me out."

"No," he conceded. "Not that way."

Futility swept him, made of a feeling that he was wast-

ing minutes; for there was Beulah yet and his hour with
Caleb Trumbull and that deadline at dawn when Sam Block
would keep his word and bring in the longhorns. He smiled
down then, seeing a way by which this girl might be
moved; and he said, "Stay if you wish." He reached out
and got his arms around her and drew her close. He kissed
her, pressing his lips hard against hers and making the kiss
long and savage and possessive. Then he released her. "Are
you staying?" he asked.

She stepped back from him, the breath bruised out of
her. She looked at him with loathing, but there was also a
certain sadness in her eyes. "Now I know what Sam Block
must be like," she said and turned and scurried through
the doorway.

He took a step after her, suddenly deeply ashamed of
himself, for all about him in this cabin was the evidence
of what she'd done to keep a bright faith burning. Hoof-
beats rose, and he realized that she must have had a horse
tethered on the far side of the cabin, beyond his sight when
he'd ridden up. He stood in the doorway and glimpsed her
quirting her horse up the coulee's gentle slope.

He called, but she paid him no heed. He turned back
into the cabin but was at once possessed of a desire to be
gone from here. Owen Kirby's gentle presence might have
been in this room, calling to him across the void of the
years; and he didn't want to hear what Owen Kirby would
be saying, after what had happened.

III

Riding northward, he looked for Nan Trumbull; for he supposed she would be heading toward Beulah; but he failed
to glimpse her. The valley's floor, which had seemed so
flat from the rim, rose and fell in gentle swells; and thus
he had no view very far ahead. He rode warily, remembering that Nan might encounter others of the colony and
spread the news of his presence; and he damned himself
as a witless one who had fouled up his own chances. He
knew what Sam Block would think of his having ac-

quainted the enemy with his intentions. He remembered Big Sam's observation that twenty men might ride into Beulah, and he supposed he could still turn back and get Hashknife's crew. But he had chosen to ride alone, and that choice was still his.

He came to Beulah at the end of the afternoon, crossing a bridge that spanned the creek that curved around the town. He rode along a false-fronted street that might have been the main one of any central Montana town except that it was laid out with greater precision than most and had some cottonwoods to throw their shade. Saddle horses stood at gnawed hitchrails; a few buggies and buckboards were here. Tod recognized most of the buildings—the blacksmith shop, the mercantile, the livery stable, the community granary, this last a huge block of a building rearing high. But there were new structures as well, a restaurant, a jail building, a printing shop, and a saloon that bore the unseemly name the Haven. This was doubtless the place of simple pleasures that Caleb Trumbull had promised his flock.

The jail building interested Tod, too. It appeared to be no more than a two-room cabin, distinguishable only by its glassless barred windows; and Tod smiled wryly as he passed it. If Trumbull had given his people a saloon, he had also given them a reminder of where too much revelry might lodge them. He was a thorough man, Trumbull.

The man's own house stood behind the main street on a slight rise and was bigger than Tod remembered it, a two-storied structure of clapboard that showed Trumbull's planning and personality, a square, drab house with little nonsense to it. No shutters adorned the gaunt windows; no vines broke the bleakness of the walls. But there was a broad, deep veranda from which Trumbull could look down upon his town. The veranda hadn't been there in Tod's day.

To this house Tod Kirby rode and dismounted in its yard. He came striding toward the veranda along a flagstone walk, and he saw that scrawny rose bushes grew beside the porch steps. Trumbull's wife lay buried in Missouri; and Tod, looking at the bushes, thought: *Nan's*. He raised a boot to the first step, and a man materialized from the dim recesses of the porch, a grizzled Missourian who said, "What do *you* want?"

Tod supposed he'd known this one in the old days, but there's been a dozen faces like that, brutalized by toil yet retaining a native shrewdness, a native good humor. None of the humor was showing on this one, though.

"I want to see Trumbull," Tod said.

"Git along. He's not seeing anybody this afternoon."

Tod took a hipshot stand, hooking his thumbs in his gunbelt. He thought: *She's told them!* and, remembering the kiss, he supposed that made them even, him and Nan. He said, "It's his hard luck if he doesn't see me. I'm going to stay in your village just long enough for a bite to eat and a drink to wash it down. You can tell him if he wants to talk to Tod Kirby, he's got just that long to do it. Do you savvy?"

"I'll tell him," the man said. His eyes showed a hard brightness.

Tod walked back to his horse, hauled himself into the saddle, put his back to the one on the porch with contemptuous carelessness, and rode to the livery stable. He left the mount here with instructions for its care, then crossed over to the restaurant and ordered a meal.

He ate silently, watching the comings and goings of people; and not one of them greeted him. He remembered some of the faces vaguely, but many were new to him. He judged that Trumbull's colony had nearly doubled, and his thought was that Hashknife was outnumbered. He thought of Big Sam Block saying, "There's only one thing I need to know, and I'll find that out soon enough: Will Trumbull fight?" The real question, Tod decided, was whether these men of Canaan would back Trumbull in a fight.

He measured the men; some had the look of being dedicated to the plow and peace, but some looked as though they were used to saddle and six-shooter. Trumbull had been experimenting with blooded cattle a dozen years ago, prophesying that the day of the longhorn would soon be done. He'd wanted men in his valley who would raise fancy stock, and he'd wanted others to till the soil, providing food for the people and the cattle. Tod recalled the haystacks that hadn't been needed that first winter. Supplemental feeding had been one of Trumbull's fetishes, part of his belief in raising superior beef. Had he also fashioned a superior people, instilling in them his own loyalty to the colony and its future? That was what interested Tod, and the question persisted: Would they fight?

His meal finished, he came again to the street. Dusk was now descending, mellowing all things, rubbing out the rawness of the street and making the cottonwoods masses of darkness. A cool breeze flowed down from the hemming hills, holding the threat of winter in it. Tod lifted his eyes to Trumbull's house; only one light showed, in a second-story window. He wondered if that was Trumbull's own room, if the man was keeping himself in it this evening. He had waited so long for the hour for facing Trumbull that his stomach now knotted with the thought that he might be denied that hour.

He turned toward the Haven and shouldered its batwings aside. He walked to the bar and leaned against it and said, "Whiskey."

There were few men in the place at this hour. An indolent barkeep held forth behind the planking; three townsmen were at one of the half-dozen tables; a houseman sat idle behind the curved blackjack table, riffling the cards, his fingers busy, his eyes vacant. Tod took his drink and held it in his hand, not wanting it really; and the barkeep retired to the far end of the planking, leaving him to his own devices.

Tod swirled the whiskey, looking into its amber depth. "Friendly place," he said aloud.

He tasted the whiskey and judged it to be no local product, and this disturbed him. He looked at the row of bottles on the backbar; they bore labels he'd seen in Dodge City and Cheyenne on the trail north. He remembered the signs of travel along the road leading down from the south rim; he'd noticed that some people in the restaurant hadn't been wearing homespun. Already there were cracks in the wall Trumbull had reared around Canaan, deviations from the idea that a people might be sufficient unto themselves. Tod remembered his fear on the south slope; he still wanted Trumbull secure before that security was wrenched from him.

A man came through the batwings then, and Tod glimpsed him in the mirror, a tall, well-built, smooth-shaven man of nearly thirty, with a face that was both handsome and hard. He wore a dark suit that might have been any citizen's Sunday best; an elk's tooth dangled from a watch chain spanning his vest.

The barkeep grinned at sight of him. "What's up, Lou?" he asked. "A funeral, or a wedding?"

The man made no answer; he came up to Tod and tapped his shoulder. "You Kirby?"

Tod turned enough to prop his left elbow on the bar, letting his right arm hang free. "That's so."

"I'm Lou Bodeen. You don't remember me."

"I do now," Tod said. "You were one of the older boys at the schoolhouse. We had a couple of fights. You must have outweighed me by twenty pounds then. I don't think you do now."

Bodeen smiled, showing a good set of teeth. "That was kid stuff. I'm not on the prod. It just so happens that I'm the law here. Town marshal. Strangers are welcome in Canaan as long as they keep the peace. I just thought I'd tell you."

An old antagonism, long forgotten, stirred in Tod. "Who handles the ones that get out of line?"

Bodeen's smile held. "Every man in the valley is a deputy if I need him. Usually I don't. I depend on this." A motion of his right hand brushed back the skirt of his coat, revealing a holstered forty-five.

"So you've grown up," Tod said. "The last time, you were using a rock in your fist."

Bodeen's smile faded. "With you, I didn't really need it."

"Times change," Tod said and hit Bodeen.

He used his left fist, a short, chopping blow that clipped at Bodeen's chin, taking the legs from under the man. Bodeen went down, clawing at his gun as he fell; but Tod instantly bent, his fingers clamping on Bodeen's right wrist. With his free hand Tod plucked the gun from Bodeen's holster and thrust it into his own pants band. He straightened up just in time to see the barkeep coming, brandishing a bung-starter. The three men at the gaming table were now on their feet. They came converging toward Tod. Bodeen, from the floor, shouted unnecessarily, "Get him!"

In Tod then was a recollection of his earlier concern as to the loyalty of Trumbull's colonists, and now he had the answer. At least as far as those in the saloon were concerned. He veered from the bar; a lunging step took him to one of the gaming tables, and he grasped a chair and sent it hurtling into the path of the three who'd been at cards. One of them stumbled over the chair; another sprawled headlong across the first. The blackjack dealer had come from behind his curved table and was moving toward the batwings, blocking escape. Tod spied a rear door and darted toward it, expecting guns to start speaking. He got through the door and slammed it shut behind him.

He found himself in an alley, and in the gathering dusk he almost stumbled over a trash barrel. Hurrying as fast as he dared, he put a hundred yards between him and the Haven, then paused to listen.

No sound of pursuit disturbed the twilight. But a shrill cry rose at the saloon, and Tod, remembering what Bodeen had said about deputies, thought: *He'll have every man in town on my trail.* He moved farther along the alley, no real plan in him. He found himself at the rear of the jail building and smiled with the notion that here might be the best place in town to hide. He raised himself and peered through the one barred window that faced on the alley. Straining his eyes, he saw an empty cell, its only furniture a cot shoved against the wall beneath the window. He took Bodeen's gun from his waistband and thrust it between the bars and let it drop down behind the cot, smiling as he heard it hit the floor.

Drifting away from the jail, he cruised the alley, eyes alert, his ears tuned to all of the town's small sounds. There seemed to be no excitement on the street. He remembered Bodeen as a determined person whose pride had to be preened constantly. He couldn't picture Bodeen letting this incident of tonight lie. He made a fist and looked at it and supposed that he should regret fanning the old feud alive and thus making Beulah untenable. Then he remembered Bodeen's smile and was not sorry.

He couldn't just linger here. Should he ride out? Caleb Trumbull wouldn't be coming out of that big house to see him. He knew that now. Likely he'd been wasting time ever since he'd left Trumbull's house. Nan must have told Trumbull of the longhorn legion that waited at Canaan's gate, and Trumbull had evidently decided what he intended to do about that. For hadn't Bodeen known for whom he was looking when he'd come to the Haven? What chance was there of standing before Trumbull for that showdown so long deferred?

Thinking this, the old stubbornness possessed Tod, and he turned toward Trumbull's house.

He came up the rise carefully, hugging the shadows and pausing to listen for the beat of boots in the dusk. He came at the house obliquely, reaching one side of it and moving cautiously around to the porch. Remembering that grizzled oldster who stood guard, he got out his own gun and held it in his hand. The porch was a shadow maze; and Tod waited, wanting to know exactly where the man was posted. And as he waited, the front door opened and someone came to the porch.

Edging closer, Tod heard a low exchange of words, and he judged that a man had come outside to talk to the one who guarded the door. He wondered if it was Trumbull himself, and his palms grew sticky with the thought.

Then the one who'd quitted the house came down the steps, a stooped, stocky man carrying a black bag; and Tod recognized him, for this was Doc Salisbury, one of the original colonists. Trumbull had fetched a medico along on that trek westward. Trumbull was a thorough man. Salisbury went with short, choppy strides into the town.

Tod, having now a plan of sorts, pouched his gun. He

climbed to the porch and said softly, "Hey, you—?" wanting the oldster to indicate where he stood. The man moved in the murk; he came forward peering.

"Come here," Tod said, wanting him closer. "I've got something to tell you."

Bodeen said out of the darkness of the veranda, "I've got another gun and it's lined on you, Kirby. No, don't move! I guessed you'd be fool enough to have another try at this house before you quit town."

Only then did Tod Kirby see the shapes of waiting men here in the deeper shadows of the porch; and seeing them, he knew the futility of either fight or flight. Bodeen's voice held a restrained savagery that was warning enough. The man would welcome an excuse to shoot. Knowing this, Tod raised his hands.

IV

Three had come with Bodeen, and they converged upon Tod and lifted his gun from leather and ran hard hands over him in search of other weapons while Bodeen hovered near, his teeth showing white in the darkness. Bodeen was both pleased and angry. He said, "It's jail for you, bucko."

Tod canted his head toward the door of Trumbull's house. "All I want is a talk with him."

"Not tonight."

They hustled Tod down the rise and into Beulah's street to the log jail building. The first of its two rooms proved to be the town marshal's office holding a desk and a chair. Upon the desk stood a lamp. One of the men with Bodeen—Tod recognized him as the houseman from the Haven—lighted the lamp, and Tod saw that a barred door separated the office from the single cell. Bodeen thrust Tod's gun into the desk, lifted a key from a drawer, and unlocked the cell door. Tod was thrust inside.

"What did you do with my gun?" Bodeen demanded.

"Threw it away."

Bodeen locked the cell door and tossed the key to the desk top; he motioned to the men who'd accompanied him and they drifted out of the building. Tod, listening to their footfalls, wondered if they were lingering just outside and couldn't be sure. He backed up to the cot and seated himself upon it; he could have reached down and touched the gun he'd planted here, but the thought of those three gnawed worriedly at his mind.

Bodeen looked at him through the barred door; his face was composed but his eyes were calculating.

"What's the charge?" Tod asked.

"Disturbing the peace. Assaulting the town marshal. Any name I want to give it."

"How long do I sit here?"

"That's for Trumbull to decide. He does the judging."

Tod said, wanting to know the extent of Bodeen's knowledge, "Then he'd better hold his court soon or there'll be a few Texans peeling this building off me."

"I wonder," Bodeen said and smiled. "I was for jailing you on any pretext, but Caleb's orders were to warn you and let it go at that. Then you got tough and gave me my excuse. Now we've got you where we want you. I think we've got a dickering point with Big Sam Block. He'll think twice about moving in if your hide is the price."

"You don't know Sam Block."

"I know that you're supposed to be the same as a son to him."

"I see," Tod said. "Then she *did* tell you everything."

"Of course," Bodeen said, his smile widening.

Again Tod thought of that gun so close at hand, and he wanted mightily to wipe away Bodeen's smile by throwing down on the man with his own gun. He fought against this impulse, knowing he must wait till a safer time. He said, "Have some supper sent in, will you?"

"You ate before you came to the Haven."

Tod's eyebrows lifted. "You know that, too. Just the same, I'm hungry again. Send in some supper."

Bodeen frowned. "I'd rather come in there and give you a taste of my fists!"

Tod said, "Why don't you?"

Bodeen made no answer. He turned on his heel and blew

out the office lamp, leaving the building in darkness. He went out the front door, and Tod heard him speak to someone outside. Those three *had* waited! Boots beat along Beulah's planking, and at once Tod was probing for the hideout gun. He slipped the weapon inside his shirt and sat waiting. He congratulated himself on the impulse that had made him put the gun here against the possibility that he might be caught and jailed, but his satisfaction was tinged with a worry that was at first nameless.

Then he thought of Doc Salisbury coming out of Trumbull's house.

Here was an indication that Trumbull was a sick man, sick enough to be under the doctor's care. Tod wondered about that; he supposed Trumbull must be in his seventies now, and even the stoutest oak had some day to fall. Did that explain why Trumbull had not answered his challenge by seeking him out in the early evening? Tod didn't know; he only knew that he was distressed by the evidence that Trumbull might not be well. When you waited for your chance to pit yourself against a man, you wanted that man sound and whole. This was like his finding cracks in the wall Trumbull had reared around Canaan. This meant being cheated after all the years.

He took to pacing the cell, sometimes moving to the rear window and listening to the night sounds of Beulah. The Haven, he judged, had filled with trade; its clatter spilled out and reached him. He could hear boots on the boardwalk and the jingle of bridle chains as men rode the street; voices drifted to him, fragments from which he sometimes separated coherent words. Someone cramped a wagon hard in the street and called out a good-bye that came clearly to Tod. "So long, Sully. Morning comes early in these parts."

Tod began to fret, wondering if Bodeen would send a man with food, thus giving him, Tod, his chance to use the gun. He wondered if he still might be here when morning came and Big Sam Block moved into Canaan. He had pictured himself riding at point position when that hour arrived; he had treasured that picture across many miles.

Then he heard the outer door open, and someone made vague movement in the office. He slipped his hand inside his shirt; the feel of the gun was reassuring as he stepped softly toward the barred door. He was a still and ready man in that moment. But it was Nan's voice that came to him, asking softly, "Tod? Tod Kirby?"

He peered. His eyes had become accustomed to the gloom, and he saw that Nan was wrapped in a dark cloak. She groped to the door and grasped the bars and her cloak fell open. Beneath it she wore a white satin gown, frilled at neck and wrists; and seeing this, he remembering Lou Bodeen's Sunday suit and the barkeep's asking, "What's up, Lou? A funeral, or a wedding?"

"No!" he cried, not wanting to believe what he must now believe.

"The gown?" Pride was in this girl and a forthright honesty, and no darkness could hide these things. "I had to come like this. We're to be married tonight."

"Not you and Bodeen," he said, his voice brittle.

"It's best, Tod."

He was strongly moved, too strongly moved to ask himself why he should be concerned. "In heaven's name, why?"

"Because my grandfather wishes it."

This struck him hard and brought his anger flaming. "He tells his people where to build their cabins and how many rooms they should have," he snapped. "He tells them whether they are to plant wheat or raise cattle. He does their thinking and their planning. Now I'm told he even orders who should marry and when. And still you cannot understand why I've counted the days till I could come back and put an end to his power!"

Her face, a white flower in the darkness, was composed; the only sadness was in her voice. "He's an old man, Tod, and ailing."

"I saw Salisbury come from the house. What's wrong with Trumbull?"

"Old age mostly. Yet a lot of men live to be ninety. I suppose he wore himself out building this colony. Some men have lived for an idea; perhaps he's dying for one. I only know that he's terribly sick.''

''But not too sick to stage a wedding.''

''There's no time to be lost, Tod. You said yourself that Hashknife's herd was on the south rim.''

''What's that got to do with it?''

''Everything. You also said that starting tomorrow, this would be Sam Block's range. Whatever stand Canaan takes will have to be taken when the first longhorn moves down the slope. Canaan will need a leader then, a strong man. My father was Caleb Trumbull's son, but Dad is dead, and that makes me the last of the Trumbulls when my grandfather goes. The name means something in this colony; it means enough so that the man I marry will be accepted as leader because he has married a Trumbull. Lou is a strong man, Tod.''

''I felt his strength a long time ago,'' Tod said. ''It's a bully's strength, and he still uses it in a bully's way. Can't Caleb Trumbull see that?''

She sighed, and her shoulders moved slightly in what might have been an involuntary shudder, and this was her one unguarded moment. ''Some are too old; some are too young. Some are newcomers who do not fully understand my grandfather's dream. There hasn't been a wide choice. There is only Lou.''

Tod said, ''And it's on my head because I brought Sam Block here. Is that what you came to tell me?''

''No, Tod,'' she said. ''I came to turn you loose. I didn't mean to talk about myself and Lou.'' She looked over her shoulder toward the desk where the key lay. ''I've moved your horse from the livery stable without anyone knowing. It's tied out behind in the alley. I've only a few minutes to spare.''

He said, ''I'll stay here.''

Her face showed that she did not understand. She said, ''You can be beyond Beulah in five minutes.''

''And why do you want me gone?''

She shook her head. ''I can't tell you why I'm doing

this. Do you always quarrel with those who bring you help?''

His voice softened. ''It's good to have found a friend in Canaan. But I hate Caleb Trumbull; he made it so. You stand by him and will always stand by him. For that, I admire you. But if I let you use that key, there'll be a price tag tied to it, even if you don't mean to have one. Sometime soon I shall come face to face with Trumbull. I don't know how I'll manage that, but I will. When I do face him, I don't want to have to remember that I owe you something. Can you understand how it is with me?''

Nan drew back. Once before, at Owen Kirby's cabin, he had seen this stricken look on her face, this sadness. She asked faintly, ''It never leaves you for a minute, this hate of yours?''

''Never.''

''And you wouldn't use the key, even if I were to toss it into the cell?''

''I'm afraid not.''

''That's your final answer?''

''Thanks, Nan.''

''I am sorry for you, Tod. Very sorry,'' she said. She drew her cloak about her and fled across the office and through the outer door.

He stood there with a strange disquietude in him, once again feeling that he had been too ruthless with her. He thought of her offer and her refusal to say what had prompted it; he knew that her reason had been an honorable one, free of any selfish calculation. He thought of the wedding gown and Lou Bodeen; and he turned his mind from such thinking, a strong revulsion in him. He thought, *''Damn such a deal!''* and was surprised to find that he'd said it aloud. Here was another wrong to be laid at Caleb Trumbull's door.

He began pacing again; he wondered what time it was and got a look at the stars from the cell window and was surprised to find it only midevening. He was striding the cell when footsteps sounded in the outer office.

His first thought was that Nan had returned; and he wondered at the fierce jubilation that rose in him, even though he knew his answer must be the same.

But the voice that spoke out of the darkness was masculine. "Here's your grub."

Tod hoped that his own voice held even. "It's about time."

The man was one of those three who'd waited with Bodeen in the darkness of Trumbull's porch. He sat the tray on the desk and fumbled for the key and came forward and got the cell door unlocked. He turned then to pick up the tray; and when he faced about with it, Tod held the gun in his hand.

Tod said, "Just step inside," and he saw the man's mouth go slack with amazement.

Here was one who'd found the tiger unleashed, but he was brave, and his eyes showed a readiness to fight. Tod gestured with the gun and repeated his command; and the fellow obeyed, moving into the cell.

"You can eat that supper yourself," Tod said.

He stepped through the doorway and closed the barred door and turned the key in it. He knew this man would raise a cry the minute he was free of the gun's menace, and Tod considered tying the fellow and improvising a gag but decided not to waste the time. These walls were stout, and the cell's one window faced on the alley. Better to gamble that it might be many minutes before anyone would hear the man. Tod tossed the key into a corner and took his own gun from Bodeen's desk and restored it to his holster. He laid down Bodeen's gun.

"Your marshal was worried about this iron," Tod said very solemnly. "You can tell him I've returned it."

The man in the cell said, "We'll have you back in here before the night's through."

"Maybe," Tod said, and slipped through the outer doorway.

He stood for a moment on Beulah's street. Overhead the stars glittered coldly; night's breeze rustled the cottonwood leaves, and the light splashed from many windows. But here before the jail building there was darkness, and he moved in this darkness, going around the building. Already the man inside the cell was shouting; his voice came clear in the alley.

Tod spied the murky silhouette of a saddled horse, a deeper shadow among the shadows; and he came to the mount and found it was his own. He owed Nan for this, and he regretted the obligation, but she had given him no choice. The one in the cell was shouting, "Help! Help! Help!" spacing out that single word and putting a lusty effort behind it. The horse showed spookiness at that constant voice. Tod said, "Easy, boy," and lifted himself into leather.

He looked up toward Trumbull's house; the one light still burned. He frowned, thinking he might have a third try at the place, and then boots pounded toward him as someone came from the rear of the Haven, stumbling along the alley and crying, "I'm coming!"

They'd heard that man in the cell, and now Tod knew a real regret for not having bound and gagged his prisoner. But a new thought erased the regret. Lou Bodeen was going to be a pretty busy man on his wedding night. Grinning, Tod swung his horse about and walked it around the jail-building before using his spurs. He had lifted the mount to a high gallop as he hit the bridge leading out of Beulah.

V

In Caleb Trumbull's house, a bare hall led from the front door to a living room scanty of furnishings and dominated by a big-bellied stove forlorn in its unlighted emptiness. The only carpeting was a huge bearskin, flung haphazardly upon the floor. Tables and chairs were homemade, crude creations of lumber and rawhide; and upon the wall were crayon portraits of Trumbull and his wife, both looking staid and severe. To this room Nan Trumbull had come after her talk at the jail with Tod Kirby; and here she sat, tired and rebellious and a little sad.

She had not bothered to light the lamp, which stood on the largest table. She liked the darkness and the aloneness;

she felt sheltered here and remote from the night and the town and the cross-purposes threading them.

She was thinking of Tod Kirby; she had been strangely stirred by him at the colony school those many years before, but she had been a child then, and she supposed that his loneliness and shyness had touched some mothering instinct in her. Today she had met him again, and as a woman she'd tasted his kiss. She had hated that kiss, knowing that he used it as his only weapon against her; but she had awakened at that moment, awakened to remorse for a bargain long made with Lou Bodeen, awakened to question for the first time her loyalty to an old man's dream and the precedence of that loyalty over all else.

The old man was lying upstairs in this very house, his life running out. Doc Salisbury had muttered vaguely about age and a heart taxed too heavily, but he had given no exact answer as to how long Caleb Trumbull might live. A week, perhaps. A month. Time enough for Nan really to face a decision she had dodged, a final decision concerning Bodeen. But now a longhorn legion stood at Canaan's gate; and Trumbull, hearing of this from her, had stated his wish. Time had run out.

Lou Bodeen came into the house; she at once recognized his footsteps, and she called his name, and he loomed in the doorway of the room. He said, "Get a lamp burning, will you?" and she obeyed. In the glow, she saw that excitement had fired his cheeks and his eyes were angry. He moved to the window and drew down the shade. She sensed that his had been an afterthought and judged by his manner that fear had prompted it, and she wondered about that.

He inclined his head toward that upstairs room. "The preacher here?"

"I thought you'd be bringing him."

He made an impatient gesture. "Kirby broke out of jail. He had a gun in there—my gun. He must have planted it earlier. He threw down on Tom Heflin when Tom fetched him supper. I've got men on his trail. I'll be deputizing others and riding with them. Perhaps I'll be gone most of the night. Tell Caleb that the wedding will have to wait."

"And then, Lou—?"

"We'll be married tomorrow morning." His glance searched her; he was seeing her wedding gown for the first time, and she knew there was some superstition that forbade this. They should be standing before the preacher at this moment. He said, very slowly, "If you still intend to marry me."

"I'll keep the bargain."

He said with a show of regret, "Is that what it will always mean to you, Nan? A deal made by an old man?"

He could be charming when he wished; his eyes took on now a look of soft pleading, and his smile was gentle. Had she known him less well, she would have been moved by him. As it was, she said, "Tomorrow you'll be head of the colony, and I will be your wife, but people will remember that I'm a Trumbull. A leader less unselfish than my grandfather could take many things for himself. He could make his power pay him; he could use favoritism as a club. I will always be at your side, Lou, to see that you never use your leadership to line your own pockets."

Anger flared again in his eyes, but he controlled it. He said softly, "So that's it. You'll be Caleb's watchdog after he's gone."

"Yes, Lou," she said. "I want you to know that."

More than the width of the room lay between them then; they were separated by two ways of thinking, and it would always be thus. She saw the surety rise in Bodeen, and she could have spoken his thought for him. *I'll have my way when the time comes.* Against his ambition she would forever be pitted, and this was part of the realization that had grown on her tonight and made her tired and rebellious and a little sad.

He turned toward the door. "I've got to be on the trail," he said brusquely.

She said then, "I hope you don't catch Tod."

This brought him around, his anger naked. "He's no friend of Canaan's."

"Are you, Lou? Or are you first, last, and always an opportunist? I've just got my eyes completely opened to you. You pointed out to Caleb that we could hold Tod as hostage against Sam Block. It wasn't that Tod roughed you up tonight that counted, though that must have hurt your pride. I could have respected you if your wish to jail him had been more personal and less calculating. I'd have turned him loose if he'd let me, rather than see him used; but his principles were higher than yours. As it is, you'll not be able to play him as you'd play a card."

He strode toward her, but she did not flinch. He stood looking down at her, his anger drawing his jaw tight; and for an instant she was sure he was going to strike her. Then some new mood stirred in him, and he laughed, his laughter filling the room. "It will be very interesting, being married to you," he said. "It will be exciting, every day of it. I would not want it otherwise."

He turned again and strode from the room and the house. After he'd gone, Nan fought for composure; she had in that last instant with Bodeen glimpsed all the years ahead and what they would hold for her. She had done the one thing for which he would never forgive her; she had drawn a comparison between him and another man and proved the other greater. She knew Bodeen's vanity and his ambition, and she had challenged both.

She arose and blew out the lamp, but she found the darkness no longer soothing to her. She made aimless movements with her hands, feeling like one tied tight while all about her events rushed to their completion, sealing her own doom. She thought of Tod Kirby, riding somewhere in the night with Canaan's men on his trail. She thought of him standing so defiant in Beulah's jail, his eyes somber with his hate for Caleb Trumbull. Out of this thinking, a resolution came that stirred her to sudden activity; and she left the room.

To the old man who lingered always on the porch, she said, "If my grandfather asks, tell him Lou had to ride out on law business. I'm going riding, too. We'll both be back before morning."

From a lean-to tacked on the back of the house, she got her own horse, the one she'd ridden to the Kirby cabin that afternoon; and when she'd saddled, she found the wedding gown an encumbrance as she lifted herself to the leather. She might have gone back to the house and changed to her riding skirt, but the need that was sending her into the night had now attained an urgency that made her fretful of delay. Drawing her dark cloak about her, she skirted the edge of the town, boomed across the bridge, and headed south into the valley.

The night made a velvet canopy, softened by starlight and the promise of a moon over the eastern hills; but Nan rode with the familiarity of one who had come often in this direction, one who knew the landmarks and could measure her pace by them. Wind touched her, promising winter, and she was glad for the cloak. She rode through an emptiness unbroken by any ranch light; but she knew this to be a peopled night, remembering those who'd taken Tod Kirby's trail; and she rode warily, not wanting to be found out here and questioned about her presence.

Once she thought she heard guns racketing far over by the western hills, and she drew to a stop and keened the night. The sound came again, fainter this time, illusive and lost. She reminded herself that Bodeen had wanted Tod Kirby alive, but alarm touched her with the remembrance of Bodeen's anger. But perhaps those shots were made by possemen signaling to each other.

After an hour she was in the vicinity of the Kirby cabin; and she wondered if Tod, hard-pressed, might have taken sanctuary there. She decided he would be too shrewd for that, recalling Bodeen's account of how Tod had contrived to hide a gun in Beulah's jail. She smiled, for she knew that although Tod had proved himself reckless and stubborn, he had also shown foresightedness when he'd taken time for thinking. He had strength in him and the makings of a good man, except for his constant bitterness. She would like to see him one day with the bitterness washed out of him, but she supposed she never would. This brought to mind her reason for riding tonight; and she pushed the horse harder, galloping it awhile, then letting it walk awhile.

The moon was showing when she came to where the hills pinched together at Canaan's south end and saw the campfire ahead. As she rode toward it, she distinguished men limned against the blaze, and the tilts of a chuck wagon, and was soon able to read Hashknife's brand smeared with axle grease upon the canvas. Someone called out, "Tod—?" and she halloed the camp, and that same voice said in mild astonishment, "Why, it's a girl!"

She rode into the rim of the firelight and saw Hashknife's crew standing, a full score, she decided, of bearded men, gaunt from the long trail out of Texas. Yet in the midst of these six-footers, Sam Block's squat figure was the dominant one; he stood peering from beneath his tufted brows, his leathery face revealing nothing. Then he said, "Will you light, miss?"

She slipped from the horse and held its reins loosely. "You're Sam Block?"

He nodded.

"I'm Nan Trumbull."

The wind had blown her long black hair, and her cloak had fallen open to reveal the wedding gown beneath; and Block said with a certain wry humor, "Do you always dress this way for riding?"

She said, "I hadn't time to change. I want to talk to you."

Suspicion was here and a slight antagonism, and she supposed these things came from her having named herself a Trumbull. For a moment she regretted coming, but she didn't want fear to show, or uncertainty; so she donned defiance. She said, "Are you still of a mind to move your cattle into Canaan?"

Block frowned, "Either you've talked to Tod or heard him make his say. Where is he?"

"He'll be along when he's ready to come. I'm here to ask you to take Tod away. Find graze somewhere else, Mr. Block."

Block said slowly, "Now I don't think that would be any kind of deal."

"Tod says you're like a father to him. Does that work two ways?"

Block took a hipshot stand, and his face closed her out. "Tod wouldn't be wanting me to talk about that to a Trumbull," he said.

Nan said, "I was kind to Tod long ago. I've tried being kind to him since his return. If he were here, he'd tell you that I've proved my friendship in spite of my name."

Block looked at her with new interest. He said, very slowly, "Once a long time ago, I drove a herd of Hashknife beef north out of Texas to the railroad at Dodge. We hit the town and checked our guns with the marshal and bought us a bath and a shave. Then we started out to drink the place dry. In a saloon I found a dying gambler and a boy with big eyes that burned through a man. Those eyes did something to me. The gambler died before we cleared town, and that left the boy on his own. I took him back to Texas with me."

"Why, Mr. Block?"

He looked at her and she had the feeling that he did not see her; he was suddenly impervious to the night and the men around him and the hush that had fallen over the camp. He said, speaking inner thoughts long kept locked, "A man broadens his acres and increases his herds, but there has to be something more than that. Each year as he turns older he comes closer to understanding. What of Hashknife when I'm gone? I wanted a son. I got one."

"Then he means something to you? A great deal to you?"

Her intentness compelled him. Block nodded. "Yes, miss."

"Then take him and your cattle out of here." Her voice rose, becoming impassioned. "Don't you understand? Take him where he can watch Hashknife's acres spread and Hashknife's herds grow and have no concern but that. He will be only half a cattleman here, for every move he makes and every thought he thinks will be colored by his need to destroy what Caleb Trumbull built. He'll tear down the colony, yes; but what is just as bad, he'll destroy himself doing it. His hate will be with him sleeping and waking. Take him away, Mr. Block. Time will dull the bitterness in him on another range. If he means anything to you, you'll do as I say.''

Block turned this over in his mind; and she stood with her breast rising and falling; she stood spent with speaking. She watched Block; she could almost see the slow workings of his mind, and she recognized him as an unimaginative man best able to grasp only such things as could be put in his hand. She knew despair then.

Block said at last, "He wanted an hour with Caleb Trumbull. Maybe he's had that hour. It was little enough to ask. I want graze for my longhorns. In this valley we'll both get what we want.''

She had failed in her mission, and she sensed that her argument had touched Sam Block no more than spring's beauty touches a grizzly bear. She mustered another argument, one that might reach through to him; and she asked, "Suppose Canaan fights you, Mr. Block?''

"Then we'll fight Canaan,'' he said. "I'll come peaceable if they'll let me. I'd rather not spend my lead and my men. That's for Caleb Trumbull to decide.''

He was an imbedded boulder, unmovable by anything save force, and realizing this, she saw him as Tod Kirby had briefly seen him, a man not to be swerved. She had ridden in vain, and she climbed to her saddle and said, "Good night, Mr. Block,'' and turned her horse northward.

He called after her as she rode away, some question about Tod's whereabouts. She was tempted to answer, for she was remembering those racketing guns; but twice tonight, in Beulah's jail and Hashknife's camp, she had placed her loyalty to Canaan second to the needs of Tod Kirby. She started home at a slow walk and was riding this way when she heard the hard beat of hoofs down out of the north.

She supposed that Tod was coming, free of the riders Bodeen had put on his trail; but because she couldn't be sure, she pulled her horse over to a thicket of trees and sat her saddle in the shadows. Thus she saw Lou Bodeen gallop by, headed for Big Sam Block's camp. She watched him thunder past, wondering what brought him here, what new calculation, what new scheme. No answer came to mind, and she rode northward again with this fresh worry to keep her company in the night.

VI

To Tod Kirby, riding out of Beulah after his jailbreak, there came a growing sense of regret; for he had failed in the purpose that had brought him to town, and he'd lived too long with that purpose to surrender it readily. A mile beyond the bridge, he drew to a halt, hipped around in his saddle, and had a look behind. He could make out Trumbull's house on the rise and see that one light burning. He watched the light; it was a magnet drawing him, and he was of a mind to turn back when he sensed some faint disturbance in the night that sharpened his wariness. Dismounting, he put an ear to the ground. At least a half-dozen riders were hard after him.

He climbed into the saddle, a calm man. Around him the valley glimmered in the starshine, no moon showing yet; and all the valley was his to ride in. He knew how badly Bodeen would want him back, for he would be to Bodeen a shield against Big Sam Block. He knew the pursuers would be expecting him to head south to Hashknife's camp; likely Bodeen's posse would ride that way to overtake him. Grimly he continued west to where the walling hills bulked against the night sky.

He rode at an easy gallop, following a wagon road that meandered through the grass, leaving this road when it angled abruptly to cut north. He taxed neither himself nor his horse, and an hour's riding brought him to the shadow of the hills. Now the moon was just beginning to show to the east; and he paused and strained his eyes in every direction, a sense of uneasiness suddenly taking hold of him.

To the southeast he thought he saw vague movement, and he wondered if cattle grazed there. No rancher had been located below Beulah in the old days. Then a gun sounded, the report dimmed by distance, and another gun, nearer, made reply, and still a third spoke. He knew then that his ruse had failed. Those Beulah riders hadn't galloped blindly to the south. They had cut his sign and guessed his intent and spread themselves out, playing a wary game. And now they were signaling one another and making ready to draw their net tight.

He rode again with a sharp carefulness, knowing he must keep constantly attentive if he was to elude them. He was remembering that they knew these hills better than he. He had explored much of the valley in his boyhood, but the cabin had been the base of his operations, and he had never ventured this far. Still he kept faced toward the hills, and soon he was into timber and crashing through brushy thickets.

He thought: *Enough racket to wake the dead!* and listened then and heard the movement of a horseman not too far distant and was sure that his commotion was drawing the man. Dismounting, Tod began leading his horse. It seemed that he groped along forever; he had lost track of time; and the stars, the cowboy's clock, were hidden from him. The moon rose high enough to filter light down through the treetops; by this light he found a game trail.

Along this, he climbed upward, riding the horse again, dismounting whenever the pitch turned abruptly steep. The timber became thicker, a tall stand of lodgepole pine, the interlocked branches shutting off the sky; and he rode through layering darkness feeling lost. A regular maze of trails crisscrossed the slope, and he explored these endlessly and became aware that men were all around him. He'd guessed they were a half-dozen; now he wondered if the first bunch had been reinforced. They called to each other and signaled with guns; and he got his own gun into his hand, then pouched it again. There was no desire in him to use his gun against these men; he felt a personal animosity for only one, and that one was Lou Bodeen. He made a wry face, reflecting that the posse might have no such compunction regarding Tod Kirby.

It came to him that he had not recognized Bodeen's voice when he had heard men calling, and he wondered if Bodeen had stayed in town after all. This worried him; he thought of the scheduled wedding.

The trail leveled off; he found himself moving northward along the shoulder of the hill. Sometimes the timber thinned, and he could look down upon the moonlit valley floor and see the distant lights of Beulah. He even thought he could make out the light that burned in Trumbull's house. That house still drew him strongly. He looked for an intersecting trail that dropped downward and, finding one, began descending. He felt as though he had been forever on the hill; the stars, when last glimpsed, had told him that midnight was past. Now he was in darkness again; and he wended through this darkness, moving carefully and hoping he'd eluded pursuit. Then he came to where his trail crossed another, and a horseman loomed before him so close that he almost crashed into the man.

He saw the fellow lean forward in his saddle. "That you, George?"

"Yes," Tod said, speaking deep in his throat. He made a fist and struck at the man, knocking him from his saddle, and he fell from his own horse atop the man. The fellow threshed wildly; Tod struck him again and again until the man went limp beneath him. Tod stood up, breathing hard and looking down at the unconscious figure. The man's horse had shied from the struggling pair; it snorted and showed signs of bolting.

All about Tod the woods were coming alive with horsemen. A sense of desperation in him, Tod leaped quickly, grasped the reins of the fallen man's horse and got the mount headed along the lateral trail the rider had been following. Slapping the horse hard across the rump with his hat, Tod sent the mount galloping. Then he piled aboard his own horse.

His impulse was to plunge wildly down the hill, heedless of low-hanging branches and uncertain terrain; but he fought down the urge. Yonder he could hear that bolting horse crashing along; he listened intently and judged that the rest of the posse was converging upon it, sure that it bore the fugitive. He looked again at the man on the ground and saw that the fellow was stirring to consciousness. Tod whispered softly, "All in the night's work, friend," He kneed his horse, descending again, holding as silent as he could.

He came unchallenged to the foot of the slope, and only then did he raise his mount to a gallop.

Now the moon was lowering over the western hills behind him, and the stars were beginning to fade. The darkness before dawn would soon be on the land. Tod felt the weight of all the miles and all the hours and the hard tension of dodging through the night. He looked back at the slope where the posse still stumbled about; and he judged that his ruse had worked, confusing them long enough for him to gain this much distance. He was far north of Beulah; a few lights still showed in the town, and he headed toward them, riding hard. He was thinking of sunrise and Sam Block. He was thinking that here was his own last chance at Trumbull, and this made him reckless of consequences.

The moon was gone when he hit the wagon road and began following it toward the bridge. Now he'd finished out a vast triangle; he was riding where he'd ridden hours earlier. He came over the bridge and pulled his horse down to a walk. Not far ahead loomed Trumbull's house; he had failed twice to gain access to that house, and thus he had learned wariness. He circled wide and came upon the house from behind, and in the darkness he dismounted and stood peering.

He saw the lean-to built against the rear of the house. He stalked cautiously toward that lean-to and heard horses move restlessly inside. He dropped the reins and anchored his own horse, afraid that it might neigh. Coming closer, he looked up and saw a second-story window above the shed. He got hold of the eaves of the slanted roof and pulled himself up and stood precariously, elation growing in him, for he could now reach that second-story window. Its sash, he discovered, had been raised slightly; he got his fingers under the sash and lifted. Then he hoisted himself till he could get a knee on the sill. Panting hard, he clambered into a dark, uncarpeted hallway and saw that lamplight streamed from under one door.

That door opened, and Nan stood peering along the hall, fetched, he supposed, by the sound of his entry. She stood hesitantly in the gloom, and then she recognized him, for her voice held surprise rather than fear. "So it's you, Tod," she said. "Come in."

She backed into the lamplighted room, and he stepped after her. There were few furnishings here, and the bed was the largest thing in the room. Doc Salisbury sat beside the bed, looking worn from a long vigil; but it was the man in the bed who held Tod's attention. He sat propped up against pillows; he wore a flannel nightgown, and his silvery hair was awry, and his patriarchal beard looked straggly. His face was drawn by illness until it was only the ghost of the face Tod Kirby remembered, but the eyes were very much alive, and they were the eyes of Caleb Trumbull. Thus had the long circle been finished.

Trumbull said, his voice even and surprisingly strong, "You are persistent, Tod. I would have had you admitted yesterday afternoon, but this despot of a doctor forbade it. Will you sit down, boy?"

Nan had seated herself. Only then did Tod realize that she'd changed from the wedding gown to a simple dress of calico. She sat with her hands folded, her face composed, her face sad. She looked at Tod, and her eyes said resignedly, "And now you are here."

Tod said, "I'll stand for what I've got to say. I've come to talk about Owen Kirby."

"Ah, yes," Trumbull said.

"He asked you for a place in your colony, and you gave it to him," Tod said. "He tried to abide by your rule, but it was too much for him when he saw people starving that first winter in the valley. He fought his way up over the south road to Nugget and fetched back supplies. He left the valley without your permission, and you never forgave him. He'd broken your rule, so you forbade your people to touch his supplies, and they were fools enough to obey. Most of the supplies are still in the cabin. You exiled Owen Kirby right here in Canaan; you passed the word that none of the colony was to speak to us. He lived until spring with every face turned from him. Then you won. He rode out of here with me sitting behind his saddle. He never came back.''

''I know,'' Trumbull said.

''But you don't know all of it! He went back to the only life he knew, a life he'd hated, a life he'd escaped from in Canaan. He went back to gambling. We were in Cheyenne a while and then in St. Louis and finally in Dodge City. But, you see, he'd got pneumonia that winter he'd fought the snowdrifts to Nugget. I nursed him through it alone; no man of Canaan dared come near us. His lungs were weakened after that. It took him four years to die, but what really killed him was that trip he made to try to save your damn' colony from starving. I've come to tell you that I hold you to account for that.''

Nan's breath caught; the sound was like a sob. Salisbury's old face turned angry. ''Can't you see that you're talking to a very sick man?''

Trumbull raised a bloodless hand. ''He's to have his say, Joel.''

Tod found his throat dry. ''That's all there is to say. You've already learned the rest from Nan. I've come back with a new father and five thousand longhorns and a fighting crew behind me. I just wanted you to know why I brought them here, Trumbull.''

Trumbull said, ''Now I shall speak.''

Tod shook his head. ''I think the time has passed for talking.''

Trumbull said, ''No man can fashion what I've fashioned here without making errors. If Canaan was to live safe from the world, there had to be a rule that closed us out from the world. Owen Kirby broke that rule. I was aware even then that he followed his own fancy for the greater good of us all. But I had to be adamant, if the rule was to stand, and so I had to punish him. Perhaps I was afraid, boy, that one exception to the rule could be the beginning of Canaan's end. I was not always sure of myself in those days. But I could let no man see my uncertainty."

"All I know is that you're alive and Owen Kirby is long dead," Tod said bitterly.

Trumbull waved a hand. "I've told you that I made mistakes. It has taken these many years of living to teach me that my basic idea was foolish. No people can live unto themselves; in such a notion there is a selfishness that I had overlooked. Canaan has changed since that day. Perhaps because of the wrong I did Owen Kirby. I've always hoped that sometime he would return to see the changes, to see the best of my idea preserved but tempered with broader understanding. You will find a happy people here, Tod. A people who have learned to live for each other. I wish that you'd come back to be one of them. That is why I ordered your cabin kept as it was."

Surprise touched Tod. "*You* ordered it?"

Trumbull nodded. "A waiting gift for the man I once exiled."

Nan said, "It's so, Tod. I could have told you that this afternoon if you'd given me a chance."

Tod shook his head. "Now I don't know what the hell to think!"

Trumbull said softly, "Think of Canaan. Think whether you want the old rule changed to Sam Block's rule."

Tod turned away. He'd had his hour of fulfilment, but the taste of it was ashes in his mouth. The old hate for Trumbull persisted; he'd lived too long with that hate to relinquish it so readily. Yet his certainty had been shaken, so badly shaken that the satisfaction was gone for having led Big Sam Block here. He thought of Owen Kirby dead in Dodge City, but he could not reach out to that gentle, vanished presence. Not in this bewildering moment.

He looked toward the window and saw the gray of dawn against the pane. Nan looked also and moved to the table where the lamp stood and blew out the flame. In the harshness of the half-light, Trumbull's face was old and seamed and tired. Trumbull said, "I can't expect you to grasp at once what took me so long to understand. Just try, boy."

Salisbury stirred. "Someone on the stairs."

Nan said, "Old Zeke," and crossed to the door and opened it.

The one who'd guarded the porch stood there, his face twisted with excitement. He saw Tod and recognized him, but the oldster was beyond being astonished that Tod was here. He cried, "Look out the window and see what I saw from the porch. Longhorns! Thousands of 'em! Coming across the flats toward town!"

Tod said, "Not yet!" He moved to the window and looked from it over the rooftops of Beulah and saw the murky mass of Hashknife's herd spilling up out of the south, spilling toward town. He knew then that Big Sam Block had jumped his own deadline, and he couldn't understand why. But the strangest thing was his own feeling of despair.

VII

Nan moved to Tod's elbow. She, too, looked beyond the town to the advancing herd, and then she faced her grandfather. She put out a hand feebly as though reaching for support; her face was chalky white. She said in a voice that threatened to break, "This is my doing!"

Trumbull was the least shaken of them all. "How could that be?" he asked.

"I had a talk with Lou last night. My eyes had been opened. I'd guessed that he wanted leadership for his own gain, and I warned him that I'd be watching. He laughed at me, but he was scared just the same. I think he decided then to find a way to rule Canaan without me. Instead of riding with the posse after Tod, he went to Block's camp. I know; I'd gone there myself. Never mind why. Now Hashknife is here. Don't you see? I drove Lou to some kind of bargain with Big Sam Block!"

"You feared Lou was the wrong man for the leadership? Why didn't you tell me, girl?"

"It wasn't news for a sick man."

Anger grew in Caleb Trumbull's eyes, and he sat bolt upright. "Lou Bodeen has overstepped. Any deal he's made with Block is not Canaan's deal. Block shall know that." He threw aside the blankets and swung his legs out of bed and came to a high, tottering stand, an emaciated old man in a nightgown. Yet he was not a ridiculous figure; no one, seeing his face, would have laughed.

Salisbury was instantly on his feet. "Get back into that bed!"

"No," Trumbull said and walked carefully to a closet and opened it. He took out his trousers and tugged them on over his nightgown, pulling the suspenders into place. He found a pair of boots and struggled into them. He was a man tapping some hidden reserve of strength. He looked at the astonished Zeke, who still stood in the doorway. "I shall need a horse," Trumbull said. "Get one saddled."

Salisbury made an impotent gesture with his hands. "Are you crazy, Caleb? This will be the finish of you!"

Trumbull said calmly, "Better that, Joel, than the finish of Canaan."

Salisbury appealed to Nan. "You've got to stop him!"

"No," Nan said, and her voice told Tod that she was close to tears. "He has to do this. All of us know that." She faced Tod, her eyes pleading. "Will you ride with him? If I know Lou, he'll turn desperate if his scheming is blocked. Grandfather has never carried a gun."

Tod said, "I'll ride along."

Trumbull gave him a quick glance. "I think your allegiance is with the other side, boy."

"Then," Tod said dryly, "I'm no colonist; you can't give me orders. I'll ride along."

Trumbull made an impatient gesture and moved toward the door. "Come then. We're wasting time."

He went into the hall and Tod moved after him, having a last look over his shoulder at Nan. She was smiling faintly, but this was merely a movement of her lips. She was sick with a great fear for Caleb Trumbull, but her pride was sustaining her, and that too was for Trumbull. It was as though she had known across the years that sometime there would be such a moment as this. She lifted a hand and let it fall; her lips quirked but no words came.

Tod said, "He'll be back soon."

On the stairs Trumbull lurched and almost fell; Tod got him by the arm. They came to the porch, and here Tod left the man and went around back to get his horse. Zeke was just leading a saddled mount from the lean-to. Tod took the reins of both horses and brought them to the porch. From here the view of the oncoming herd was limited, but Tod got a glimpse of them between two buildings and judged that the longhorns were hardly more than a mile away. Their bawling made a discordance in the dawn; the raised dust stood above the flatland in a cloud.

Trumbull stood peering, his face showing nothing. He came down off the porch and caught hold of a saddle horn. He had a hard time lifting himself; Tod moved to help, but Trumbull waved him away. Grimacing with pain, Trumbull got into leather; and Tod rode beside him as they headed down into the town.

That distant bawling had awakened Beulah; men gathered in excited knots on the street, some wearing guns. A few were here who stood by spent horses; and these gave Tod hard, appraising looks; and he judged them to be the possemen who had harried him through the night. One had a lump on his jaw, and Tod recognized him as the man he'd felled on the slope. Seeing Tod with Trumbull, they made no move; their real astonishment was that Trumbull was riding; and they converged upon him, their questions rising.

Trumbull said, "There is to be no shooting, understand. Not unless I order it. Every man of you is to stay here until I return."

He reined his horse along the street, Tod riding with him. In the doorway of the jail building Lou Bodeen stood. He still wore his black suit, a faint beard stubble showed on his cheeks, and he looked as though he needed sleep; Tod supposed his own eyes were a red-rimmed. Bodeen's glance flickered with brief surprise to find Caleb Trumbull astride a horse.

Trumbull said, "I have a question to ask, Lou: Did you ride to Sam Block's camp last night?"

Again there was that flicker of surprise; a moment's calculation showed on Bodeen's face, and then he chose to be defiant. "Suppose I did?"

"Another question: Is yonder herd moving upon Beulah because of a deal you made?"

Bodeen showed his teeth in a smile and became a sure man, done with pretense. "Hell, Caleb, those Texans are my friends!"

Trumbull grew in his saddle. He said in a great and terrible voice, "I am giving you exactly one hour to be on your way out of Canaan. At the end of that hour, if you are still here, I shall drive you out with a horsewhip!"

Bodeen's eyes moved to Tod. "So you made a deal, too, Caleb. You're counting on Kirby to change Sam Block's mind. It won't work."

Trumbull said, "I'm counting on my people not being such fools as to back you in whatever bargain you made. One hour, Lou."

He rode on. Tod touched his heel to his horse and moved after Trumbull, but he kept his eyes on Bodeen, seeing the man as one who'd staked everything on his surety. Temper colored Bodeen's face, an explosive temper that shook the man; but he merely fingered the elk's tooth on his watch-chain, keeping his hand away from the skirt of his coat. Trumbull picked a passage between two buildings, Tod following; and thus Bodeen was lost from their sight.

Now they were clear of the town and riding across the dawn-flushed flats. They lifted their horses to a gallop, and meadowlarks flew from the grass before them complaining at this violation of the morning's peace. Tod could make out the man riding at the point of the oncoming herd; that man loomed larger as the distance narrowed, becoming recognizable as Big Sam Block. Halfway to him, Trumbull drew to a halt. "This is far enough," he said.

Block also reined up; he peered, and then, because he

must have understood a parley was wanted, he lifted his hand, signaling his crew to hold the herd. At once the swing and drag riders began circling, working to stop the herd's movement. Some of the cattle fell to grazing; others tossed their horns and moved restlessly. *They're skittish,* Tod decided, the thought instinctive, a cattleman's. He remembered all the mornings on the long trail north when he had watched for such skittishness, tasting the drover's eternal fear of a stampede.

Block came spurring forward; he reined up again, his leathery face puckered. He said, a genuine concern in his voice, "Tod, I've been worried about you!"

Tod said, "No need. Sam, this is Caleb Trumbull."

Block's bushy eyebrows bunched. "Hell, man, I thought you were sick abed."

Trumbull said in a grave voice, "Not too sick to speak for my people, Mr. Block. I'm the leader here."

Block frowned. "I heard different. A man named Bodeen told me you'd picked him to take your place."

Trumbull shook his head. "Last night, that was half-true. It is no longer even that. Your dealings must be with me. Do you propose to take over my valley, Mr. Block?"

Block said with a show of anger, "Let's quit this fiddle-faddling. My deal's with Bodeen. He said there's room in the valley for me and the colony both. He said he'd run the town and I could run the range. I'll scratch his back, if he'll scratch mine. He asked me to bring my herd to Beulah to show folks I meant business and be on hand to back him if there was trouble. I spent the last half of the night getting these longhorns down into the valley. They're tired and spooky, and I'm not going to turn them back now. My deal with Bodeen stands. That's the size of it, Trumbull."

"Then," said Trumbull, "I shall not move from here. If you bring on those longhorns, you will have to trample me under."

Block's broad shoulders lifted in a shrug. "Your misfortune," he said and fingered his reins. "Coming, Tod?"

But Tod was looking at Caleb Trumbull, and he was

seeing a man straight in his saddle, an old man, a sick man, yet one who still clung to this desperate attempt to stave off disaster. Tod remembered those gun-hung men who waited along Beulah's street, waited for the word. Trumbull had made no mention of them, had not threatened to call upon them to defend the town and the valley; and Tod knew now that Trumbull would never do so. He would make this lone, stubborn, futile stand before he would unleash the very kind of violence from which he had long ago fled. He had taken the responsibility upon himself alone, and that made him both magnificent and mad.

Tod glanced over his shoulder toward Beulah and now saw the town not as just another scatteration of buildings but as one man's handiwork, embodying his principles and therefore dearer to him than anything else. Trumbull had given to that town his own greatness; and in the defense of his town, his greatness turned clear in Tod's eyes. Less than an hour ago Tod had listened to Trumbull claim a regret for what he had done to Owen Kirby, but Tod had found it hard to believe Trumbull. Now he saw Trumbull as a man too big for petty deceits, too brave to deal in lying.

Block said again, impatiently, "Coming, Tod?"

"No, Sam," Tod said. "I'm staying here with him."

This hit Block like the blow of a fist. His face puckered, and disbelief came into his eyes. "You and me made a deal, too, Tod. I kept my end of it. You had your chance to ride in. You wanted this man pulled down. Come along, and we'll start pulling."

"I've changed my mind, Sam."

Temper tugged at the corner of Block's mouth; he was now a troubled man dealing with the unexpected and angered by a thing beyond his understanding. He looked about him at the fairness of Canaan and the avarice that Tod had witnessed briefly yesterday afternoon, the lust for grass, took a hard hold on Block. His gaze swung back to Tod and turned troubled.

"You ain't leaving me, Tod? What about the last eight years? Doesn't Hashknife mean something to you?"

"I rode for a brand that was too big to deal with the likes of Bodeen, Sam."

Block said, "That's your final word, Tod?"

"Thanks, Sam. Thanks for everything."

Trumbull said, "I will make you a deal, Mr. Block. The south end of Canaan can be yours. If this boy goes with you, I think that your people will live in peace with mine. Will that satisfy you?"

The struggle in Block was visible to Tod; he could see it on Big Sam's face. Decency was there, but greed was there also, making him all men in one. Block looked at Tod, but Tod kept his own face grim, and that was the breaking of Big Sam Block. He said, "I told that girl last night there had to be something besides Hashknife." He lifted his arm and made the circling motion that ordered his crew to turn the herd about. He faced around and said, "You win, Trumbull."

Trumbull's eyes were on Tod, and this was the only time Tod was ever to see Caleb Trumbull smile. "More than you know, Mr. Block," Trumbull said.

Ahead of them Hashknife's crew spurred into action and went about turning the herd. Tod knew that those in Beulah would see this and understand what it meant, and a fierce elation blossomed in him.

Trumbull said, "Go help your crew, Tod," and wheeled his horse about and faced Beulah.

He looked old and spent, a man who'd lived on borrowed strength until the need for strength was gone. He looked sick, but his eyes were warm. And then suddenly his eyes turned stricken, and he pitched from his horse. Tod heard then the report of a rifle and saw a faint puff of smoke lift from atop the community granary in town.

Bodeen! he thought and remembered Nan's prediction that Bodeen, his scheming bested, would turn desperate. Then he was spurring forward to the fallen man, Big Sam hard after him. Dismounting, Tod saw blood on Trumbull's flannel nightgown, and he judged the man to be badly wounded. But Trumbull's eyes held life. Tod said, "Help me get him onto his horse, Sam."

Block swung down. "Easy with him," he said.

Together they hoisted Trumbull; and the man clutched hard at the saddle horn, reeling. The rifle began to speak again, the bullets geysering dust close by. Temper showed in Block's eyes, but his hand was steady enough. He got out his gun and fired toward the granary.

"Get moving," he said to Tod.

Tod lifted himself to leather; some warning brought his head about. He had his look and felt the roots of terror strike deep within him. "Sam!" he shouted. *"The herd!"*

Block looked, too, and was at once piling aboard his horse, his face gone gray. The gunfire had put panic into the longhorns; and that panic had become a contagion, stampeding them. And because Hashknife's crew hadn't yet turned the cattle, the herd was thundering toward these three out here in the openness; the herd was spilling hard across the flats toward Beulah.

VIII

Tod's fear was for Caleb Trumbull. Events had piled up with such rapidity as to give a man no chance for thinking. Thus instinct sent Tod spurring across the openness toward town with the herd behind him, and he spurred with the stark realization that he must gain the town before the herd engulfed him. The real problem was to keep Trumbull in his saddle. Tod rode beside the man, an arm out to steady Trumbull; he rode awkwardly, sure that Trumbull would fall at any moment. He shouted, "Hang onto the horn!" but he wasn't sure Trumbull heard him. The stampede made a roar in Tod's ears; the stampede filled the world and shook it.

Looking back, Tod saw that Big Sam had deliberately fallen behind. Block had let the van of the herd overtake him; he was batting at the head of one of the leaders with his hat, trying to turn that fear-crazed steer and thus perhaps turn the herd. Let Block's horse once stumble, and he was done for. Knowing this, Tod averted his eyes, a crawling sickness in him.

Trumbull was listing in his saddle; Tod plucked hard at the man's arm, straightening him. His horse crowded Trumbull's, slowing them both. The distance to Beulah had been cut in half, but still this seemed an endless race. Tod looked up at the granary and marked the rifle's flash. They were moving too fast to make good targets.

Then they were into the town; driving between two buildings, they came upon the street. Already men were scattering, running to whatever shelter they could find. But some, bolder than the rest, now dropped to one knee and began firing at the oncoming herd. Realizing that Block might be hit in the excitement, Tod shouted, "Aim at the steers! Aim at the steers!" He looked over his shoulder and saw the vanguard of the herd come spilling into the street. A townsman fired, and the first steer buckled at the knees and went down.

Caleb Trumbull croaked, "Run for cover!" He teetered in his saddle then; before Tod could get a hand on him, he fell. Townsmen rushed at once to Trumbull.

Tod shouted, "Carry him to his house," and ready hands lifted Trumbull and bore him away. Tod turned to look behind, and the stampede was into Beulah.

The panicked steers came pouring into the street to run aimlessly, some plunging one direction, some another. Beulah's people broke in panic; Tod saw several shinnying up the cottonwoods; others darted into doorways; one was climbing the front of the Haven. The longhorns were everywhere, a turbulence of bony brown backs; a steer caromed against Tod's horse, and then he was engulfed by cattle. He fought against this sweeping tide, all the while worrying about that gun atop the granary. Bodeen, his cause lost, had nothing left now but to kill.

Tod looked about for Sam Block; he couldn't see the man, but he could hear him shouting. Tod recognized a couple of the Hashknife crew who must have been riding in swing position. They were now trying to chouse the herd on through the town. The herd's bawling added to the bedlam; steers crashed against buildings and glass tinkled and wood splintered. Dust rose chokingly. A Hashknife rider materialized out of the dust close to Tod. Dirt and sweat streaked this one's face, making it a weird mask. He grinned brokenly at Tod and shouted, "It's hell, ain't it!"

Around them guns were speaking. That Hashknife rider held one in his hand, and Tod guessed that Block had shouted the word to break up the stampede at any cost. But that would have to be the others' job. Tod had his own chore to do; and he was bucking the careening cattle, working toward the far side of the street, his objective firm in his mind. The thought of Bodeen's gun nagged at him; he was glad for the dust and the confusion.

A horn grazed the rump of Tod's horse, and the mount pitched violently. Tod, caught off-balance, kicked free of the stirrups and went out of the saddle. He landed on his hip, rolled, and was at once on his feet. A longhorn came charging at him, looming out of the dust; but he dodged and managed to gain the Haven's porch. He ran into the saloon; it was full of men, some firing at the longhorns from the broken windows. Tod gained the back door and got into the alley and ran along it. Cattle were here; Tod dodged among them recklessly and got to the rear of the community granary. He found a ladder nailed to the building; he swarmed up this ladder and came to the flat roof. Here he saw Bodeen.

The man had lain prone to the front of the roof to do his shooting. He had his back to Tod and was still busily working a Winchester, firing down into the street at the cattle. He was a trapped man, held here by the herd his rifle had stampeded; this was an irony Tod could appreciate. If any townsmen had marked Bodeen's presence, they in turn had been kept from him by the cattle. Tod was thankful for that, too.

Bodeen fired twice more, then levered his rifle angrily, finding it empty. He fumbled in his pockets and began to reload.

At that moment, Tod said, "Bodeen—!"

Bodeen turned and saw him and very carefully laid down the useless rifle and came to a stand. His face was unreadable, not even surprise showing; it was as though Bodeen had expected Tod to come here.

"Trumbull won't live," Tod said. "Not with the wound you gave him. But your scheme wouldn't have worked anyway. The townspeople would have torn you to pieces. You can't shoot an idea. I've come to square for Trumbull, Bodeen."

Bodeen showed his teeth. "And you came back hating him!"

"He made his mistakes; I made mine, Bodeen."

"What a sentimental fool you turned out to be!" Bodeen said, and his hand moved to brush aside the skirt of his coat.

Tod let him get his gun out of leather before he shot him. He saw Bodeen's gun barrel come up, and the finest target in the world was that elk's tooth dangling from Bodeen's watch chain. There was a skill in Tod acquired from Big Sam Block, a skill that was a Texan's heritage. He had never used this skill against a man, but it was an easy thing to do now. He felt the buck of his gun against the heel of his hand. Bodeen looked at him and shook his head as though what was happening was beyond belief. Bodeen's eyes turned vacant; the man's knees came unhinged, and he slumped down.

Tod turned then and walked back to the ladder and descended to the alley. He came around the corner of the granary and found the street almost free of cattle. A few dead ones lay scattered about. He stood feeling used up; he stood without conscious thought. People were beginning to venture into the street. Down by the Haven someone had tied up Tod's horse. He rubbed his fingers across his cheek; his face felt grimy, and he had the beginning of a beard. He'd shaved last at yesterday morning's campfire; that seemed very long ago. Walking to a horse trough that hadn't been overturned by the stampede, he washed his face, then looked up to see Big Sam Block come riding from between two buildings. Block had lost his hat; his right trouser leg was torn, and blood showed.

Block rode to where Tod stood. Block's broad face had

aged in the last half hour. "The boys have got 'em choused beyond town," he said. "These steers got a bellyful of running." He looked about him. "They sure played merry hell."

Tod said, "Your first job will be to fix up this town."

Block nodded. "Yes, I know."

Tod said, "I'm staying here, Sam. It's where I belong. They even kept the cabin ready for me."

Block sighed. "A wise man knows when he's beat, son. If these folks will take cash payment for the damages, I'll be out of this valley before sundown."

"No," Tod said. "I'd rather you'd be in the south end than anybody else. Trumbull's offer still goes. I reckon Nan will want it that way."

"The girl?" Block shook his head. "She came to camp last night, son. She wanted one thing bad."

"Canaan saved?"

"No, you saved. She was afraid of what hate would do to you. I've been studying on that ever since. She was right, boy. But I couldn't see how right she was, not with all that graze before my eyes."

Tod said, "I'll go see her."

Block stirred in his saddle; he was, for him, strangely humble; he had a new hope in his eyes. "Tod," he said, "we'll be neighbors?"

Tod smiled at him. "Within a hoot and a holler. But there's going to be a fence between your cattle and mine, and you'll keep your bulls inside that fence. You see, I'm going to try my hand at raising the blooded stock Trumbull always talked about."

Block was suddenly a contented man with some last fear washed out of him. "I made a cattleman out of you, eh, son?"

"You made a cattleman out of me, Sam."

Block started to neck-rein his horse about. But a last puzzlement was still in him. He said then, in the manner of a man talking to himself, "He'd have sat right there in his saddle and let the whole herd roll over him before he'd have budged. He'd have done that, wouldn't he?"

"Yes," Tod said. "And that's what licked both of us, Sam."

"It sure as hell did," Block said. He frowned again. "That fellow with the rifle—?"

"He's dead, Sam."

Block lifted his head. "Be seeing you," he said and rode away.

Old Zeke stood on Trumbull's porch as Tod came toiling up the rise, leading his horse behind him. Zeke peered, then stepped aside, no longer barring the way. He said, "She's inside, waiting for you."

"Trumbull—?" Tod said.

Zeke's lower lip twitched. "Dead," he said, his voice breaking.

"So's Bodeen, Zeke," Tod said.

Zeke shook his head. "It weren't much of a trade."

Tod jerked a thumb at his horse. "He got scratched. You got any salve, Zeke?"

"I'll fix him up fine," Zeke said. "Caleb always claimed he never had a better hand with horses." He came down off the porch and took the reins from Tod.

Tod went on into the house. Finding the door open from the hall into the big living room, he made the turn and saw Nan standing upon the bearskin rug. He removed his hat and laid it on a table and looked at her across the space of this room. He saw that grief, like the stampeding herd, had run its course and spent itself. She was wholly composed; she was beautiful in her wildling way. She was someone he'd known long ago and known again for less than a day, but he was not so blind as he'd been. It came to him that there was all the world to be rediscovered now that hate was gone. Strangely, he felt at last the gentle vanished presence of Owen Kirby in this house, and he was at peace.

He said gently, "Zeke told me about your grandfather."

She nodded. "He was still alive when they fetched him here. He told me what happened out on the flat. He was pleased, Tod; he knew at the end that you understood."

He said, "I've talked to Big Sam. He'll stay in the valley, but he knows how it must be. I have made that clear to him." He was suddenly conscious of the weight of his gunbelt, and he unlatched it and laid belt and holster upon a table. "I'll not need this again."

She moved to the table and picked up the gunbelt and brought it to him. She shook her head. "The difference between you and my grandfather is that you will use this when there is need. He wanted a strong man to lead us when he was gone. The strong man is the ready man, Tod."

He was somber for a moment, taking what she offered him. He put the gunbelt about him again, and then he smiled. "You still have the wedding gown?"

"I burned it after I rode back from Block's camp last night."

He said, "I like calico better." He remembered that there would have to be a funeral for Caleb Trumbull. "Can you be ready in a week?"

"I'm ready now, Tod," she said.

He opened his arms to her then. She came into them, and he kissed her gently and hoped that his arms didn't hurt her. She was warm in his arms. The goodness of this moment grew and encompassed him, and all the bleak, lost years faded and were forgotten. This was the moment from which he would mark all future remembrances. This was the beginning. . . .

About the Editors

Bill Pronzini has written numerous Western short stories and such novels of the Old West as FREEBOOTY and THE GALLOWS LAND. He lives in Sonoma, California.

Martin H. Greenberg has compiled nearly 100 anthologies, including Westerns, science fiction, and mysteries. He lives in Green Bay, Wisconsin.

FAWCETT ROUNDS UP THE Best of the West